THE YELLOWSTONE MURDERS

DANIEL ROSENFELD
LAURA WELDON

The Yellowstone Murders By Daniel Rosenfeld and Laura Weldon.
ISBN: 0-9799114-8-6
ISBN: 978-0-9799114-8-4
Published 2010 by Rosenfeld Book Publishing, U.S.

Printed in the United States of America.

ALSO BY DANIEL ROSENFELD

WHAT IF
THE FALL OF THE SPANISH INQUISITION
CODE NAME: AMNON
THE JERUSALEM CONSPIRACY*
THE SWORD OF JERUSALEM**
MEIN KAMPF AGAINST HITLER**
ELEANOR AND KAHINA: WOMEN WARRIORS**
CHASING NASRALLAH**
TREACHEROUS LIAISON**
WICKED FATE**
RANDOM THOUGHTS**
SURVIVAL**
JAMES JAY JONES**
FOR THE LOVE OF?**
THE BOLIVIAN PRIEST**

Co-authored with:
*   Anne Steinhardt
** Laura Weldon
To order any of these books please visit our website:

www.rosenfeldbookpublishing.com

1.

Frank Galitson was in shock. He had just risen from a deep slumber. His friend, Julia Rendel, had held a party in his honor the night before. He staggered into the kitchen, blearily turning on the Lavanzza coffee brewer Julia had given him for his 28th birthday. His head ached, his eyesight blurry. He had to blink several times before he was able to make out the time. It was already 11:30.

While the coffee was brewing, he picked up the Sunday New York Times delivered right to his apartment door. He dug through the mammoth stack of paper to retrieve the Book Review section. For the past two months, two of his mystery novels had been top of the bestseller list. Today there was no sign of either. "The Murder of Jessica Stone" and "The Mystery of Xonda" had both disappeared. He flipped the pages, fingers shaking, looking for the promised review of his latest book, "The Art of Murder". It wasn't there. His heart was pounding so hard he could hear it.

He sank to the sofa, thoughts swirling. What happened? "The Art of Murder is the best book I've ever written," he told himself over and over, voice a pathetic whisper. He picked up the phone to dial, then slammed it back down. "Today is Sunday. Harry won't be in his office." He called information for Harry's Connecticut number. He knew he had it somewhere but he was in too much of a hurry to figure it out.

"Is Harry there?" His voice was rough and unfriendly, even though he'd known Harry's wife, Mary, for years.

"Is that you, Frank? What's the matter? You sound awful." She spoke with both surprise and concern.

"Where's Harry? I must speak to him. Get him."

"He's busy barbequing on the patio. We're entertaining Barbara Stein of the New York Times and her children. He'll call you later this afternoon."

"All the more the reason to talk to him. Get him on the bloody phone." His tone was that of an army sergeant ordering his troops.

"Frank, I don't like your attitude. Are you drunk?"

Frank slammed down the receiver so hard it broke in two. He was furious. He dressed hurriedly, grabbing up clothes he'd dropped in a heap the night before. He thundered downstairs from his penthouse apartment to the 17th floor where he repeatedly pressed Julia's doorbell, cursing savagely under his breath. There was no response. He banged on the door, loudly calling out Julia's name. A neighbor poked her head around her door, but seeing what looked like a mad man in the hall she slammed it shut.

Finally, the door cracked open. Frank pushed it with great force, but it held on to its security chain. Julia peered out. "Oh, it's you. What's the rush? You got me out of bed. I'm not decent. Please, wait." The door slammed in his face, serving only to escalate his fury. He paced the hallway, slamming his fist against the wall. He was completely distraught.

Minutes later, the door opened. Julia was dismayed by her friend's angry face and unkempt appearance. She was appalled at the words he was muttering. "What's the matter, Frank? You look terrible. Come in." She stepped back as Frank rushed in her door. She got as far away from him as she could in the narrow hallway.

Frank entered Julia's apartment at parade-march speed. "The New York Times dropped me from the bestseller list, and the review of my book, which Barbara promised to publish this week, isn't there either." He dropped onto the sofa as if he were a rock.

She stared at him, trying to figure out why this news had sent him into such a state. "That's terrible."

"To top it all off, Harry is entertaining Barbara Stein at his home in Connecticut. Mary refused to get him to the phone."

Julia hid a small smile. She hadn't known Frank to be as dramatic before. "You must calm down, Frank. There has to be a reason. Perhaps it was an accidental omission." She sat next to him, placing her small hand over his knotted fingers.

He shook her off. "There was no omission. Other books are now on top of the list."

"Frank, did you really expect to be on top of the list forever? Come on, you know there are a lot of other good books on the market."

Frank wouldn't listen. "You don't understand. I'm ruined." He grabbed his head with both hands. "I'm finished."

Julia almost laughed aloud at this. Was he kidding? "That is the most stupid thing I've ever heard from you. You are far from finished. First, you shouldn't have expected to stay at the top of the list forever, and second, you know you have a following. People will buy your books even if you're third or tenth on the list." She tried again to get close to him but he leapt from the sofa.

He turned to Julia, a queer look on his face. "I'm going to Connecticut. I pay Harry to deliver." He rushed out without another word, slamming the door violently behind him.

Julia remained seated, baffled. What had gotten into her best friend? Had his pride gone to his head? Had he forgotten how long and difficult the path was to success? What else was going on to provoke such an extreme reaction.

Frank completely forgot about his coffee. He took the elevator to the lobby, brusquely ordering the doorman to bring around his Mercedes. The doorman shrugged, used to the rudeness of the tenants.

Frank shot away from the curb with no word of thanks, leaving Manhattan at an alarming speed.

****

Frank Galitson had been born in Manhattan, son of a renowned professor of English literature at the New York University. Frank had many wins as a remarkable athlete during his school days. He started out playing little league baseball, then went through soccer and basketball, ending up playing hockey at Sanford, where he received his Masters Degree in English literature. Frank was just over 5-11", his body firm and muscular, his face a lean oval shape with dark brown eyes. He was the envy of other male students who wished for his good looks. Girls were always after him, but he showed no interest, his mind set on a writing career. Mysteries had always attracted him, so he decided his long term goal was to become the best mystery writer in America.

Frank was able to afford his luxurious, multi-million dollar penthouse at 7889 Park Avenue, Manhattan after his first book, "The Murdering Judge" was published. It had been a mystery about a judge who perpetrated a murder conspiracy. The book was snapped up by the thousands. Prior to publishing his first book he'd written stories for mystery magazines and had gained some recognition. Harry Simner, owner of the well known Simner Publishing House, liked Frank's work. His company did an outstanding job on promotion and marketing. Since then, Harry had published all of Frank's books.

Frank met Julia in the elevator the day he moved in. She was an executive assistant to her father, president of Help Foundation, a well known charitable organization for the promotion of artistic talent. They became friends immediately. Julia was an avid reader and a supporter of the arts. She often hosted gatherings for up and coming personalities and celebrities, hoping to promote one art or another. Frank became one of her projects.

****

Harry Simner, like many affluent New Yorkers, lived in Kent, a small picturesque town next to the Connecticut River. Route 7, which led to Great Barrington, Massachusetts, ran through the town center. Frank sped down the two-lane Merritt Parkway, going 80 in a 45 mile speed zone. A persistent State trooper gave Frank a long chase before pulling him over two miles outside Fairfield. "What's the matter, young man? Is someone chasing you?" The officer was polite, voice neutral while he scanned the interior of Frank's car. His gaze finally settled on Frank's mottled face and his white knuckled grip on the wheel.

"Can you believe this? The bastards took me off the bestseller list." Frank's voice was nearly a scream.

The officer realized he might be dealing with an unbalanced person, or someone under the influence. "Sir, have you been drinking?" He leaned down to look more closely at Frank's face.

"I must get to Harry Simner before it's too late." Frank spoke harshly, his tone high. He completely disregarded the officer's question.

"Your driver's license please." The officer spoke calmly. "What driver's license? What do you want? I'm in a hurry. They dropped me, can't you get that?" Frank had saliva bubbles at the corners of his mouth from the intensity of his speech.

The officer moved back, pulling his gun from its holster. "Please, step out of the car sir. Keep your hands where I can see them." He spoke firmly, but politely.

Suddenly Frank jerked his car into reverse slamming into the front of the trooper's car. He accelerated forward, spewing dirt and gravel as the car lurched back onto the pavement. Immediately the officer radioed in for help, giving his location and Frank's license plate number. He started chasing Frank, by now far ahead of him. Minutes later all traffic came to a stop. The Fairfield police had created a road block.

As Frank approached the barrier, he drove off the road into a nearby field. The officers ran back to their cars, wanting to capture this crazy driver. They were stopped in their tracks as the front right tire of Frank's car plunged into a hole and the car flipped over. Unbeknown to Frank, his airbag was defective. His head slammed into the steering wheel and he knew no more.

****

Frank struggled to open what felt like glued shut eyelids. The dim light in the room hurt his eyes. He wondered where he was. He could see Julia through rails on the side of his bed. There were tubes and equipment all around. Julia's eyes were closed. She was leaning back, trying to nap in a most uncomfortable position. He blinked several times, his mind racing, but nothing rang a bell for him.

With difficulty he touched Julia's arm, waking her from her sleepy trance. "Where am I?"

Julia was upset, impatient with him. "You idiot, are you out of your mind? What's the matter with you? Can't you take a setback? Do you think life is nothing but a perfectly smooth road?" She flooded him with questions. "The police are out to get you, you idiot."

"Where am I?" He squinted at Julia, not even remotely comprehending her questions.

She exhaled loudly, almost snorting. "You're in a hospital, you idiot… you were driving like a lunatic."

Frank remained silent for several moments, trying to digest Julia's words. He winced as the memory of his recent misadventure crashed back into his mind. "Oh… I was mad as hell. Have you heard anything from Harry? Did he call back?"

"Why would I have heard from Harry? He doesn't even know you're here."

"Where are we?" He sounded like a fretful child.

"At the Fairfield Hospital." Julia was upset, seething with anger at him for his foolishness. She swept hair off his forehead with a less than kind hand.

"What did the doctors say?"

"You're just shook up. You'll be alright by tomorrow."

"What about the New York Times?"

Julia felt like slapping his face. "Wake up to reality. It's not the end of the world, you know."

"I'm finished."

"I told you before, that's the most stupid thing I've ever heard. You're young, a brilliant writer. Someone didn't like your last book, so what? You'll write others."

Frank stared at Julia as if she were a complete stranger. Julia stayed quiet, trying to cool off. "Can I get you anything? Are you hungry, thirsty? I'm going to go home soon and get some sleep."

"What time is it?"

"After nine."

"Will you come back tomorrow?"

"Yes, you idiot. I still love you, God only knows why." She kissed his cheek tenderly, trying to avoid the bruises which were starting to show.

As Julia left, Frank's mind spun into a new cycle. The words 'I still love you' rang through his head like church bells. Why did she say that? Love? What love? I've never said a thing to her about being in love. It's never even entered my mind. I like her a lot, she's a great friend... but love? Deep down maybe I do love her. She said she loved me. When did that happen?

Frank grabbed his head, shouting out loud, "Stop... stop... stop."

He sank back into the pillows, mind returning to his anger at the New York Times. "The bastards... I'll show them who's best. I'll write a book that will knock them off their feet." He spoke loudly, not realizing his internal dialogue had become external.

A young nurse passing by the door halted her progress. "Why are you shouting? Are you in pain?"

"My head is full of pain. I'll show them. They can't drop me just like that." He snapped his fingers.

She was used to the incoherence of head injury patients. "Would you like a couple of Tylenol tablets? I can't give you anything stronger because you hit your head so hard." She was leaning over the rails, trying to ascertain the level of Frank's injuries.

He raised his hand as if to strike her. "You fool... tablets won't help. I'm going to get back on the bestseller list even if I have to kill someone to do it."

The nurse fled to summon the resident. "I think the patient in 304 needs psychiatric attention." Her voice was high pitched with nervous anxiety.

"Come now, he just has a slight concussion from a car accident. He'll be released tomorrow. Don't worry about him. Just check in on him every half hour."

Julia decided to spend the night in the hospital rather than drive home. She was exhausted. No one was in the waiting room so she lay down on a long lumpy old sofa, covering herself with a blanket left behind by another visitor. She dropped off to sleep almost immediately. The noises didn't bother her since she was used to the street noise of Manhattan.

She rose early the following morning. Frank was awake, sitting up in bed, mumbling to himself. "You have to appear in court next week," handing him the summons left on his bedside table. "You've been accused of speeding, reckless driving, insulting a police officer, disturbing the peace, and endangering the lives of other people."

"Is that all? I'll pay the fine and it will be all forgotten."

Julia gaped at him. Who was this callous stranger? "I'm afraid it'll be more than a mere fine."

"I'll hire the best lawyer in Manhattan. He'll get me off completely." Frank spoke complacently, sure of himself. He knew the power of fame and wealth.

Julia sighed. "I wish you'd put your optimism to your work and stop this grudge against Harry and the New York Times."

They left the hospital to head back to Manhattan. Julia maintained a strained silence all the way home. As they approached their apartment building, they saw several police cars parked in front. A policeman stood sentry at the entrance. He stopped them, inquiring about their business in the building.

"We live here. What's going on?" Frank blurted out his words, unheeding and uncaring about his tone. He made as if to push by but the officer held him off.

"A tenant on the second floor was murdered last night. Wait here, the homicide detective will want to see you."

Julia paled. She grabbed Frank's arm, stuttering, "Murder? In our building? How odd?"

The detective, a blob of a middle aged man, his face too long for his small body, came toward them. His brown eyes, deep in their sockets, darted side-to-side as if he had to observe three things all at the same time. "Which apartment do you occupy?" He thought them to be husband and wife.

"The penthouse."

"Where were you last night?" He was watching them thoughtfully, busying his hands with a small notebook and pen.

"At the Fairfield Hospital. We've just come from there."

"Did you both know Ms. Smith?"

"Vaguely. I've seen her in the elevator on occasion. We had nothing in common, being of different age groups."

"Was your wife with you the entire night?"

Frank laughed heartily. "Oh… this isn't my wife."

The detective turned his attention to Julia. "Where were you last night?"

"At the hospital with Frank."

"Where do you live?"

"Apartment 17A."

"In this building?"

Julia looked at him, eyes ablaze. "Do you have a problem with that?"

"Listen, lady, I'm only doing my job. No need for sarcasm. How well did you know Ms. Smith?"

"Not at all."

"How is it you never saw her?"

"You ask too many questions. Just because we live in the same building…" She moved to brush past him.

The detective raised a hand, stopping Julia in her tracks, saying in a firm voice, "You're going to get in trouble talking to me like that. Simply answer my questions. Is that clear?"

Frank was the one to respond as Julia remained mutinously silent. "Ok… Ok, don't get bent out of shape. We weren't here at all last night and we hardly knew the woman."

The detective turned to Julia. "What were you doing at the hospital?"

"Frank was in a car accident yesterday. I got a call from the Fairfield police, and left immediately to join him."

"Are you two engaged?"

Frank rushed to answer. "No, no, we're just good friends."

"How come the police called you?" He looked Julia straight in the eye.

She stared back, not a bit nervous. "They found my card in Frank's wallet."

"I'll have to check both your apartments."

"Then you'll have to get a search warrant." Frank's limited store of patience had run out. "I've already had enough trouble for one day."

"What kind of trouble?"

Frank bit his tongue. He'd opened Pandora's box. "The New York Times dropped me from their bestseller list." He instantly became angry all over again.

"Ah... a writer? What do you write?"

"Mysteries."

"So maybe you created a mystery in your own building."

Frank couldn't figure out if the detective was trying to be funny, or this was part of his interrogation. He responded, irate. "We told you we were at the Fairfield Hospital. You can easily verify that. Now, can we go?"

"Don't leave town until you hear from me." He stepped aside, a signal of permission for them to enter the main door.

"Police detectives must be the dumbest people on earth," Frank spoke loudly as they walked through the lobby.

The detective heard Frank. Immediately he shouted at him. "Get back here, I'm not finished with you." He was furious. Frank stopped in his tracks. The detective approached him, nose only an inch away from Frank's face. "So we are the dumbest people on earth, hey? And the detectives in your mysteries are geniuses. No wonder the New York Times dropped you."

Frank pushed the detective away, saying impudently, "I don't need to breathe your stale air."

"You're under arrest for assaulting a police officer." Forcibly he turned Frank around, handcuffing him. Then he pushed him out of the door, calling to an officer standing next to his car. "Book this man for assaulting a police officer."

Frank was speechless. How could he be under arrest just for mouthing off? He was rudely pushed into the back seat while Julia apologized, pleading for his release. Her words fell on deaf ears. As the car left, the detective grabbed Julia's arm. "Better educate your friend. He has a big mouth. Now, what time did you receive a call from the Fairfield police?"

Julia was upset. She remained silent while her mind spun. She felt like hitting the detective in the nose, but she quickly realized that any such movement on her part would land her at the police station as well. She mumbled, "I think it was around four."

"Speak up. Was it yesterday afternoon or this morning?"

"Yesterday afternoon."

"What did the Fairfield police ask you?"

"How I knew Frank and what type of relationship we had."

"Your answer?"

"I told them we were neighbors and close friends."

At that moment a plain clothes officer approached the detective, pulling him aside. They spoke in low voices. Julia tried to eavesdrop but she couldn't make out what they were saying. She swayed in fatigue, mentally pleading for this to be over and done with.

The detective returned. "What made Frank drive like such a lunatic yesterday?"

"He was extremely upset when he found out he had been dropped from the bestseller list."

"What's that got to do with Connecticut?"

"His publisher lives there."

"He'll have to be in court next week and he'll likely spend several months in jail. You may go."

Julia didn't budge. "Where have you taken Frank?"

"Twenty-fourth precinct."

Julia was shocked. "Isn't that in Harlem?"

"Yes, it is."

"They'll kill him there. Couldn't he have been taken to a midtown location?"

"He needs to be taught a lesson. Good day, Miss." He turned his back on Julia, still standing with her hands pressed to her cheeks. She wasn't at all accustomed to someone treating her with the disrespect she so easily turned on others.

Julia returned to her car. She checked to see if she was being followed. No one seemed to have any interest in her. On the drive to Harlem she wondered why it had occurred to her she was being followed. She laughed at herself. It was odd to hear a laugh coming out when she felt closer to weeping.

The police officer at the front desk was uncooperative. "He can't see anyone." She pleaded, telling him she wanted to consult with Frank about what attorney to use, but her words were to no avail. Her next request was to see the police inspector in charge of the precinct but this was also turned down. "Young lady, when you've assaulted a police officer, you're in deep trouble."

"He's entitled to at least one phone call."

"He'll be allowed to call anyone he wants. I suggest you go home. Maybe one of his calls will be to you."

Julia left, completely disappointed. She knew Frank had caused himself more trouble than he could even imagine. Driving back home without having been able to help Frank in any way brought tears to her eyes. She became aware how deep her love was for him. Dismayed by everything that had gone on in the last two days she let herself into her apartment and poured herself a very stiff drink. Sleep was a long time coming that night.

2.

The morning following Frank's arrest he was taken to the Manhattan Municipal Court. The judge read out the charges, to which Frank responded, wearily, 'not guilty'. The detective was called to the stand by the prosecutor. He told the court about the events of the previous day, concluding, "After being pushed by the defendant, not knowing what he might do next, I had him arrested."

The judge turned to Frank. "Did you touch the detective?"

"Yes, but…"

The judge didn't let him finish. "This court is inundated. My calendar is full. Since you have no other convictions I sentence you to one week in jail and a $500 fine. If you're brought here again for disrespecting an officer of the law, you'll spend six months in jail. Next case."

Julia had returned to the 24th precinct to try once more to see Frank. She was told he'd been taken to court. By the time she reached the courthouse the case was closed and Frank had been removed. She was furious with the system. Her request to see him in jail was turned down. She was a seething mass of emotions as she tried to determine what to do next.

Julia wasn't able to see Frank until he appeared in the Fairfield Municipal Court. A special police car delivered him there from his cell at the Harlem jail. She was able to get a front row seat behind the railing, facing the back of the defendant's desk. Frank looked haggard. He'd lost a lot of weight and his overall appearance made him look like a hobo. He stared at Julia momentarily but there was no sign of recognition. His face remained blank. The lawyer representing him was dressed in Armani, like he was in attendance at a high society wedding.

The case against Frank moved swiftly. The judge read out the charges and Frank pleaded guilty. The judge reprimanded

Frank for being overtly rude, for disobeying a State trooper, and for reckless driving. He sentenced him to three months in jail and a $5,000 fine. The judge asked Frank if he had anything to say, but Frank was mute, shoulders hunched forward. The entire affair lasted only eight minutes and he was led away in cuffs.

Julia tried to speak to him as the two court officers took him away, but he showed no sign of interest. Julia was saddened, distressed by his behavior. What had she done to deserve such a frigid response? Her eyes welled. She returned to New York an emotional wreck, vowing not to see him till he came home from jail.

Frank was badly depressed during his stay in jail. He was reluctant to participate in any of the prison functions. He barely spoke to anyone. He was released after two months for good behavior. The day before his release he was allowed to make a phone call. He called Julia, asking her to pick him up. She hung up on him. He couldn't even muster up the energy to feel hurt.

The few dollars he was given was enough to pay for a train ride to Grand Central Station. He walked up Park Avenue to his apartment building. The doorman was shocked when he saw him. "Where have you been? Are you alright, sir?"

Frank didn't respond, walking right by him as if he hadn't seen anyone. The doorman stared at him, scratching the back of his neck. What's the matter with this guy?

Frank went up to his apartment. He shaved, showered, and put on his favorite blue jeans and a long sleeved white shirt. He went down to Julia's apartment, gently knocking on her door. There was no answer. He looked at his watch – 3:30 p.m.

Frank sat alone on the sofa in his apartment, wondering why being dropped from the bestseller list had driven him to exhibit such irrational behavior. His mind spun. Was he mentally unstable? Why had he viewed a setback as the end of the world? There were no answers. He thought long and hard about whether he needed a therapist.

His thoughts were disturbed by a loud knock at the door. He rose slowly. He opened the door to see Julia standing in front of him, face dour. "I knocked on your door but you were out. I wanted to see you and see how you were."

"Can I come in?"

"Of course."

"Frank, would you please get me a glass of wine." She sat down, lighting a cigarette, taking a deep draw, only to extinguish it seconds later. She was nervous, full of anxiety.

"Here you are." He tried to caress her cheek but she brushed his hand aside.

She took a long sip. The glass trembled in her hand. "There's something I must tell you. I've been having restless nights. I must get this off my chest."

Frank looked at her gloomy face, wondering to himself, is this another love talk? He sat down across from her. "What's the matter? You look awful. Are you upset because of me?"

"Well... indirectly." She remained silent for a few minutes, not sure how to start. She took another huge swallow of wine for liquid courage.

"It can't be all that serious. Come on, talk to me." He leaned toward her, urging her on.

"You'll never understand." She began sobbing.

"Try me, will you. My mind is much clearer now. I know I behaved like a fool."

"I... I... I killed Mrs. Smith."

Frank leaped up. "What? Are you crazy? Why would you say such a thing? You were with me all night at the hospital." He gaped, eyebrows crawling up almost to his scalp.

There was a short pause before she could continue. "Not all night. I left after midnight and came back two and a half hours later. No one saw me leave or come back."

Frank stared at Julia, mouth still open, mind spinning. "What were you doing?" He stopped, staring at her with a look of incomprehension. The disheartened look on her face changed his line of reasoning. "You are serious, aren't you? Why the hell did you want to kill Mrs. Smith? You hardly knew her." Frank was so overwrought he knocked his own glass of wine to the carpet where the stain spread out like a small lake.

"I killed her for you."

Frank collapsed beside her on the sofa. "For me? Are you nuts? How could killing her be good for me? That is, if your story is true."

"Yes... yes... it's true enough."

"Why, why?" Frank was beside himself. He heard himself shouting and fought for self control.

"I know how you love mysteries. I thought a murder in your own building would be a good plot for a story." She wiped tears away with the back of her hand.

"Julia, that's insane. Do you have any idea what you've done?

"I love you so much. I'd do anything for you." Her eyes blazed with intensity, as if willing Frank to be pleased.

Frank closed his eyes, furrows starting on his forehead, hands beginning to shake. "This must be a bad dream, a nightmare."

"Frank, you mean everything to me. I'd give up my life for you, if needed." She leaned into him, hand on his left knee.

"I can't understand this. I've never encouraged you. I like you a lot and you're a wonderful friend. I care for you, but I don't love you. Why would you think that?" He pushed her hand away roughly, getting up to pace the room.

Julia sank back into the cushions. "You've been my one and only for almost two years. You've never gone out with another woman that I know of. I thought I was your woman." She looked at Frank in complete incredulity

Frank stopped pacing only long enough to shout at her. "Julia, I like you a lot. I felt no need for companionship with other women. That didn't mean I loved you."

Julia's sobbing increased. She wiped tears away with both hands. "I knew I loved you from the first day I saw you, but I only realized the depth of my love when I saw you in the hospital bed so bruised and battered. I realized then that I couldn't live without you. Please, Frank, have you no feelings for me?" She spoke in desperation.

Frank reseated himself, leaned back, closing his eyes. After a while he said, "What are we going to do now? You've put me in a very difficult position. If I call the police you'll be taken away and I'll never see you again. On the other hand, if I remain silent, I'm an accomplice to murder." He shook his head, not knowing what the best option was. "I must sleep on this. I need to think."

"You've written many mysteries. You're an expert at these things. Work with what I've given you."

Frank remained silent a long time. He was searching his feelings, trying to determine whether he had even a shred of love for her. She'd been a devoted friend. She'd admitted her love, expressing its intensity by going so far as to kill someone to provide him with a subject for a mystery novel.

Suddenly he hit his forehead with his hand. "Didn't the doorman see you when you came in so late at night?"

"No one saw me. I came in from the back. I have a key to the rear service door."

"How did you enter Mrs. Smith's apartment?"

"It was surprisingly simple. I saw light through her transom and gently knocked on the door. She cracked it open, asking who was there. She let me in. I... I... strangled her with my belt." Julia made a retching noise as the sights and sounds of the murder came back full force.

"Oh, my God. Did you touch anything?"

"Not a thing."

"You must have closed the door when you left, didn't you?"

"I used the edge of my scarf."

"You're sure no one saw you."

"Positive. What do you think I should do?"

"Take a leave without pay for several months. You can come up with a good excuse for your father. We'll move to Wyoming until this case is officially closed by the police." Frank was shocked by his own words. The thought had crossed his mind with no decision.

Julia was surprised. "Why Wyoming? What's there?"

"Lots of quiet and plenty of nature. I'll be able to write without interruption, and you can help me."

"I'll do anything, Frank. Thank you." She moved to hug him, but he turned away. "Let's go out for dinner. I haven't had a decent meal in a long time."

3.

Frank and Julia's flight from New York to Jackson Hole in Wyoming was uneventful. Frank buried himself in a book the moment they boarded the plane. He didn't want to discuss their problem in case unwanted ears might be listening. Julia was still edgy even though the New York detective had given them permission to leave. Although her nerves were causing her to chew at her fingernails, a habit left over from childhood, part of her was excited to be spending time with her lover.

Frank rented an SUV, then drove directly to Yellowstone National Park using the 55 mile Roosevelt Parkway. The cabin he'd reserved at the Old Faithful Lodge was ready for them. From the small rear window he could see the most famous geyser in the United States, erupting every 45 to 60 minutes.

Frank was pleased. The cabin was large and airy with updated conveniences. Apart from a king size bed and a private bathroom, it had a large desk where he set up his laptop and printer. He unpacked, placing his clothes in a chest of drawers.

Julia stood at the bedside, watching him. Finally she broke the long silence. "Aren't you going to talk to me? You haven't said a word since we left New York."

"Sorry, I've been preoccupied." There was no warmth in his voice and he refused to look her in the eye.

"Preoccupied with what?"

"Oh... I don't know... this whole situation, I guess"

"You're the one who suggested we come here to this isolated place."

"I know... I wanted to get away from the world... from the injustice that had been done to me."

"Injustice? What injustice? You behaved like a lunatic."

"Obviously you don't understand what my loss of prestige has done to me. In fact you don't seem to care." His voice was argumentative.

"That's ridiculous. I understand the shock, but 'loss of prestige', don't be such a child. The reading public doesn't expect your books to be at the top forever. There are many authors as good as you and some better. I'm sure no one expects you to be the king of writers forever. Grow up. Keep producing excellent novels like you have in the past and your books will continue to sell in huge numbers. The public likes your writing, and you'll make good money. What else do you want?"

"Thanks for the lecture. Maybe I did behave stupidly, but being at the top of the bestseller list meant more to me than you'll ever be able to understand."

Julia, realizing the impossibility of changing Frank's view, reverted to another subject. "Frank, we've been soul-mates for over two years. I fell in love with you right away. Why can't you accept it? Why are you trying so hard to hide your love for me?"

"I'm not trying to hide anything. I just know I'm not in love with you or with anyone else. Don't misunderstand me. I like you a great deal. You're a good friend and neighbor just as I am to you."

Julia winced at the good friend comment but went on doggedly. "We've been enjoying sex together ever since we met. As far as I know you're not seeing another woman. There must be some feeling for me in your body if not in your heart."

"Yes... you're a great sex partner."

"Is that all you have to say?"

Frank heaved a huge sigh, shaking his head. "Julia, grow up. People can have sex without being in love."

"You're such a cold fish. My heart is bursting for you and you don't give a damn. I'm so deeply in love with you I even killed for you."

Frank stared at Julia's sad face, and her tear filled eyes for several long moments. "Come... come now... We've been a good pair till now. Let's not spoil it." He took her in his arms, hugging her warmly, then continued softly. "Why did you kill

Ms. Smith? What made you go overboard? Help me understand why you did what you did."

"I don't know, Frank. Your situation drove me to extreme measures. I thought a murder case in the building where you lived would inspire you to write your best mystery ever. I suppose I was as foolish as you were, perhaps more so."

"Well… it didn't. It's created just the opposite effect."

"I'm so sorry." Julia's small voice turned to broken sobs.

Frank wasn't interested in continuing their conversation. "Let's go eat. I'm hungry."

Julia stifled her sobs, washed her face and reapplied some makeup while Frank paced. They walked to the Old Faithful Lodge around the corner from their cabin. The parking lot in front was full. A huge crowd of people of all ages stood on the plaza on the east side of the lodge facing Old Faithful. Another group stood near the geyser. All were waiting to see the next eruption. The backdrop scenery was amazing.

They crossed the carpeted front lobby where a large souvenir store and a wooden registration counter were located. That led into a huge hall with an enormous window directly facing the geyser. A variety of sofas and comfortable chairs had been set up to accommodate visitors. A cafeteria was located on the north side of the hall but Frank was unhappy with the limited food selection, plus, there wasn't any place to sit and eat. There was an outdoor patio which operated on warm days only, quite rare in Yellowstone.

As they left the cafeteria, a forest ranger standing by the entrance stared intently at Frank. A moment later she rushed to overtake him. "Aren't you Frank Galitson?" She had a huge smile on her face. "I thought I recognized you from the picture on the cover of your books."

Frank grimaced. "I didn't think those pictures were so good. I'm surprised you knew who I was."

"My name is Lisa Warrenton. I've read all your books. I love mysteries. I'm a great fan of yours."

Julia eyed the attractive young ranger, dressed in form fitting khakis, a thin red scarf tied around her neck. "Can you recommend a good restaurant in this area? The cafeteria here isn't very inviting." She tried a smile but it was far from heartfelt. She felt her jealousy begin to stir immediately.

"Sure. Let me drive you there. It's close by."

"Don't bother. We can walk if it's not too far." Julia's response was abrupt and unfriendly.

The young woman paid no attention to Julia's impolite response. "No trouble at all. It's getting dark and you might get lost. I have to go there anyway." She grabbed Frank's elbow, propelling him ahead. She made no effort to keep Julia close.

Frank didn't seem to mind. Julia was furious but said nothing more, simply following them to the parking lot. Lisa drove her SUV south on the lower Yellowstone loop, exiting on the next ramp. The Old Faithful Inn, a huge log structure, stood proudly on the left.

Both Frank and Julia were awestruck as they entered the inn's main lobby. The magnificent woodwork, from the ground floor to a ceiling eight floors above, took their breath away. The entire interior, walls, railings, floors, and staircases, had been crafted from logs carefully sculpted and carved.

The dining room was crowded. Due to its popularity, reservations had to be made days in advance. Lisa pushed her way in, emerging minutes later arm-in-arm with the manager. She introduced Frank as one of the greatest authors of the day. Like magic a table was arranged for them. There were angry murmurs from those still waiting as they moved to the front of the queue.

Gracefully, Frank invited Lisa to join them for dinner. She accepted with glee. Julia was enraged. She didn't want to start anything new with Frank. Her wine tasted bitter as she watched Lisa paying homage to Frank.

Lisa couldn't stop talking about Frank's books. She knew each mystery by heart, and could discuss the detective work, the criminal activity and the final solution of each crime. Frank was amazed by her thorough knowledge of his writings. He soaked up the attention, neither noticing nor caring what Julia was doing.

After dinner, while Frank and Julia walked around the immense fireplace, observing its unusual structure and height,

Lisa attended to her business at the inn. She took them back to their cabin, still voluble about Frank's novels.

Frank thanked Lisa by offering his hand. She shook it, then impulsively leaned forward to kiss him on the cheek. She waved all the way back to her car. She said nothing to Julia.

"The audacity of that girl," Julia blurted out, voice harsh. "She's a bitch."

Frank laughed. "She was excited to meet me. Obviously, she loves mysteries."

"Her behavior was disgusting. She has no manners whatsoever."

"Come on, don't be so mean. She loves my stories. That's all there is to it."

****

The following morning Frank went out alone. He drove around the entire southern loop of the park. Just after Norris Junction a dilapidated sign pointed to Firehole Canyon Drive. He parked at the end of the drive which led to several tiny, bubbling geysers of steam. Frank sat on top of a flat rock, trying to develop an idea for his next book. Nothing came to mind. His eyes remained glued to the constant small eruptions of steam while his mind went in circles.

Thoughts about their hasty departure from New York were bothering him. Why the hell did I leave my comfortable apartment? That thought kept coming to him time and again. Why did I want to save Julia? Is it possible I have some deep seated love for her? Frank finally got up, completely disgusted with himself. I must mend my relationship with Julia. After all, we're going to be here together for a long time. As that thought passed through his mind, a picture of Lisa crept in, as if a frame had changed on a roll of film. She's so pretty, so young, so exciting in her approach and behavior.

Frank quickly dismissed this new vision, questioning his sanity. What would he do with another woman in his life? He walked briskly to his car, driving off in a hurry.

Julia was sitting in a lounge chair in front of the cabin, tanning herself in the bright sun. "Where did you get the chair?" He asked this question quite gingerly, trying to initiate a friendly discussion after having left earlier without a word to her.

"From a cowboy passing by on a wagon. He's renting all kinds of stuff to cabin guests. I have a chair for you too. Bring it out. It's such a beautiful day." Julia responded as calmly as she could despite being upset by the way Frank had left her behind.

"I went out for some solitude to try and develop a subject for my next book but nothing came to me." His tone was that of a weary, dejected man.

"Sit down, close your eyes, relax and enjoy the sun. I'm sure something will come to you."

"Look Julia… I'm sorry I've been so hard on you. I've been giving a great deal of thought to my irrational behavior. Unfortunately, I have no explanations or excuses. My behavior lately has been unforgivable."

"It seems that I too acquired a momentary insanity. I feel awful about Ms. Smith. I can't even begin to imagine how I took such a step, strangling her to death. Fortunately, I didn't see her face. There's no way to undo what I did." She sounded sorrowful.

"Well… luckily, so far, you have a solid alibi."

Julia was startled. "Frank, what do you mean by 'so far'?"

"Maybe I shouldn't have said that. But what if someone shows up in the future, telling the police they saw you in the building after midnight? Your alibi may be forfeit."

"I'm sure no one saw me."

"That's good."

"Frank, you are worried for me. It's all over your face."

"I'm worried for both of us."

"You do love me but you're afraid to admit it."

"For God's sake, Julia, stop yammering on about the love angle. I've never loved anyone in my life." Frank spoke with irritation in his voice.

"I can't believe that. How can you have sex with me two or three times a week, kissing me, hugging me, arousing me with incredible foreplay and not have the slightest feeling of love? It makes no sense." Her voice rose as emotions washed over her.

"Julia, I realize this is a painful subject for you, but the truth is the truth. Love is in your heart, in your soul, and in your mind. Love takes over your entire body. It reflects itself in your eyes, in your behavior, in your decision making. It engulfs you completely. It's a warm and enchanting feeling toward another human being."

"That's how I feel about you."

"But that's not how I feel about you. I like you very much, but I hear no bells ringing. Please, don't be angry. I can't change the chemistry. I'll know when I fall in love with someone just as you know you love me now."

Julia remained silent. The thought of leaving Frank crossed her mind only to quickly vanish. Despite the fact he had explained his lack of feelings, a glimmer of hope still rang in her heart. What could she do to win him over completely?

The evening air cooled significantly. Despite the breeze they decided to walk to the Old Faithful Inn for dinner. This time they settled in the Bear Paw Deli section, with a delightful, rustic, English atmosphere. A huge half-circle bar was completely filled with tourists seeking a drink with their meal. Frank and Julia sat near a large window overlooking the garden at the back of the inn.

They didn't talk much. Both were thinking about their earlier conversation. Frank ordered a bottle of Pinot Grigio, sipping the wine between bites of a chicken and vegetable wrap. Finally, Julia spoke, placing her hand over his. "Frank, we mustn't behave like strangers. I want us to go back to being good friends. Let's talk about your next book." Julia knew full well that Frank's self absorption could be manipulated by talk of his writing.

Frank hesitated for a moment. "I've been racking my brain but nothing seems to come to me. I think I have writer's block."

"Why did you choose Yellowstone?" She toyed with her wine glass as she spoke. She didn't really care but she wanted to keep the conversation going. She took another sip.

"I don't know. The idea of coming here just popped up in my mind. I knew we had to get away. This place is far from the hustle of New York, peaceful and relaxing."

"But, Yellowstone is loaded with tourists."

"They'll soon be gone."

"There's almost three months before the end of the season. Are you thinking we'll both stay here until October?"

"Yes... why not? Hopefully, an idea will soon strike me for a good mystery."

Julia sank deeper into her chair. She wasn't excited about Frank's comments. She didn't want to be stuck in the middle of the wilderness for so long. She missed her artistic activities and her many friends. "I already miss my social life," she blurted. "I'll be bored stiff here."

"I brought you here for your own good. I want the business of the murder to die out."

"Ok... I'll try. But it's going to be hard for me."

"Let's do some sightseeing while we're here. Yellowstone is home to a great deal of wildlife, as well as incredible landscape and rock formations. We've never been this close to nature."

Suddenly, Frank sat up, a smile on his face. "Look, Lisa just walked in. She seems to be looking for someone."

Julia turned to face the entrance. "So what?"

At that moment Lisa spotted Frank. She came running toward him. "Frank, a terrible murder took place this afternoon in the Mud Volcano area. My supervisor is away as his wife is critically ill. I need all the help I can get. This is a real mystery. Could you help me?"

Julia spoke in a surly tone. "Why Frank? Where are the police?"

"Forest rangers are the only police in the park." She turned back to Frank, speaking with desperation. "You write about crime. You know all the angles. Please, will you help me?"

"Of course." He winked at Julia. "This could be a plot for my next book. Let's go." He grabbed Julia's arm, propelling her toward the door before she had a chance to respond. Lisa dropped

Julia at the cabin as she had shown no interest in the murder case, then drove on to the Mud Volcano area.

"What can we see in the dark?" He sat next to Lisa, almost radiant with excitement

"Not much but I'd like you to see the area before the body is removed."

The twenty-one mile drive took less than fifteen minutes. A night curfew on vehicular traffic in Yellowstone facilitated their drive. As they arrived at the scene of the murder, they saw two other ranger cars and an ambulance parked nearby. Lisa introduced Frank to the two rangers. Neither had any experience in police business. Frank was tingling with nerves.

At Frank's request, the three cars were moved so their headlights were directed at full beam to illuminate the victim and the surrounding area. He tread slowly, carefully checking the ground around the body. He found nothing out of order, just dirt, pebbles, and trodden down grass. His dinner sandwich almost came up when he looked at the woman. Her face had been badly cut and bruised, as were her arms and hands. Her flowery dress was torn as if she had been clawed by an animal. Most of the blood had already congealed. It was impossible to see what her face might have looked like before the attack. Frank bent down to examine the body more closely. Suddenly he looked up at Lisa. "It looks like there's a bullet hole in her neck."

"I thought so too, but I wasn't sure. If that's the case the killer shot his victim, then clawed at her viciously to make it look like an animal attack."

"Did you find the woman's handbag or any other belongings?"

"Not a thing."

"Her dress seems expensive. I'd like a look at the label after the examiner undresses her."

"I, too, wondered about the dress. No one tours the park in this kind of outfit."

"Who reported the crime?"

"A man called the northern ranger station. He refused to leave his name. He said he was a tourist and didn't want to get involved. He hung up within a minute. We traced the call to a booth next to Lake Yellowstone cabins. Where we are now is about halfway between the Lake cabins and the Grant Village Hotel, about fifteen miles in each direction."

"I wonder why he called the northern station and not the southern, which is much closer. I guess he wanted to create some confusion. Let's assume he isn't staying at the Lake cabins. We'll check the Grant Village Hotel first, then the others."

Lisa nodded, glad to have some decent advice to follow. "The ambulance driver took pictures with his Polaroid, but I doubt they'll be of much use. I've notified the sheriff and the coroner in Jackson Hole."

"Let's go. How many hotels are there in Yellowstone?"

"Nine. Five are within a twenty-five mile radius and four are much further to the north."

"We'll have to check all the hotels and cabins."

As the ambulance driver and the paramedic removed the body, Frank walked around the murder scene once more, carefully looking for clues. There were no signs of blood on the ground underneath the body, leading him to conclude that the murder had taken place elsewhere and the body moved to this location. The fact that most of the blood was congealed confirmed his thinking.

"Do you have any idea when the murder was committed?"

Lisa responded sheepishly. "I haven't thought about that. I made a note regarding the outside temperature. It was 45°."

"That won't be of much help if the murder took place elsewhere, which I strongly believe it did. The pathologist must check her dress and her hands carefully, particularly under her fingernails. He may find a clue that'll lead us to the location of the murder and to the murderer."

The hotel named Yellowstone Lake Cabins was situated in a small village known simply as Lake. The main building was an old, thoroughly unimpressive structure. Its outer walls were wooden planks that hadn't seen a coat of paint in decades. The hotel was surrounded by some two dozen cabins, similar to others in the park. They were about 20'X16', made of wood planks or logs, all painted a dull brown. A parking space was provided at one side of each cabin. A large, secure, steel garbage container, inaccessible to bears, was situated in front of the cabins.

They awakened the manager. "Has there been any unusual activity in your complex this afternoon or evening?"

"Unusual? What do you mean?" The man rubbed his eyes, fatigue shadowing his features.

"Any arguments, fights, disturbances?"

"I don't know what goes on in each cabin." He was plainly puzzled by such questions.

"Did anyone report a disorder of any kind? Have you seen anything unusual?"

"No... we're fully rented. I only see people when they check in. Why are you asking all these questions?"

"A murder was committed at Mud Volcano. A woman was killed."

He stared at them in some consternation, trying to figure out what else he could tell them.

"Did anyone ask for change to make a call from the phone booth up front?"

After a brief pause, scratching at the back of his neck, he said, "Yea... a woman asked for some change."

"What time?"

"Oh, I don't know... maybe around five."

"Was she a guest?"

"I don't know. I don't usually see all the guests, just the people who come in to register. I don't even pretend to remember them."

"Think man... what was she like? What was she wearing?"

"I don't know... I couldn't tell you what I wore this afternoon."

"Was she white, black, oriental, blonde, brunette, what? You must remember something about her." Frank was becoming more and more agitated. He wanted something to happen.

"Yea... yea... yea... she was blonde, about my height. She gave me a five dollar note to change."

"Was she pretty, attractive, average? Did she strike you in any way?"

"You ask too many questions. I'm not good at these things."

Lisa interrupted. "If you see her again, call me right away. Do you understand?" She gave him her official card.

Frank wasn't satisfied. He stopped at every cabin, even though he had to wake people up. No one had heard a thing or seen a strange woman. Lisa followed him like a baby lamb. They returned to the main building. "Please, check all of your registration cards carefully. If anything comes to mind, call me right away."

Lisa was silent most of the way to Grant Village. Her mind was spinning with thoughts about the murder. Before entering the village she said, "This hotel is right on the lakeshore. Should we make different inquiries here?"

"No... the same. You need to stimulate that man's memory. He's being stupid. Did you notice he was shaking like a leaf when being questioned?" Frank neglected the fact that he had awakened the man from a sound sleep.

Their visit to the hotel produced nothing. Due to the late hour, guests were upset and uncooperative. According to them no one was missing. No guest had left. "Investigation of a murder is a very tedious job, particularly in a national park of this size where most of the people are tourists simply passing through. I'm curious, has there been a murder here in the past?"

"I've never heard of one. From time to time we have people who don't pay attention to warning signs and get hurt by wildlife."

It was 4:00 a.m. when Lisa finally dropped Frank off at his cabin. They were both too exhausted to do anything but murmur good night to each other. Julia was sitting on their bed, staring blankly at the wall. "What took so long? You like younger girls, don't you?"

Frank hadn't expected that kind of welcome. He responded angrily. "What's the matter with you? I was helping her in a murder case. It's given me a great idea for my next mystery."

"Ha! Till four in the morning? Do you take me for a fool?"

Frank laughed. "You're jealous. Grow up, woman. Lisa and I have nothing in common."

"Get out of here. I don't want to see you again." Julia jumped out of bed, lunging at Frank, punching his chest.

Frank grabbed her by force, shoving her back on the bed. "Have you gone mad? What's the matter with you?"

"Get out... get out." She was screaming, burrowing herself into her pillow.

Frank was bewildered by Julia's outburst. At first, he stood next to the bed wondering what to do, then touched her shoulder, saying gently, "Julia, what's gotten into you? I've just been out helping Lisa to investigate a most bizarre murder case. Nothing else."

"You have no feelings for me." She was muttering into the pillow, face still buried.

"Oh... so you're back on that old subject. I'm really disappointed in you. I can't tell my brain who to love and who not to. When love comes, I'll know it, I'll feel it, it'll engulf me head to toe. You can't fault me for not being in love with you. I'm not doing this intentionally."

"You're a beast." She turned on her side, as far away from him as she could get.

Frank could hear her sobs but could do nothing more. He undressed, climbing carefully into bed, doing his utmost not to disturb Julia. He turned the light off, then turned on his side to face the wall. "I'm tired. Goodnight."

Frank had a sound sleep despite being so upset. He slept till noon. When he woke Julia wasn't in the cabin. He quickly washed and dressed. He found Julia sitting on a sofa in the lodge's recreation area, calmly reading a newspaper. "Have you had anything to eat?"

Julia looked up, face somber. "No."

"Come on, let's get something, then drive to the murder scene."

Julia rose silently. They picked up sandwiches and coffee in the cafeteria, then sat down on one of the benches facing Old Faithful. Frank hoped Julia would say something about the previous night, but she ate in complete silence. He tried a couple of openers but Julia would not respond. He gave up with a sigh.

The twenty minute drive to Mud Volcano took them almost an hour. Herds of bison were sighted on the way, several closer than six feet from the road. Scores of cars had stopped on both sides of the road for picture taking.

The huge circle of Mud Volcano was bubbling, steam shooting into the air, causing curious tourists to move back. Many visitors stood in the location where the victim's body had been found the previous night.

Frank broke their lengthy silence, pointing to the spot. "This is where the body was found. There was no blood on the ground. I strongly suspect her body was dumped here long after the murder."

"Was she pretty?" Julia refused to look at Frank and her voice was sullen.

Frank wondered why she asked that question. Not only pretty people get killed. A funny thought flashed through his mind; were ugly women targeted in greater numbers? "I couldn't tell. Her face was severely cut and bruised with dried blood all over it."

"She must have been killed by a bear if she was out here at night."

"I doubt it. There were signs on her neck that looked like strangulation, and a possible bullet hole."

Julia shuddered at the word 'strangling'. She trembled for a moment. "Please, don't use that word."

"Let's check the ground for clues. It was difficult to do that last night."

Frank led the way, slowly checking every inch of the ground. His mind was active as he moved. Lisa's picture surfaced, her young, innocent, beautiful face. He felt a twitch in his heart.

"Did you check the parking area?"

"No... it was dark and the truth is I didn't think of it. Thanks." He quickly walked to the large cul-de-sac about a hundred feet away. Several cars were leaving, almost immediately replaced by new arrivals. Suddenly, a girl about five or six years old came running toward her mother, shouting, "Look mummy, I found a purse on the ground." She held a small leather bag high, beaming at her treasure.

Frank grabbed Julia's hand, pulling her toward the girl. "It's my wife's bag. We've been looking all over for it." The little girl stopped dead in her tracks. "I found it, it's mine," she screamed. "You can't take it."

"Where is your mother?"

A young woman ran toward the girl, shouting, "Let go of my daughter." The look on her face was one of both anger and fear.

Frank forcibly grabbed the handbag from the girl's hands. "Lady, don't get excited. This isn't your bag." He yanked Julia away. The woman shouted at his back, "I'll call the police." Her arms protectively cuddled her weeping child.

"Please do," Frank shouted back. He and Julia ran to their car, climbing in quickly to drive away. Anxious to see what was in the bag, Frank drove off the road to park in an open field. A thin fabric wallet contained a driver's license in the name of Margaret Anne Swansen, 32 Central Park West, New York. There were several credit cards in the same name, $274 in cash and a well used lipstick. He examined the picture on the license carefully, then shook his head. "I doubt this is the dead woman. This face is round. The victim's face was long and narrow. This bag could belong to the killer, or it could easily have been lost by a tourist."

"What are you going to do now?"

"The hotels and cabins in the area have to be checked for this name. I'll have Lisa do that."

"You talk like you're running the show here."

Frank heard the hostility in Julia's voice. "The rangers in Yellowstone don't have much experience in police work. A murder in this huge park is about as common as a rose growing in the Sahara Desert. That's why Lisa asked for my help."

"You don't have to be so generous about it."

Frank decided not to get into another argument. "I have to deliver this bag to Lisa." He drove back to the lodge. A message awaited him from Lisa. He immediately called her.

She sounded very excited. "You won't believe this. I couldn't sleep so as the sun rose this morning I drove back to the Mud Volcano. I walked through the entire area thinking we might have missed something in the dark. I found a handbag on the far side of the circle where people usually park. The wallet contained a driver's license in the name of Elizabeth Anne Swansen..."

Frank interrupted her, "of 32 Central Park West, New York."

Lisa's disappointment was audible. "Do you know her?"

"No, but this morning I found another handbag belonging to a Margaret Anne Swansen with the same address."

"Oh my God," Lisa's voice was a scream. "It must have been underneath one of the cars. That's why I missed it. This is getting more complicated by the minute."

"Not really. I think it may be of great help in solving the murder."

"Are you sure?"

"Absolutely. You can depend on it." Frank tried to be reassuring.

"I'm coming over to the lodge. Please wait for me." She hung up before Frank could add a word. He turned to Julia. "Lisa found another bag belonging to another Swansen woman. This case is becoming more interesting with each passing hour. What a story this will be."

Julia tried to engage Frank in conversation but he was too deep in thought to notice. His mind was racing; twins? Sisters of different ages? Mother and daughter? Had one killed the other? If the victim's body was left there sometime after the killing, how did the bags get lost in two different locations? Had a New Yorker deliberately come to Yellowstone to kill another, far away from home?

Julia was irate with Frank shunning her. She walked away to browse in the large souvenir shop across the hall.

4.

Lisa spotted Frank as soon as she arrived. He was sitting in one of the large armchairs in the lounge. She poked his shoulder. "You must have the same thoughts as mine. Let's compare our two pictures." She didn't think to ask about Julia, watching them balefully from the shop.

Frank leapt up from his seat as if he'd been stung by a bee. He looked at Lisa, a big smile on his face. He touched her arm, directing her to a desk situated right next to a wood-paneled wall. It would give them a little privacy. "Place all the contents of your bag on the left. I'll put mine on the right."

As they finished emptying the bags, Frank said, "These bags are identical in design, but one is black while the other is brown. Both seem fairly new."

"These are Gucci bags. I couldn't even guess their value." Lisa looked over both bags in amazement.

"These bags would easily cost $500 each. Let's compare the pictures on the drivers' licenses."

Frank laid down both licenses, one next to the other. It didn't take more than three seconds for him to burst out. "They're twins... there's no doubt about it."

"What do we do now?"

"Several things need immediate attention. Get a professional photographer to create decent pictures out of each license. The Jackson Hole Sheriff can contact his counterpart in New York City to make inquiries about the Swansen family, especially those with an address on Central Park West. The FBI will have to be notified if this is an interstate crime. Meanwhile, check back at each hotel with the picture, both Yellowstone and in Jackson Hole to determine if anyone by the name Swansen was registered there, or if anyone saw them. Assign these jobs to other rangers so we don't lose any time. Also, I suggest you check on nearby car rental agencies."

Lisa was busy making notes while Frank spoke, not wanting to miss a thing. "I know a good photographer in Jackson. Let's go."

"I have to find Julia. I can't leave without any notice."

Frank set out to look for Julia. She wasn't anywhere in the grand lobby, the souvenir store, or the cafeteria. He ran out to check the grounds facing Old Faithful. Hundreds of people crowded the area around the geyser. Lisa drove him to their cabin, but Julia wasn't there. He left a note saying he'd gone to Jackson in conjunction with the investigation. "OK, let's go. I can't imagine where she is. I've left a note." He felt a sense of relief at not having to face Julia's anger.

It was dark by the time they arrived in Jackson. The door to the photographer's place of business was closed. Lisa walked around the building where a light shone from inside his studio. She gently knocked on the window.

They took a moment to get reacquainted before Lisa explained what she was in need of so quickly and at such a late hour. "Sorry to bother you but I need an urgent job done. There was a murder in the park." She handed him the two drivers' licenses. "I need the best pictures you can make out of these. 5 X 7's will do. Make ten copies of each. When shall I come back for them?"

"It will require a lot of work, but I can have them ready by ten tomorrow morning."

"Thanks." Turning to Frank she said with a weary little sigh, "I'll have to stay in town tonight. There's no point in me going back and forth."

"I have to go back. I'm concerned about Julia. She's been acting odd ever since we arrived here."

"Then let's visit the morgue before you leave. It's located at the back of the hospital. I'm sure the doctor will be working on our victim after his office hours."

The doctor performing the autopsy wasn't pleased to see them. His uniform was stained, his hands encased in plastic gloves, his face lined with fatigue. The interruption meant an even longer night for him. "There isn't much I can tell you right now except about the stuff I pumped out of her stomach. There's evidence she ingested some kind of poison or dope. I'll have it checked by the lab tomorrow."

"Is the hole in her neck from a bullet?"

"I haven't gotten to that yet. I'll need another day."

"Do you have an idea when she was killed?"

"I can't confirm that she was killed. She may have committed suicide. Either way, right now it'll be impossible to give you a reasonable estimate of the time of death. I'd just be making an uneducated guess and I don't want to do that."

Frank took Lisa's arm as they left the morgue. "It's obvious this doctor isn't a pathologist. We'll just have to make do with what's here."

"He's the best in the city."

"Where are you staying? I have to get back."

"I'll stay at the police station across the street. They always have a spare bed."

"I'll take your car, if you don't mind. I'll be back to meet you tomorrow at ten."

During the drive back to the cabin Frank's mind was laden with conflicting thoughts. On one hand he was concerned for Julia, on the other he despised her behavior, particularly her constant declarations of love. He thought he might be a little bit afraid of her, a feeling he'd first felt after she admitted killing Ms. Smith, ostensibly for his sake. Was it possible love could drive you to insane behavior? Apparently so in Julia's case. Why was she trying so hard to force her 'love' on him? Could she succeed? Would he be strong enough to withstand her? Did he want to withstand her? Why couldn't they just remain good friends as they'd been in the past? If indeed she loved him why hadn't she said a thing until he went berserk over the matter of the bestseller list? She could have hinted at it earlier, perhaps shown it in some small way.

His thoughts became more and more frenzied. He stopped the car on the shoulder of the road. "I have to cool down," he spoke aloud to himself. He leaned back, closing his eyes, making every effort to stop torturing himself.

Suddenly, a picture of Lisa surfaced. It was the second time he'd seen her subconsciously. Her innocent, beautiful face, her smile, her devotion to duty all stood out for him. "I like her. She's the kind of woman I could fall in love with." That thought went through him as if it had been shouted into his ears. Maybe he felt this way because she had praised his novels. He hoped he wasn't as shallow as that.

It was close to midnight when Frank arrived at the cabin. The light was on. Julia was leaning back against the headboard, reading a magazine. "You finally found your way back from wherever you've been," was her sarcastic remark.

"I told you before, and I'm telling you again, I'm helping in a murder investigation."

"Till midnight? Do you think I'm that stupid?"

Frank felt his stomach roil. He decided he could not afford to get upset by her attitude. He responded softly, "For an educated woman your mind works like that of a child. Get off it."

"Make love to me."

Frank stared at Julia, wondering whether she was completely normal, with all this jumping from one extreme to the other. "I'm not in the mood for sex."

"That proves it!" Her sharp tone sounded like that of a defense attorney in court. "You had sex with that slut."

Frank couldn't hold back anymore. "You sound like a slut. You're mentally ill. I'm tired of your insinuations. You say you love me, yet you torture me with your behavior. Now I know I will never love you. You've just killed our friendship. Go back home." He left the cabin, slamming the door behind him.

The clerk on duty at the lodge's front desk was sound asleep on a couch. Frank didn't have the heart to wake him. He stretched himself out on one of several long, overstuffed sofas in the grand hall. It took a while, but finally he fell asleep.

The noise of cafeteria workers preparing breakfast woke Frank. He was cold. He got himself a large cup of coffee which he downed in one gulp, ate two muffins and left the lobby feeling like he'd been through an old fashioned wringer washer.

Frank approached the cabin slowly, wanting only to get a change of clothes and be gone. The light was on. He noticed his car wasn't there. The cabin door was unlocked. Quietly he slipped in through the door. Julia wasn't there and all her belongings were gone. "Bitch," he said as he slapped his hand on the desk top. "Good riddance."

After a quick shower and a change of clothes Frank returned to the lobby. He called the police department in Jackson Hole, asking to speak to Lisa.

"My friend left while I was sleeping."

"Don't you know where she is?"

"I think she's gone for good. She was very upset, and all her stuff is missing."

"Are you OK?"

"I'm fine. I'll see you at ten."

Frank wondered why he'd called Lisa. He could have told her the news when he saw her. He had no answer for that, just that he wanted to hear her voice.

Frank called the car rental office to find out that the SUV had been returned early that morning. At first, he felt saddened by Julia's departure but his feelings changed quickly after he thought about her latest behavior. A new thought came to him. For the first time he thought what a shame it was they lived in the same building in New York.

Frank had some time to kill before going to meet Lisa so he sat outside on a bench, waiting for Old Faithful to erupt once more. He didn't have to wait long. Water began to shoot up into the air, slowly at first, then the eruption strengthened until it reached a height of about 150 feet. The huge crowd assembled around the geyser screamed excitedly. Hundreds of cameras clicked over and over throughout the process. There was a collective sigh when the spectacle was finally over.

Frank picked up Lisa at the designated time. She looked tired but cheerful. "I've never been involved in a murder case. This is exciting."

Frank smiled at her. "Yellowstone Park isn't exactly the place where the average murderer would kill someone."

"Who do you think killed this woman?"

"It's too early to say. There's no guessing during an investigation. First, you have to identify the victim, which it looks like we're getting close, then we need to follow every connection to her to uncover a motive and thus the killer. Second, we need to determine what instruments or weapons were used for the killing, and find it or them. We also need to uncover as many clues as we can to help us come to a final decision. Right now we're close to identifying her. We suspect her death was caused by a bullet wound in her neck. There were no clues on the ground, except that there was little blood. What blood there was had already coagulated. That means she was killed elsewhere, some time before her body was left at the scene of the crime. Right now we have little else to go on. We have to wait for the autopsy report. I'm anxious to have her picture taken after the doctor cleans up her face so we can compare it to the two driver licenses we found."

"I had other rangers check every hotel and cabin in the area. No one seems to know a thing. We'll have to repeat the process as soon as we have decent pictures."

"Since the body was dropped so close to the park's south entrance, I have reason to believe the crime may have been committed in Jackson Hole or its vicinity. The distance to the east, west, or north entrances is too great. I'm curious to find out the approximate time of death. That'll tell us a lot."

As promised, the photographer had the pictures ready. He had been so intrigued by the project he'd stayed up late. He said, "These women are definitely twins."

Frank turned to Lisa. "Please call the doctor and ask him if he's cleaned up the woman's face. If he has, we'll need to take some good pictures of her too."

The doctor confirmed that the victim was ready to be photographed. Assuming the police would want a picture he'd used makeup to hide the worst of the cuts. The three of them rushed to the morgue.

Lisa said, "Who is she?"

"The Swansens may help lead us to that knowledge."

"What's next?"

"Send rangers back to the hotels with pictures of the victim. Hopefully, someone saw her. We need as much information about her as possible. I'll call a friend of mine who's a detective with the New York police."

"Sounds good."

Frank called his friend before they drove back to Yellowstone. Frank was observing the scenery along the parkway when he noticed a road sign for Marina and Restaurant. "Let's take a look."

The narrow, badly paved road ended in a gravel lot in front of two brick buildings that were connected by a narrow path. Marina services and management occupied the one story building to the right, while the other was a two story restaurant with a large outdoor patio that overlooked Lake Jackson. The two buildings were surrounded by perfectly manicured lawns. Red, white, and pink impatients and begonias formed a colorful edge. Several sparrows were looking for worms. The lake shimmered in the sunshine.

"According to the signs this is a pizza place. Let's go eat. I'm famished."

Lisa didn't object. The sun was high, the temperature comfortable with a light breeze blowing. They sat outside at a scarred wooden table facing the lake. Frank commented on the magnificent view. Dozens of boats of all sizes were moored at the marina, many others cruised the lake. It all looked idyllic to this boy from the city. Lisa, who saw sights like this every day, enjoyed his enthusiasm for the beauty of the place.

Two hot and hearty pizzas were delivered, along with soft drinks. While eating hungrily Frank became thoughtful for a moment or two. "You know... the killing may have taken place right here, maybe on one of the boats."

"What makes you think that?" Lisa looked at him with wonder. What would he think of next?

"I don't know... that woman's dress was an expensive one... a dress worn by someone wealthy. It's been on my mind. Not that many people would be wearing a Stella McCartney original in Yellowstone."

"I thought you wanted us to wait for the autopsy results."

"Of course, but in a murder case you can't afford to stop thinking. You have to examine and re-examine everything you've seen and heard. Maybe we missed something. Let's talk to the marina manager when we're done lunch."

They finished their meal in a companiable mood, making small talk, smiling often at each other.

Frank showed the manager pictures of the twins first. "Have you seen these two women?"

The manager's face lit up. "Oh yes. They rented a boat from me several days ago. They had the proper licenses... State of New York... I believe."

"Was there anyone with them?"

"No, just them, but they may have had guests."

"Did you check the boat when it was returned?"

"The boat was never returned."

"What? Never returned? Did you see them again?" Frank was astonished.

"Oh yes. They paid full price for it. I still have their check."

"Did they say what had happened to the boat?"

"Yea... they said they had accidentally crashed into a tree on the other side of the lake, and the boat sank. They were really sorry."

"Did you check on their story?"

"No. They apologized profusely and offered payment without me even suggesting it. I still have their check as I told you."

"How did they get back to the marina from the other side of the lake?"

"They returned in a boat I rented for a day to a man."

"I'd like to see his rental papers."

"There aren't any. He told me he was an FBI agent."

"Did you see his badge?"

"Yea... he flashed it. He said he was in a great hurry."

"Please make a copy of the check for us. It's needed for a murder investigation."

The marina manager was obviously shocked. "Murder?" He ran to his office to make the copy. Nothing like this had ever happened to him.

A smile showed on Frank's face. "Well... it seems the plot is getting thicker."

Lisa's mind was elsewhere. She abruptly changed the subject. "Frank, are you married?" There was a hint of red in her cheeks, her eyes downcast. It was as if she was afraid of what the answer might be.

Frank laughed. "What an odd question. Are you?"

"Answering a question with a question is very clever. Are you hiding something?"

"No... don't be silly. I'm not married now nor was I ever."

Lisa giggled. "Me either."

"What made you ask?"

"I was curious about that woman I met with you."

"That's a long story."

"What made her leave so abruptly? Is she angry at you? You said she was upset."

Frank looked into Lisa's innocent face. A small smile appeared on his own. He told her what had happened, leaving out, of course, the part about Ms. Smith.

"Wow! What a story." She clapped her hands. "I've only read about such life experiences in books."

"Looking back... I think I acted pretty stupidly."

"I can understand how losing a prestigious position could hurt you, but I wouldn't worry... you've written wonderful stories and you will again."

"I have a feeling a good story is developing right here."

"I'd like to be part of it."

"You are, my dear."

The manager returned with a copy of the check. Frank took one look at it, saying, "My God... look at this... the check is drawn on an account named as part of the Julius Swansen Estate."

"What does that mean?"

"The twins must be the trustees. The murder may be related to a dispute between heirs."

5.

Julia left the cabin early. She had been restless ever since Frank's mid-night return. Her thoughts flew in various directions, ranging from the love she felt for him to a sense of hatred. She loathed how abruptly he had left her, a grave insult. She had every right to suspect him. I should have bashed in his head, she thought, then I should have caressed him and kissed him.

Her riotous thoughts included a picture of the strangulation of Ms. Smith. Her mind was so confused that suddenly, in the middle of visualizing this awful picture, she flashed on to one of Frank reporting the murder to the police. She shuddered, her entire body shook like a leaf in the wind. Her mind became paralyzed.

"He wouldn't do that," she spoke aloud, as if to quiet her inner voice. Her mental debate continued for a long while. Finally she got up, and began packing her belongings. He hates me despite how I have loved him. He's found someone else. She left the cabin, gently closing the door so as not to make unnecessary noise at that hour of the morning. She drove away without a backward glance.

Julia drove to Jackson Hole where she returned Frank's car. She went to another rental company where she rented a compact car for herself, then checked into a nearby Motel 6. Her mind eased as she made the momentous decision to completely change her life.

After a late breakfast at the famous Bubba's restaurant named Bubba's, she walked across the street to the offices of Dunnely & Rogers, real estate agents. She told them she wanted to rent a small furnished apartment. Several were available. The agent, a pleasant young man, drove her around to see all of them.

Julia selected a large studio, located on Glenwood Street, several blocks from the city center, overlooking Jackson's ski slopes. She purchased a newspaper to scan the jobs available section in the classifieds. She knew her father wasn't expecting her back for months. She was also aware that Jackson Hole was an important art center in the west of the country.

An advertisement by Trailside Galleries caught Julia's eye. She wasted no time. With city map in hand, she strolled four blocks to the gallery located on East Broadway Avenue.

The manager was very impressed with Julia's knowledge of the art world. He explained that Trailside was the premier western art gallery in the city, specializing in works by leading contemporary western artists for the discerning collector. They billed themselves as a hallmark of excellence, representing only the finest painters and sculptors in the United States. Their collection represented several genres; Western Art, Native American Art, Impressionism, Figurative, Landscape Art, Southwestern, Wildlife Art, and Western Sculpture.

After a thorough tour of the gallery they agreed on a salary. Julia accepted a position as assistant manager, responsible for supervising six sales personnel. In fact, she didn't need to negotiate much on the salary as her financial position was strong.

Being satisfied with her accomplishments, she drove to Albertson's, main supermarket in Jackson Hole, to buy food and drink. Then, on to Walgreen's to purchase some needed cosmetics. She had not been one to wear much makeup but she was determined to present a new Julia to the world.

She rose early the following morning. She dyed her hair dark brunette, departing from her natural light brown color. She changed her hairstyle, letting more hair fall to the left side of her face. Then she donned the latest model Prada eyeglasses, checked herself in the mirror, and stood smiling, pleased with what she saw. She was ready for day one at the gallery.

6.

Lisa handed Frank a copy of the autopsy report. Glancing at it, before even reading it, he commented, "This is just about the most unprofessional report I've ever seen. Look at it."

> *Murder victim: identity unknown*
> *Gender: Female*
> *Age: 35 – 40*
> *Race: Caucasian*
> *Hair: black (dyed blonde)*
> *Cause of death: a) rat poisoning*
> *b) suffocation/strangling*
> *c) bullet in the neck/carotid rupture*
> *Other: cuts on face and hands -- bear attack?*
> *Time of death: 12 noon – 5:00 p.m.*

Lisa smiled at his expression of disgust. "We'll have to make do with this. There's no medical examiner in the area."

He shook the page at her. "The big question is why was the victim poisoned, strangled, and shot, when any one of those acts would have killed her. And, why would two sisters lose their handbags in the general area where the victim's body was dumped? At least this primitive report confirms that the killing must have taken place elsewhere."

"For my first murder case this one certainly has become very complex. I'm glad I found you. Without your help I'd be totally lost." She aimed a look of gratitude at Frank, who felt a swelling of pride at her words.

"I'm delighted to be of help. I was looking for a subject for my next book and here it is. I've never thought about including three killings in one novel. It reminds me of Agatha Christie's book, The Orient Express, where eleven different people stabbed the same victim."

Frank became pensive, his mind churning in a new direction. Was it possible three different people had attacked the victim? One who strangled her, one who poisoned her, and another who shot her. So far he had discovered the twins. Was there a third killer? If so, where was he or she? If the twins were licensed to pilot a boat why had their boat crashed and sunk? Had the third killer been eliminated? They'd willingly paid for the boat. Such odd behavior might be attributed to heirs fighting among themselves.

A sudden outburst from Frank shocked Lisa who had also been doing some deep thinking. "We have to get back to Lake Jackson. I suspect that another person has been killed."

Lisa was appalled. "Are you sure? How can you possibly know that?" She was disconcerted by his intensity.

"We need to find the sunken boat."

"In that case I must contact the commander of the State Troopers."

They went back to the police station. While Lisa was busy on the phone, Frank called Joe Caputo, the New York City detective who had helped him before. "Joe, what did you find out about the Swansens?"

"Julius and Adela Swansen died two years ago in a plane crash. He was the major shareholder and chief executive officer of the Swansen Metal Company, as well as the biggest partner in Global Real Estate Enterprises. His wealth has been estimated at around five hundred million dollars. There are four children; the youngest twin girls, an older sister and an older brother."

"Any of them married?"

"No. They all live at home."

"Have you been able to find the older sister and brother?"

"None of them are at home. The housekeeper told me the oldest sister, Sheila, was vacationing in Jamaica with her boyfriend. Paul, the middle child, is traveling, checking on various properties. He's vice president of his father's company."

"Check with the company about his whereabouts. I must speak to him. What about the twins?"

"The housekeeper wasn't sure. She said they've been in and out every day. She said she overheard some talk about them traveling to the west, but they hadn't yet left."

"Joe, I have to find out as much as I can about the Swansen estate, particularly if the heirs are fighting among themselves. Find out who the lawyer and the accountant are who are handling the case. I need details of the wills, the estate, and the trust. Since an estate account exists, papers must have been filed with the court. I have a copy of a check the twins signed for the estate. That means they must be trustees."

"Has the victim been identified?"

"Not yet. It wouldn't surprise me to find out she's the older sister. Could you find a picture of her and e-mail it to the Jackson Hole police, attention Lisa Warrenton."

"Sure."

"Thanks, Joe."

****

Frank and Lisa drove to the marina to investigate the boat crash. They spoke little, each busy thinking about the case. At one point a small smile appeared on Frank's face. He felt quite satisfied. To his mind he had fortuitously come across a murder case more bizarre than any story he'd written. The words for the opening lines of his new novel surfaced as they arrived at the marina, parking next to a beat-up van.

The marina manager refused to give them any help, citing the busy season, but Lisa threatened him. "If you don't help us with this investigation you'll be prosecuted as an accomplice." She used her sternest look and a voice that brooked no option.

Frank bit his tongue trying hard not to laugh at the way Lisa spoke; a young kid talking to a man twice her age, just like an experienced police officer. He decided it was time to intervene. "Better be quick about it. Take us to the scene of the crash. There's no time to lose."

He gave in ungraciously, slamming shut the door to the office and stomping off. They followed him to one of the docks where a 20 foot speedboat was moored. "I don't know the exact location of the crash." His voice was guttural, his face a mask of anger.

"The twins told you their boat had crashed into a tree and sunk. Let's examine the other side of the lake."

It was painfully obvious the manager was reluctant to help. "There are hundreds of trees by and in the water." He stood, arms clenched at his side, legs spread as if to indicate he was going no farther.

"If there are trees in the water I assume that the lake is quite shallow in that area. We should be able to see the sunken boat."

With continuing ill humor he motioned them into the boat, taking off with no care for their safety. As they neared the other side of the lake Frank instructed him to slow down. The speedboat crawled up beside a group of trees. Frank and Lisa each bent over a side of the boat, carefully checking the water. There was nothing to be seen but weeds and tiny fish, glimmering in the sun.

Frank looked up ahead. "There's another group of trees further to the north." They sped away, repeating the exercise unsuccessfully.

Frank was impatient. "Drop us off here and go get someone with diving experience. We must find that boat."

The manager was mutinous. "There isn't anyone," was the curt response.

"Do you know how to dive?" Frank tried staring him down.

"Yes, but..."

"No buts. Go get your equipment."

Frank sat down on the bank, his mind racing. He looked up at Lisa standing facing the lake. He wondered why she hadn't said a word. Her mind must be racing just like mine, was his conclusion. Frank had been so self-centered for so long he couldn't conceive of anyone not acting just like he did.

The manager returned after 45 minutes. He donned his diving equipment. "Where do you want me to go?"

"Go out about 200 feet. Zigzag your way out."

Without a word the manager dived in. He soon disappeared. Frank called to Lisa. "You've become so quiet. I thought you'd have hundreds of questions. What's going on?"

"I guess the anxiety of the search is making me wonder why people kill each other." She was looking away, voice somber, face drawn.

Frank didn't respond. He tried to figure out what her statement meant as it made no sense to him. Before he could sort out his thoughts the manager popped up out of the water, shouting, "There's a boat down here."

Frank leapt up. "Can you get to it?"

"I'll try." He vanished, leaving only a trail of bubbles behind.

Ten excruciating minutes passed before he resurfaced. "Yea, that's the boat the twins rented. There are no signs of a collision but there's a heck of a big hole in the bottom."

"Did you see anything else amiss?"

"I didn't really look."

"Dive back down and search the area around the boat."

"For what? What are you looking for?"

"I don't know. Let me know if you see anything that you think shouldn't be there."

"How far out should I go?"

"200 to 300 feet from the boat."

Finally Lisa turned, saying, "Frank, isn't this a waste of time?" She sounded tired and anxious. There was a small tic under her right eye.

"In a murder case every possibility, no matter how remote it seems, has to be examined."

"What are you looking for?"

"Clues… maybe another body?" He spoke with some hesitation, brow furrowed, index finger to his lips as he stared out at the lake.

Lisa shuddered. "Another body? Who do you expect to find?"

"Well… I can't say this with any conviction, but… if the woman at Mud Volcano is the twins' sister, perhaps their older brother has also been killed."

Lisa's face turned paper white. "Are you sure?"

"No, at this stage it's only a supposition. Remember, every angle has to be investigated. We're using a process of elimination."

The manager emerged, shooting up like a bullet out of the water, rivulets cascading off his gear. He was shouting almost hysterical, "There's a dead man on the bottom."

After a momentary shock, Frank yelled, "Pull him up." He was stunned that the manager couldn't think that through on his own.

"He's tied to something."

"Use your brains, man. Cut him loose and pull him up."

Frank turned to Lisa. "If this man isn't the twins' older brother, I'll eat my hat." He wanted to add something more but seeing how shocked and pale Lisa looked he stopped. "What's the matter? You look like you've seen a ghost."

Lisa could barely speak. She mumbled something incomprehensible. Frank gently touched her face. "What has shocked you so much? Is it because there's another corpse?"

"Yes… no… I don't know. It's all so awful." Her voice was like a low hiss.

"Pull yourself together. This isn't the time to get carried away by emotion."

Suddenly Lisa lurched forward, grabbing Frank and hugging him with a ferocity that was nearly overwhelming. Frank didn't object, thinking that a warm touch would help her calm down. Shouts from the lake woke them both. The manager, exhausted by the ordeal, was breathing heavily as he dragged the body close to shore. Frank helped him pull the body up on the bank.

Lisa stood, immobile, while Frank searched the dead man's pockets. He retrieved a wallet, a key chain with several keys, and a small handgun. Impatiently he dropped the contents of the wallet to the ground. A huge smile appeared on his face. He looked up at Lisa, still standing with a bewildered look on her face, saying, "Well… I was right. This man is none other than Paul Swansen. We're lucky to have found him so soon after his sister's murder. His body hasn't started to decompose yet."

Lisa gathered her senses, speaking weakly. "Who do you think killed him?"

"Everything points to the twins." Frank began to check the body carefully, finding no external signs of violence. He was flabbergasted, scratching the back of his neck. Then it hit him. He turned to the marina manager, struggling out of his diving suit. "You'll have to go down there again. I want you to search the boat thoroughly. Bring up everything you find inside the boat."

Realizing that no argument would change Frank's mind, the tired, grumpy man readied himself for another dive. He disappeared into the lake without a word.

Frank's mind was spinning. Everything pointed to the twins. They controlled the family trust. It seemed that in order to own all of the assets of the trust they had decided to eliminate their brother and sister. Their handbags had been found near their sister's body. But, that made no sense. How or why had the two sisters lost or deliberately left their handbags behind? The gun found in Paul's pocket must have been the one used to kill the sister. But, who or what had killed Paul Swansen? Why go through such an elaborate scheme? Was this amateur hour? Where were the twins now? Still in the area, or back home?

Suddenly a different train of thought started rolling through his mind. What was wrong with Lisa? She had been enthusiastically investigating the murder with him, then had become stunned by the whole affair. She seemed to have lost her equanimity. At times she looked completely shocked.

Finally the diver emerged from the water, breathing heavily. He carried a briefcase and an empty champagne bottle. "I'm not going back there anymore. I've had it."

"I have news for you. You'll have to dredge the boat. The local police will need it as evidence in a murder case."

"Let the police bring it up. I've been paid for it."

"Dream on. Everything that has to do with the murder will be taken as evidence. I suggest you make an effort to cooperate with the police. You may need them in the future. They'll remember your efforts in helping them."

Lisa startled him by breaking her long silence. "Let's get the body back to the marina. I must call the Jackson police."

Frank was anxious to look through the briefcase but decided to wait until the police were present. The speedboat, carrying its new cargo, returned to base. Very little was said during the short trip, except for comments from Lisa. She seemed not to care about a reply from Frank or the boat captain. Frank had a feeling that this bizarre murder case was about to become even more eerie.

7.

Paul Swansen's body was laid out on the dock, covered by a dirty tarp. Jackson Hole's police chief, Richard Crawley, arrived accompanied by a police officer. Two state troopers arrived moments later.

Lisa introduced Frank, explaining his presence, then immediately reported the latest developments. Chief Crawley removed the tarp, staring down at the corpse for a moment, face still. He surprised everyone by saying, "This man looks familiar. I'm sure he was at the police station last week." He held his chin in his hand, head slightly bent, thinking. "Yes... he was requesting police protection. We sent him away, telling him that there were too many tourists in our jurisdiction and we weren't equipped to provide personal security. He was quite upset when he left. He looked like a man used to getting whatever he wanted." He continued to stroke his chin while staring down at the corpse. Lisa kept a respectful silence around the officers, standing slightly behind Frank.

Frank wasn't surprised. "Did he say who he was afraid of?"

"No. We never got to that."

"Was he hysterical, frightened, unbalanced or agitated when he asked for help? What was his approach?"

"He seemed calm and composed. I saw no signs of hysteria."

"Let's check out the briefcase."

Chief Crawley opened the case on a nearby picnic table. The sight of ten bundles of $100 bills shocked everyone. Frank quickly calculated that Paul Swansen had carried with him about $50,000. Underneath the money was a folder containing a copy of the Julius and Adela Swansen Trust along with an unsigned amendment.

"I had a feeling this case was related to a fight over the estate. I'd like to study these documents. I'll stop at your office tomorrow morning, if that's ok with you." Frank felt he should give the police chief some time to perform his duty.

Lisa called her office before leaving the marina. "Rangers have checked all of the hotels in Yellowstone. No one recognized the women in the pictures. The twins may have stayed in Jackson Hole. I'll ask the police to check there.

"Let's meet up tomorrow after I check the trust papers." Frank was tired, his mind restless. The murder of a single woman had been turned into a family battle. Why was Paul Swansen carrying $50,000? What was the purpose of this sum of money when the estate was valued in the millions? If the heirs were fighting each other, this kind of money meant little or nothing. Was it possible another person was involved in the scheme? Was he being blackmailed? Was the money being used to bribe somebody? The twins certainly didn't need that kind of money. The whole affair seemed to make no sense whatsoever.

It was dark by the time Frank arrived at his cabin. A note was stuck on the door, a telephone message. He rushed to the lobby. Joe Caputo had called from New York.

"Sorry, Joe, I was out in the field. Cell phones don't work in this area. What's up?"

"Are you ready for a shock? The Swansen twins never left New York. The doormen at their apartment building said he'd seen them every single day, sometimes more than once. A maintenance man working in the building has also seen them."
Frank was shocked. His mind went blank for a brief moment. "Joe, this is the weirdest case I've ever seen. How can twin sisters be in New York and rent a boat in Jackson at the same time? They issued a check, drawn on the Swansen estate. I have a copy. To top it off, this afternoon we found the body of Paul Swansen in Jackson Lake. I don't know yet what killed him. There were no signs of bodily injury. I suspect he was poisoned. I need more information about this family. I'll call you tomorrow."

Frank hung up, his thinking in complete disarray. The marina manager had identified the pictures of the twins as the women who had rented the boat. How could they have been in two different places, thousands of miles apart, at the same time? Had the doorman been bribed, or the marina manager?

Frank went to bed, forcefully kicking all thoughts out of his tired mind. He desperately wanted to sleep so he could get a fresh start in the morning. He didn't sleep long. Heavy pounding on the door, and a woman's loud voice calling his name, woke him up. He turned on the light to discover it was 4:30 a.m. "Who is it? What do you want at this ungodly hour?" He was gruff, his anger clearly evident in his voice.

"Frank, it's me, Lisa. Open the door. There's been another murder."

Frank thought he was in the middle of a nightmare. He shook his head and rubbed his eyes to rid himself of his drowsiness. "Wait a minute." He struggled to the door. "What's happened?"

Lisa's frightened face could be seen in the muted light from the cabin door. She looked completely spent. "Frank, it's awful. A ranger accompanying two international photographers to the Mammoth Hot Springs Terraces just called our hot line to tell us they've come across a dead couple on the path to one of the terraces." She held her head as if in pain, pausing for a moment, before continuing. "It was so nice and quiet in the park before you arrived."

Frank was doubly shocked. His mind raced. What did the murders in Yellowstone have to do with his arrival? Was Lisa out of her mind, or was this just an off hand comment? "Have you been to the scene of the crime?"

"Not yet. I got the phone call half an hour ago and rushed to get you. I want you to go with me. Mammoth Terraces are a good hour away."

"Are you telling me they found the bodies at this hour? That's extremely odd, wouldn't you say?"

"No... no... no... The ranger and the two photographers camped in the area so they could take pictures in the very early hours of the morning. The terraces are travertine and they are uniquely colored. They create an incredible rainbow with the first rays of the sun."

Reluctantly, half asleep, Frank put on a warm jacket, a scarf and a hat. He looked at Lisa. She, too, was completely bundled up. The temperature was in the mid-thirties, with the piercing wind making it feel even colder. Lisa drove as fast as she could, eyes scanning the roadside for potential wildlife hazards, although it seemed too cold for animals to be out hunting for food.

Frank talked a great deal during the one hour drive. He described out loud their findings about the Swansen murders, hoping to draw a clearer picture about the investigative task ahead. "What bothers me the most is that the Swansen twins have been confirmed to be in New York the whole time. Something is dreadfully wrong. It seems obvious that killing Paul Swansen and hiding his body deep in the lake was meant to simulate his disappearance. I'm going to have another talk with Joe Caputo. The problem is that he has no authority to conduct an official investigation in New York. The crimes were committed here."

Lisa gave a huge yawn. Even with her adrenaline peak her body was exhausted. "I haven't notified the FBI yet."

"That's good, because if the twins never left New York, there hasn't been any interstate crime."

"What are you planning to do?"

"I want to go back to New York and conduct the investigation on my own. There's no doubt in my mind that the Swansen killings are related to a dispute between the heirs."

At that moment they arrived at the village of Mammoth Hot Springs. The horizon was blossoming into rose as Lisa drove on to a dirt road leading to the terraces. She parked at the end of the road where they continued on foot along one of the trails. They had strong flashlights, but as dawn overtook them they shut them off and returned them to their backpacks. They didn't have to walk long. Two bodies lay on the path, one next to the other, holding hands.

Frank bent down to take a closer look. "It's a young man and woman, probably in their twenties, both shot in the back on the left side. The bullets must have penetrated their hearts, killing them instantly. It looks like they were shot at close range and they fell forward because of the incline of the path."

"They must have been killed in the evening after sunset."

"Why do you say that?"

"Hikers don't stay here at night unless they bring camping equipment."

"Good assumption. I suggest you go back to the village to get a doctor, a photographer and an ambulance. You look terrible. Are you feeling ok to go?"

"Of course. It's just that I'm shocked by this crime. Who would want to kill such a young couple?"

As soon as Lisa left, Frank carefully turned the dead man over. His wallet revealed a driver's license in the name of Eric Chandler, 589 Walnut Street, Hamilton, New Jersey. There were also several credit cards in his name and some cash. The woman's small purse contained sample sized cosmetics, a thin leather wallet with a single credit card in the name of Sandra Swansen Chandler, of the same address. She also had been carrying a small amount of money. "Damn, another dead Swansen," Frank shouted out his frustration. What were all of the Swansens doing in Yellowstone? Were there more family members in the park? Was this a family reunion? If so, had it already been held, or was it still to be held?

Frank sat down on a nearby rock, his mind spinning. What a wonderful plot for his next book. Three murders, each one different, all taking place in one of the most magnificent parks in the world, connected by one family. This could be the most exciting mystery I've ever written. Ideas began to form in his head, along with opening sentences and a vivid description of the scenery.

The ambulance bringing Jackson Hole's only doctor was first to arrive. Lisa came along with Chief Crawley and the photographer shortly after. The doctor checked both victims and pronounced them dead. The photographer took a multitude of pictures before the bodies were removed.

Chief Crawley was bewildered. "Do we have a serial killer here? All these dead people are strangers to the area. The killer can't possibly be a local."

Frank was quick to respond. "You can't really say that until a motive has been determined. It could be just a coincidence." Frank knew his words made little sense, but he wanted to test the police chief to better understand if, and how, he would deal with the situation.

Chief Crawley was openly offended by Frank's remarks. "I say that it's someone after the Swansen family, no "ifs" or "buts" about it." He sounded like an obstinate child.

Lisa sensed the change in the atmosphere and quickly intervened. "While I agree with you, Chief Crawley, I've learned that no stone should be left unturned in a murder case, even if it seems illogical." Her youth and gentleness softened him.

"Ok... Ok... let's not argue, but I can't have a civilian doing my investigative work."

"I'm not here to stop you. Lisa invited me to help her and here I am for whatever it's worth."

"I can't have a member of the public getting any more involved than you are."

"Very well. I'll investigate on my own. My real interest is in writing about this case as a novel."

The chief was aghast. "You can't write a story about unsolved murders."

Frank laughed. "Who says so?" He wanted to tell the chief what an idiot he was, but he bit his tongue to keep silent.

"Get out of my sight. I don't want you here." He turned his back on Frank, who left without another word. "The hell with him," he hissed to himself.

Lisa chased after him. "Please, Frank, don't leave. Stay with me." She held on to his arm, pulling him back toward her.

"Lisa, Chief Crawley is an asshole. When did he ever investigate a murder? You said yourself that there's never been a murder before in this area."

"It's just his pride talking. After all, he has to run for office and he needs to be seen to be effective."

"Well... I'll work with you only. Keep him away from me."

"Thank you, Frank." Lisa planted a kiss on Frank's lips. "You're the greatest. This means a lot to me."

"I'll call Joe Caputo, then I'm leaving for New York."

"You come back, you promise." She pleaded, voice sad, hand plucking at his sleeve.

"I will. I have to find out everything I can about the Swansens."

"You will call me, won't you?" Lisa sounded like a woman losing her mate.

"Take it easy. I'll be back."

8.

The doorman at Frank's apartment building was happy to see him. "Mr. Galitson, it's nice to see you. I'm delighted you're back. We've missed you."

"Thanks, Mac. Unfortunately, it's just for a short time."

"Is Ms. Rendel coming back too?"

Frank was shocked. "Are you telling me she isn't here?"

"That's right, sir. I know she left with you."

"She isn't with me. I assumed she'd returned to New York."

"No, sir, she hasn't been here since the two of you left."

Frank wanted to verify the doorman's comments. He took the elevator to the 17th floor, ringing the bell on Julia's door, calling her name several times. There was no answer. He climbed the stairs to his own apartment while his mind raced with thoughts about Julia's whereabouts. He couldn't figure out why she hadn't returned to New York.

Frank opened the windows to air out his apartment, then called Julia's father. Frank was stunned to hear that he had not heard from Julia since the two of them left. He had no idea where she could be. This was something new for him to worry about. Had she committed suicide? Crazy lovers often behave irrationally.

Lisa's face suddenly surfaced in Frank's mind. He felt a twinge in his heart. A feeling of missing her converged on him. He'd never had this kind of feeling before. He'd never missed anyone, not even his parents. Am I falling in love, he wondered out loud, then felt silly for even saying the words.

The reason for his coming to New York brought an end to his daydreaming. He looked up the Swansen name in the telephone directory. There were several; Julius Swansen, 32 Central Park West, Sheila Swansen, 1200 Broadway, and Paul Swansen, 225 East 86th Street.

Frank smiled. He was pleased to find that all of the Swansens lived in Manhattan. It would make his life easier. He planned to call on the twins first, but at that moment he remembered he hadn't spoken to Harry Simner since that horrible Sunday weeks ago. He dialed his office. Simner was surprised to hear from Frank. "Where the devil have you been? Mary told me you'd called and that you were drunk or something."

"It's a long story, Harry. I behaved like an idiot. I apologize to you and to Mary. I've been in Yellowstone, helping the park authorities in a triple murder case which I plan to use for my next book. It's going to be one of my best books ever."

"Are you going back to Yellowstone?"

"As soon as I finish my investigation in New York."

"Are these murders connected to someone in Manhattan?"

"Yes, the Swansen family."

"Julius Swansen, the guy who died in a plane crash?"

"You knew him?"

"Who didn't? He was a major industrialist, specializing in precision metal works, medical equipment, and technological components. His empire is now run by Joseph Weiserman, a well known engineer."

"How do you know all of this?"

"I read the financial papers."

"Where can I find this Mr. Weiserman?"

"Look up Swansen Metals Corporation. Their shares are traded on the New York Stock Exchange."

"Thanks, Harry. You won't hear from me for a while. I'll call you when I get back."

"Ok, Frank, good luck."

Frank still desperately wanted to find out why the New York Times had taken him off the bestseller list. They could have dropped him from first place to second or third. Why had they removed him completely? At the last moment he decided to talk to Harry about it next time he saw him face-to-face. Right now, the Swansen murders were his priority.

Frank looked at his watch. It was 6:30. The sun had set, opening up the sky to a bright full moon, along with a galaxy of stars, not usually visible in the night sky of the city. He stepped out to the large terrace overlooking Central Park. The lights on 72nd Street that crossed the park to the west side stood out in the vast darkness of the park. He loved this view.

He remained looking out for several moments, then left for dinner at his favorite restaurant, Club 57. He felt rejuvenated by being in his home town.

Frank slept late the following morning. Exhaustion from his long trip, the two hours difference in time, plus his excellent dinner had forced him to a crash landing. He thought of calling Mr. Weiserman for an appointment but decided to make a cold call instead. He thought his name might get him an interview. It felt good to be back driving his repaired Mercedes, having abandoned it for so long.

"I'm sorry, sir, but Mr. Weiserman is tied up in meetings. You must make an appointment." The secretary was insistent, her face stern and unsympathetic.

"I've just arrived from Wyoming. Several members of the Swansen family have been murdered. I doubt the news has reached him. I must see him immediately."

The woman was shocked, staring at Frank quizzically before saying loudly, "Who are you, anyway? What kind of a cockamamie excuse is this to obtain an interview with Mr. Weiserman? Are you a newspaper man?"

"Lady, this is not a cockamamie story. Paul and Sheila Swansen were killed several days ago, in Wyoming. The locals have no idea who the Swansens are. I'm a mystery writer who happened to be in Yellowstone and was asked by the authorities to help. Now, get your behind off your comfortable chair and tell Mr. Weiserman the author, Frank Galitson, wants to see him immediately in conjunction with these murders."

"You're Frank Galitson? I read The Mystery of Xonda... I loved it." A huge smile showed on her face. Her demeanor changed completely at the mention of his name.

Frank had no patience for chit chat. "Tell Mr. Weiserman that I'm here. I don't have much time. I think he'd rather talk to me than the police or the FBI."

She hurried off, returning only a few moments later. "Follow me, please."

Daniel Rosenfeld/Laura Weldon

Frank was shown into a large conference room. A man he assumed to be Mr. Weiserman sat at the head of a huge table. Three men sat with him, all examining a bundle of papers. He stared at Frank, speaking angrily. "You've got a hell of a nerve coming in here with such a story."

Frank didn't let him finish. "Get rid of your help. We have some serious matters to discuss. I haven't come here to share a fantasy with you. The fact is both Paul and Sheila Swansen are dead." Frank spoke authoritatively, careful not to use the word murder in front of Weiserman's staff.

Weiserman stared at Frank's somber face, then curtly dismissed his aides. "Sit down. What's your name?"

Frank explained who he was and how and why he had become involved in the investigation. "Feel free to call Police Chief Richard Crawley in Jackson Hole if you want to verify my statement." He handed over Crawley's card.

Weiserman hesitated, then picked up the phone and dialed. He spoke briefly, receiving the confirmation he sought. "My God, this is horrible news. Who would want to kill them?" He looked at Frank, shocked, and saddened.

Frank wasted no time on sentiment. "Tell me what you know about Margaret Ann and Elizabeth Ann Swansen, and Sandra Chandler Swansen. Margaret and Elizabeth are twins aren't they?"

"Yes. They're the youngest children. Julius and Adela had five children, one right after the other. They both loved children. They would have had more if Adela hadn't developed ovarian cancer. She had to have a complete hysterectomy."

"How long have you known the Swansens?"

"I went to college with Julius. We graduated from MIT. We were very close."

"How did Julius get into this business?"

"His father left him a small precision tool manufacturing company and he built it up."

"When did you join the company?"

"At the very beginning."

"Did you know Julius' parents?"

"Sure. I spent several summers on their estate as Julius' guest."

"Were any of Julius' children involved in the business?"

"Not one. They went their own way except for the twins, who chose to stay home and enjoy life."

"I take it they receive an allowance."

"The estate provides them with a substantial sum every year."

"Do the others also receive an allowance?"

"Yes, they all do."

"Who are the executors of the estate?"

"The twins."

"Why not the older brother or sister?"

"I don't know. That was how Julius planned it."

"What happens when the estate is settled?"

"As far as I know all the assets are to be divided between the five children."

Frank frowned. "That means the fewer the heirs the greater the piece of the pie."

"I suppose so."

"Did Julius bequeath anything to you?"

"Not a penny." Anger slipped out, to be quickly chased away.

"You must get a decent salary and bonuses. I understand the company is doing very well." Frank knew nothing about the company but decided to do a little fishing.

A look of complacency replaced the anger on the face of the man across from him. "I can't complain, but I deserve every penny I earn. If not for me this company would have died a long time ago." He preened a little, too lost in his own self-importance to resent the questions. Frank was incredulous at what he'd been able to get away with so far.

"Why? Wasn't Julius in charge?"

"Only on paper. He spent more time hunting, fishing, and playing golf than he did working here. He wanted to be known as a man's man."

Frank changed the subject. He didn't want Weiserman to feel he was being pressured. "How well do you know the twins?"

He leaned back to give the impression he didn't much care about the answers to his next set of questions.

"I know them, of course, but I rarely see them. They lead very active lives."

"Do you know if they left New York for any reason these past two weeks?"

"No idea. Why don't you ask them?"

Frank plowed on ahead. "Let's talk about Paul and Sheila. Are they married or single?"

"Both are single."

"When did Sandra get married?"

"Soon after her parents died."

"What do you know about Eric Chandler?"

"Not a thing. I wasn't even invited to the wedding."

"Now that these three are dead, what will happen to their allowances?"

"Nothing. It just means more money in the estate." Frank thought that would be the case but he wanted to be sure.

"If these crimes turn out to be interstate crimes, I'm sure you'll be contacted by the FBI. I'm going back to Wyoming in a few days. Should anything come to mind that you think could help the investigation, please call me. I'd like to help." He shook the man's hand and left before he had to answer some questions himself.

Frank left feeling somewhat bewildered. He wondered why the man hadn't asked how the victims died or where. He hadn't even inquired about memorial services.

Before pressing on, Frank called his broker at Smith Barney, asking for a complete dossier on Julius Swansen's group of companies. He wanted to develop a clearer picture of the estate to which the twins were now the only beneficiaries.

Frank's next stop was at 32 Central Park West, an old, ornate building whose brick exterior had recently been sand blasted. The façade was immaculate. A jacketed doorman stood at attention behind a set of plate glass doors. He was denied admission to the building without an appointment. Frank was surprised by the strict procedures. Even his well known name was of no avail. The doorman was unimpressed. He explained that every day the tenants provided him with the names of expected guests – no one else was to be admitted.

Frank called the twins from a nearby phone booth. No one answered. There was not even an answering machine. He walked to 1200 Broadway, several blocks away, to a thirty story all brick apartment building standing on the east side of the street. It was a plain featured building with no terraces. The main entrance was located in the center of the facade with several stores occupying the ground floor on both sides. He saw an old fashioned deli with fresh meat hanging on hooks in the window and a small, grimy windowed dry cleaning establishment.

Sheila Swansen occupied apartment 265 on the 26th floor. With a ten dollar tip as inducement the concierge informed Frank that Sheila had left on a trip about ten days ago and hadn't returned.

"I have some bad news about Ms. Swansen. She was killed last week in Yellowstone National Park. I'm part of the investigative team."

The concierge wore a look of shock. He immediately assumed Frank to be a police detective. "You'll want to check her apartment."

Frank wasted no time. "That's why I'm here."

The concierge led the way toward the bank of elevators at the rear of the lobby. The carpeting was clean but worn, wall tiles chipped in some spots. Using an internal phone the concierge called the building superintendent. He was an older man, thin and scruffy looking, who let Frank into Sheila's apartment without a question. He seemed to be more interested in how she had been killed than anything else. Frank gently maneuvered him to the door, closing it behind him. Frank made sure there was no one else in the apartment before beginning a methodical search.

It was clear from the start that Sheila Swansen had lived alone in the two bedroom apartment. Frank thought that her taste in decor was sort of childish, lots of pink lacy pillows and stuffed animals. Things in the apartment were like the lobby, clean but worn and out-dated. Apart from a bundle of letters neatly held together by a rubber band, and a single folder holding several sheets of paper, there was nothing of any significance. Most of the letters were dated years earlier, written by a Nicholas Vohn, a former high school friend if the content was to be believed.

The folder contained notes concerning her allowance, financial information about the value of the estate, and an ornately engraved heavy parchment invitation to a family reunion. Frank examined this with great interest. The date of the supposed reunion was four days prior to his initial arrival in Yellowstone. The invitation hadn't been signed. Family members were asked to meet in room 202 at The Old Faithful Inn. He pocketed the card. Before leaving the apartment he called Joe Caputo, who informed Frank that the New York police couldn't get involved in a Wyoming murder case even if a New Yorker had been the victim. However, he did say he would help Frank unofficially, if he could. Frank tried the number for the twins once more. This time he was successful. A pleasant voice informed him he had reached the home of the Swansens. Frank identified himself to the woman.

"I'd like to talk to you about your brother and sisters who've gone missing."

"Missing? They're not missing. Who is this? Why are you calling me to make such a statement? I don't have time for this."

"As I said, my name is Frank Galitson. You may know me as the author of several mystery novels...."

"You're Frank Galitson? I've read several of your books. Why do you say they're missing?"

"Is this Margaret or Elizabeth?"

"I'm Elizabeth. Are you serious or is this a new approach to ask me out for a date?"

"Elizabeth, I'm dead serious but I don't want to discuss this over the phone. I'd like to talk to you face-to-face. Can I come up to see you now?"

"Sure, why not."

"I'll be there in half an hour." Frank hung up before she could say another word. He didn't want to waste a second. He power walked back to their building, shouldering several people out of his way in his hurry.

This time the doorman and the concierge greeted Frank as if he were royalty. They apologized for their earlier encounter, explaining that the tough security measures had been imposed by the board of the cooperative association for the building. Frank shrugged off their apologies. He wasted no time with them, having no empathy or liking for what he thought of as help.

Elizabeth was waiting by the door when Frank exited the elevator. She shook Frank's hand warmly, inviting him into their apartment. Margaret sat comfortably on a plush velour sofa reading a Vogue magazine. The two of them were dressed identically in dark skirts and white blouses, flat leather slippers on long narrow feet. Blonde hair was pulled back severely into a tight chignon. After introductions, Frank sat next to Margaret while Elizabeth pulled up a chintz covered chair to sit across from them.

Frank drove straight to the point. "I understand you've been to a family reunion in Yellowstone recently." He paused for some reaction from the pair.

The twins, whose looks mirrored each other, stared at him in complete disbelief. "Mr. Galitson, we've never been to Yellowstone in our lives. Where would you get such a notion?" Both spoke at the same time, sounding like a two woman chorus.

Frank examined their faces carefully. He couldn't find a reason not to believe them. "Are you aware that Sheila, Sandra and Paul went to Yellowstone to attend a family reunion?"

"That is totally crazy. We weren't invited to any such thing and we already told you we've never been to Yellowstone. How do you know all this?"

Frank removed the invitation from his pocket, passing it to the women. They read it several times, then looked at each other, their faces questioning. Elizabeth spoke first. "Mr. Galitson."

"Call me Frank."

After a brief hesitation, she said, "Frank, let us assure you that we never received such an invitation, and that we haven't been to Yellowstone, not ever."

Frank tried to find signs pointing to a lie but could find none. The twins spoke sincerely, and their statements confirmed the report he'd received from Joe Caputo. "I have bad news for you. Forgive me for being so blunt. Your sisters, Sheila and Sandra and your brother Paul have all been murdered."

"What?" Both screamed at the same time. "Murdered? How?" Margaret fell back into the sofa cushions. She fainted. Elizabeth took one look, then ran to the kitchen to fetch water. She sprinkled a few drops on Margaret's forehead and wrists, while tears trickled down her cheeks.

After Margaret was revived, Frank went on. "I can't give you all the details. That's up to the police. I was dragged into the investigation by an inexperienced forest ranger. Since I'm a mystery writer, the events of these murders intrigued me."

"Why would anyone want to kill our brother and sisters? We've harmed no one. We all lead very quiet lives." Elizabeth stopped abruptly, then corrected herself, "Led quiet lives." The two women took a moment to mop their eyes and discretely blow their noses before clasping each other's hand and facing Frank once more. He was in a fever of impatience but for the first time ever he took someone else's feelings into consideration.

"You're trustees to your parents trust, aren't you?"

"Yes, we are, but what has that to do with anything?"

"Did you issue a check in the amount of $10,000 to a marina outside Yellowstone?"

Again, the twins looked at each other in amazement. "Mr. Galitson… Frank, we have not issued any such check. Why would we?" Elizabeth ran out, returning moments later with a large commercial checkbook which she opened. "Here, look for yourself."

Frank hesitated for only a moment, then leafed through the ledger section of the checkbook. Few checks had been written in the past several months, and certainly none to a marina or anywhere else in Yellowstone. Furthermore, there wasn't a single check even close to the amount of $10,000.

He remained silent for a while, the twins staring at him in dismay. Suddenly he rose, taking an envelope from his pocket from which he withdrew the copy of the check he'd been given by the marina manager. The copy was identical to the checks in the book. It was numbered 5261. He checked the book again. There was no entry for that check.

Frank stared at the bewildered twins, his eyes hooded. These two women may be the best actresses I've ever seen. Before he could say a word, Elizabeth burst out. "There's an odd look on your face. What is it you're holding back?"

"Is this your signature?" He handed the copy of the check to Margaret. She looked at it, completely puzzled, then handed it over to Elizabeth. "I can assure you we've never written such a check."

"This check is missing from your book. I suggest you stop this charade and tell me the truth. The police and the FBI won't be as gentle with you."

"What truth? We haven't done anything. We've never issued such a check, we've never been to Yellowstone, and we certainly didn't kill anyone. Are you accusing us of lying?" Elizabeth's voice rose almost an octave in her indignation.

"Are the signatures on this check yours?"

They looked at the copy again, then at each other in amazement. Margaret's voice was shaky. "These are our signatures, but we've never seen this check before and I can assure you neither of us issued it."

"Have either of you lost your handbag recently?"

Again, the twins looked at each other, obviously not comprehending the question. "Handbag? What does a handbag have to do with anything? Mr. Galitson, you'd better leave. You came here with some ridiculous story and we have no idea what you're driving at. Please go."

Frank didn't move. "Your drivers' licenses were found in your bags. Here are the copies."

The twins looked at the copies, then at each other. Margaret leaped up from the sofa, running out of the living room. She returned several moments later, throwing two driver licenses into his lap. She didn't say a word. Her face was flushed with anger and she was breathing heavily. Her chignon was starting to unravel from its pins.

Frank looked at the licenses – authentic New York licenses. He frowned, wondering what to say or do next. His entire visit with the twins had either been a well rehearsed farce, or was the complete truth. He looked at the twins, playing his last card. "The marina manager identified you from pictures. He told us you rented a boat for a day… then returned to tell him the boat had sunk as result of an accident. You gave him a check for $10,000 to compensate for the boat."

"Get out… you're crazy… out… out… and don't ever come back." Elizabeth was screaming, pointing to the door, spittle at the corners of her mouth.

Frank got up. "If you've told the truth, then I believe your lives to be in danger. If you've lied, you'll be arrested for multiple murders." He walked out, slamming the door behind him. He heard a muffled thud, the result of a slipper being thrown at his retreating back.

Frank crossed the street to enter Central Park. The famed restaurant, Tavern on the Green, was located immediately to his left. The weather was pleasant so he sat at a table in the outdoor garden where he ordered a glass of Merlot. There were birds singing, and a hum of voices from park visitors, but Frank heard nothing. The sun shone on his face but he didn't notice it, didn't put his sunglasses on. The wait staff left him alone.

Frank remained in the restaurant for a long time, sipping slowly. He drank two more glasses, not noticing the passage of time. He couldn't stop his racing mind. He'd written several mysteries. He'd spent hours with friendly detectives discussing all kinds of crimes, criminal behavior and patterns leading to murder, but this one puzzled him more than anything else he had in the past. He stared at his cell phone for a moment before keying in the familiar number for Joe Caputo.

Joe arrived half an hour later. Frank told him about his meetings with Weiserman and the Swansen twins. Joe listened attentively, then said, "We can check passenger lists of airlines flying to Jackson Hole from New York."

Frank nodded but added more complexity to the situation. He was running his hands over his face like a dry shave. "They may have flown in a private jet or chartered a plane. If that's the case, no one would have checked their identities. They could have easily driven to an out-of-state airport."

Joe sipped at his beer, mulling over Frank's comments. He snapped his fingers, a decision made. "I can easily check all airports in the area and nearby states, but I'll need the right authorization."

Frank paused to think about the evidence against the twins, then continued. "I have a feeling a request for extradition may be on its way. Of course, that may take several days, as the paperwork has to be produced by the Attorney General's office in Wyoming. "

Joe's mind was on another track altogether. "They may have left before dawn and returned late at night."

Frank laughed. "That's out of the question. There were three murders, each taking place on a different day."

"I'll grill the doorman again."

"I wonder if the New York police have been contacted by the Jackson sheriff."

"Not that I know of."

"Something is bothering me but I can't put my finger on it. Something I've seen... someone I've seen...I wish it would ring a bell. Meanwhile, could you arrange for someone to keep an eye on the twins? Either they're a pair of sophisticated killers or they are the next victims."

"Unless we receive a formal request from the Jackson police my chief will kick me out of his office before I even enter."

"I'll arrange the call." The two men finished their drinks and vacated the patio. Their places were immediately taken by impatient tourists.

Frank called Lisa, explaining his findings. Lisa was impatient for him to finish. "Don't let them out of your sight. Every bit of evidence points to them. While you were gone we checked all the hotels in the area. The Swansen twins stayed two nights at a Lake cabin. They rented a car from Avis at the Jackson airport. A jury will easily convict them. Don't let them fool you." She was breathless with anxiety lest her first big case go amiss.

Frank thought about Lisa's comments. She was right. They had the handbags, the driver licenses, the registration at a local hotel, the car rental record, their identification by the marina manager, check, and above all, motive – all of Julius Swansen's wealth for themselves. "Ok... you're right. Have Chief Crawley call the New York police for action."

"Will do, Frank. Chief Crawley already notified the Attorney General's office. Frank, I miss you terribly. When are you coming back?"

"In a few days. I'm not finished here yet."

"I love you, Frank."

"I love you too." Frank hung up in complete consternation. What was this sudden declaration of love? He couldn't believe such words would have come from his mouth. He knew his feelings for Lisa were entirely new to him. The words had just slipped out. Was he really in love? How would he know? His palms were slick with a sudden rush of perspiration and his throat felt tight.

Frank went to 225 East 86th Street to check on Paul Swansen's apartment. The doorman, who was also acting as the concierge, was a pleasant young man in his early thirties. "I haven't seen Mr. Swansen since last week, but Mrs. Swansen is in their apartment." He adjusted the cuff on his tunic and rubbed his right foot against his left pant leg to remove a speck of city dust.

"Does she seem alright?"

"Oh yes. She told me her husband had gone out of town to a family meeting. She expects him back soon. I know she misses him because she's down here to chat with me several times a day."

"Is she home now?"

"Yes. Would you like me to call her?"

"No. I have some bad news I have to give her. Her husband has been found dead in Wyoming. I want to talk to her face-to-face."

The doorman was shocked. "He was such a nice man..."

Frank didn't let him finish. "What apartment?"

"805," he responded sadly, still in shock.

Frank took the elevator to the eighth floor. He knocked gently on the door. It was opened almost immediately by a woman in her late thirties, wearing a morning robe. She was obviously surprised to see Frank. "I thought you were the handyman. You must have the wrong apartment."

"Mrs. Swansen, I've come to see you. I have news from your husband."

"He hasn't called me since he left last week. Is he alright? Has there been an accident?" She held on to the door handle with a white knuckled ferocity.

"May I come in?"

"Of course, please." She signaled Frank to take a seat on a nearby loveseat covered with a loose, denim weave throw. Mrs. Swansen stared at Frank's somber face for several moments, then spoke quietly. "Something must be wrong. Why hasn't Paul called me? Who are you? What news?"

"Mrs. Swansen, please sit down." He indicated a nearby chair into which she sank with a huge sigh. She sensed that something was terribly wrong. She was trembling, her eyes welling up with tears. "Is Paul ill? Was he in an accident?" She was so distraught she was repeating herself.

"I hate to be the bearer of bad news, but I was asked to help. I've become entangled in an investigation. I deeply regret to tell you that your husband drowned in Lake Jackson. There's reason to believe he was murdered."

Mrs. Swansen leaped up, knocking her chair over backward. "How dare you say such a thing? Paul hated the water."

"I'm sorry, but you must know your husband's fate." He watched her carefully. She was shaking and sobbing, hands tearing at the tie on her robe. She finally sat down in the chair Frank had set upright, tissues pressed to her face to stem the tide of tears.

"Why did your husband go to Wyoming?"

"He received an invitation, then a telephone call from one of his sisters about attending an urgent family meeting."

"Was it Sandra who called?"

"No. He said it was Elizabeth."

"What was the meeting about?"

"Something to do with fraud. He said Elizabeth couldn't elaborate over the phone." She sipped at a cold cup of coffee, her hands rocking the cup in its saucer.

"Why didn't you go with him?"

"He didn't want me to join him. He said the meeting might turn ugly."

"Do you see Elizabeth and Margaret often?"

"Only two three times a year, usually around the holidays."

"Why were they appointed trustees to the family trust when Paul was older and probably more experienced?"

She shook her head at the question. It obviously raised some strong feelings from the past. "Paul and his father weren't on good terms. Julius was very disappointed that Paul chose another profession. He had always planned for Paul to take over the business but Paul had no interest in it."

Frank thought for a moment about the whole situation. "I suggest you stay away from Elizabeth and Margaret for the time being. I suspect they'll be arrested soon."

Shock overtook her again. "Arrested for what?"

"It seems they have been involved in some kind of fraud." Frank didn't want to tell her the truth, to leave her fearing for her life. "Please do as I ask. Don't get involved. It's for your own good."

Frank left her sitting on the sofa, staring at the wall, face blank. He waved to the doorman as he left the building, then retrieved his car and drove to Hamilton, New Jersey.

Eric and Sandra Chandler lived in a single family home in Hamilton, a village better known as a New York bedroom community. The house was small but well kept, vinyl siding almost new. Frank knocked, hoping someone was home and that his trip would not be wasted. He waited several minutes and was ready to leave when the door suddenly opened. A silver haired woman in her late 70's, leaning heavily on a walker, looked at him with an apprehensive look on her face. She stuttered, "I thought it was my grandson. Who are you? What do you want? I can't stand long so you'll have to speak quickly."

"I came here to see Eric and Sandra. May I come in?"

"They're not home."

"I know. They're in Wyoming. Both of them are sick." It appeared that the woman had probably suffered a previous stroke. He didn't want to alarm her any further. "I'd like to talk to you. May I come in?"

"My helper isn't here yet. Come back in an hour." Slowly the door swung shut but Frank didn't stop her. He was afraid she might fall over and he didn't want to have any responsibility for that.

He strolled along, enjoying the shade from huge oak trees planted on both sides. They formed a leafy umbrella over the street. Every home had a perfectly manicured lawn, trimmed hedges and masses of seasonal flowers. What a difference between Manhattan with all its hassle and noise and this suburban village where life was gentle and calm. He soon came to a main street with small, well decorated and maintained shops. A sidewalk café was open for business. He sat at a small wrought iron bistro table and ordered a latte along with a chocolate croissant. He didn't often take time to relax and treat himself to some people watching.

As much as the situation seemed serene Frank's mind was hard at work, puzzling over the Swansen case. Even though every scrap of evidence pointed toward the twins, his encounter with them had left doubts he couldn't explain away. The doorman swore he'd seen them every day, sometimes more than once. How could this be? Had they paid him off?

He walked back to the Chandler residence. This time the door was opened by a young woman wearing a white nurse's uniform, something not seen in most modern hospitals. She showed him in immediately. The old woman was comfortably ensconced in an old armchair, walker beside her. "Please sit down." She greeted Frank with pleasure as she had few visitors. "You said Eric and Sandra are sick?"

Frank sat down across from her, unsure of his opening lines. He didn't want to shock her as she seemed quite fragile. "You may wonder why I'm here," he began slowly. "My name is Frank Galitson. I'm an author. I've been traveling in Yellowstone and I came across several members of the Swansen family. Did Eric and Sandra go to Wyoming for a family reunion?"

The old lady was sharper than Frank expected. "What does the Swansen family reunion have to do with you? Why are you really here? Are you related to the family? Eric knows how to reach me if he needs to."

Frank was boxed in. He knew eventually he'd have to tell her the truth. Why not now rather than later? He realized he was dealing with a shrewd woman. "Well… I didn't want to shock you… seeing that you were disabled… but if you insist, I'll get straight to the point. Eric and Sandra were murdered in Yellowstone several days ago. They were both shot. The killer or killers are still at large."

The old woman didn't bat an eyelash. She was completely expressionless. "Why would anyone want them dead?" She spoke as if she didn't believe him, but her tone was neutral rather than accusatory.

Frank, who had expected an outburst of grief or doubt was completely surprised by her unruffled attitude. After several moments of silence he said, "Are you Eric's mother?"

"Yes. This is my home. I've lived here since I got married over fifty years ago." Her eyes scanned the room, noting pictures and other pieces of art she could probably identify in the dark.

"Do you have any idea why Eric and Sandra might have been killed? Had they been threatened in any way?"

"I don't want to talk about it."

"Mrs. Chandler, you must talk about it. I'm sure the police, and possibly the FBI, will want to question you too. They won't be so nice to deal with. Please, tell me what you know."

She stared sideways as if to avoid Frank's eyes. Suddenly, she turned to him, speaking brusquely. "I don't see what any of this has to do with you. Good day, Mr. Galitson."

Frank didn't move. "Mrs. Chandler, maybe this has nothing to do with me, but I'm the only one who can help you and your family. You may not realize it, but when you do, it'll be too late."

She looked down her nose at him. "What do you mean too late?"

"I didn't tell you everything on account of your condition. I didn't want to shock you, seeing you are so fragile."

"Nothing shocks me," she spoke defiantly. "Go on." Her tone was that of an army officer ordering his troops.

"Sandra's sister Sheila and her brother Paul have also been killed. Obviously, someone is after members of the Swansen family."

She took in a deep breath, then hissed at him. "The twins. They are a nasty pair of people."

"Why do you say that? What do you base that on?"

"They're the ones who called for the reunion. They are still alive, aren't they?"

"They are, but according to my investigation they haven't left New York in the past two weeks." Frank decided to make the statement, despite his own doubts.

"The twins had a huge argument with Eric over the phone one night. Eric didn't want to leave me alone. My helper is here only four hours a day. He did not want to go to their reunion."

"It looks like they won the argument. What do you think made Eric change his mind?"

"They told him they would cut Sandra off from her trust allowance and prevent her from receiving anything from the final distribution of Julius' estate."

"Was the estate or trust discussed at any other time?"

"Yes. The twins were here soon after Eric and Sandra returned from their honeymoon. The argument then was whether to sell all of the shares in the Metal Company. The twins wanted to get rid of them, but Sandra refused. She said Mr. Weiserman was doing an excellent job, dividends were higher than market average, the company was growing by more than 5% a year and that meant greater value for them on the stock exchange."

"Did the twins say how the others felt about the sale?"

"They didn't, but Sandra called the others to find out they were of the same opinion as her."

The smile that showed itself on Frank's face quickly vanished. He knew that a clear motive for the killings had been established. But, the twin's stalwart denial that they had never left New York kept a small door open to doubts he had seemingly put aside.

"How were relations between Eric and Sandra and her sisters and brother?"

"They spoke mostly by phone. They didn't see each other often, maybe once or twice a year at holiday time."

"Do you know if there were other arguments prior to the recent one about the sale of the company?"

"Not that I know of."

Frank made his escape after thanking her for her generous assistance. He needed to keep on her good side since he might need more information.

He returned home, relaxing on a chaise lounge on his terrace, seeing leafy green in Central Park. He closed his eyes, trying to still his mind. He needed to rethink the entire scenario. He let the mild sun caress his face. He fell asleep, completely relaxed in his own little garden oasis of peace and quiet.

Frank was dragged to wakefulness by the constant ringing of the phone. He's slept so soundly he had to struggle to get to it. It was the doorman, announcing that a Ms. Warrenton wanted to visit. Frank snapped out of his somnolence at the speed of a rocket. What the hell was she doing in New York? That was all he needed. He looked at his watch – it was 7:00 p.m. He had slept for hours.

Frank opened the door to let Lisa in. She leapt at him, planting a thorough moist kiss on his lips. "I've missed you so much, Frank. You look great." She took a look at the vastness of his living room, the huge terrace glimmering beyond. "Wow! I've never seen anything like this. Look at that sight!"

Frank stopped her half way to the terrace. "Lisa, why have you come to New York? I was planning to return to Yellowstone tomorrow."

"I'm carrying extradition papers. The Wyoming Attorney General wants them delivered personally to the Manhattan District Attorney."

"Lisa, did you fabricate a reason for this trip? Did you tell them you would take on this job? It's not normally a task for a Park Ranger."

"Well... in a way. I missed you terribly." She grabbed Frank again, hugging him close to her. "I love you, Frank. I only realized how much when you left." She was smiling at him, stroking his cheek with one hand while holding tight to his arm with the other.

Frank was completely confused. On one hand he wanted to completely reject her forwardness, yet, on the other, it was certainly making him feel good. Finally, he mustered a weak response. "Lisa, I have good feelings about you, but I must admit I'm confused. I've never been in love with anyone before. This is the first time such a sensation has even touched me. I can't see through it right now, but please, bear with me." He touched her hair gently, then ran a wondering finger down the bridge of her nose to come to rest on her silky smooth lips.

"Frank, that's wonderful. I'm willing to wait as long as it takes." She hugged him, nestling into him with her head on his chest.

He pushed her away but quite gently. "So much has happened here. I have all kinds of news, some of it perplexing."

She looked at him with great eagerness, eyes shining. "I'm hungry. Can we have dinner? Then we can talk all you want about the case." She covered his hands with her own, willing him to agree.

"Sure. I haven't eaten a thing since breakfast. What kind of food would you like?"

"Anything, Frank. I just want to be with you."

He took her to Chez Maurice, on Third Avenue, an immensely popular French restaurant. She seemed overwhelmed by Manhattan but made every effort not to look like a gawking tourist. The night was balmy so they chose a table on the sidewalk, in the midst of the street theatre that was midtown.

Lisa was talkative during dinner, telling Frank about her formative years in Minnesota, about her mother who had raised her. She described how she felt not having a father around, and her jealousy of her friends who had a father. Frank asked whether she had brothers or sisters. She responded shortly that she had one sister but refused to speak any further about her. Frank didn't press her on the issue, thinking how sometimes parents tend to favor one child over the other. There would be plenty of time to investigate this touchy issue later.

Frank listened to Lisa without any particular sense of interest as his mind was busy trying to sort out these new feelings. He wondered where Julia was and struggled to understand the intensity of the deep love she had proclaimed for him, since he had never experienced even an ordinary love for anyone. He had read about cases in which people in love had taken steps that looked like madness, when they had committed all types of serious crimes. Julia had killed Ms. Smith for his benefit. Had she planned that murder or had she taken action during a momentary insanity. What was the boundary between love and insanity?

Lisa noticed Frank's blank face, and glassy eyes. "Frank, are you listening to me?"

"Yes... yes... yes... I've heard everything you said." Lisa was so enthralled she could only giggle at his obvious lie. Frank forced his attention back to the table and his engaging dinner partner.

After dessert Frank spoke of his investigation in New York and New Jersey. "Evidence clearly points to the Swansen twins, but there's one big fly in the ointment. They absolutely deny ever having left New York and the doorman backs their story."

"They can be indicted on the strength of the current evidence, which is foolproof, according to our District Attorney."

"The twins were quite hostile toward me by the time I left their apartment. I'd like you to visit them so we can compare."

"We can go there after I've delivered my papers to the district attorney."

They sipped their expressos and chatted a little bit longer. Lisa's energy was starting to flag so Frank stopped one of the battalion of yellow cabs and had Lisa delivered to her hotel.

****

The following morning, after delivering the extradition papers, Lisa phoned the Swansen residence. She introduced herself, then taking Frank's advice, said she believed their story that they had never left New York, but she wanted to hear it directly from them. The twins agreed, albeit reluctantly.

The twins were obviously distressed when they saw Frank in partnership with Lisa. She quickly explained that she had asked Frank to help, given her inexperience. She used one of her special smiles and finally they were asked to enter. Frank let Lisa do all the talking and tried to efface himself in the corner, a difficult task for such an ego driven man.

"Frank told me you claim not to have left New York in the past several weeks. There must be witnesses who can confirm your presence in the city at the time of the murders."

Elizabeth was first to speak. "I've been so upset, I hadn't even thought about that. First, there's the doorman who sees us every day, then on the night in question we attended a literary gathering at P.J. Thomson's brownstone. She's an old friend. The following night we had dinner with Mr. Weiserman at his club, and the third night we entertained a New York assembly man, Hugh Disnick. He wanted us to help raise funds for his re-election campaign. As we have already told Mr. Galitson, we were never out of the city." She wrote down the names, addresses and phone numbers of their witnesses on a sheet of paper. "You're welcome to verify this."

Frank wondered why he hadn't thought about asking about other witnesses. He looked at Lisa, then at the twins. The three were of similar height and body build. Their hair was remarkably similar in color but not style. His thoughts were cut short by Lisa's next question. He gave himself a mental kick to get focused.

"Why were you interested in selling your father's company?"

The twins looked at each other briefly, trying to figure out what this had to do with the murders. Margaret made an overt signal to Elizabeth for her to respond. "The stock market is at a peak right now. It's the highest it's been since the beginning of the decade. We've seen continual slow increases. We would have received better than 30% above the stock price by selling the company. None of us is interested in working in the company.

We felt this would be an ideal time to unload so we could maximize our profits."

"I take it your sisters and brother rejected your idea. Was there a big argument?"

Elizabeth made a face of disapproval while Margaret sat placidly, content to have her sister make all the effort. "We did, but they were the majority."

"Did you call for a family reunion in Yellowstone?"

"Absolutely not since we had agreed to leave things as they were."

"Did you two change your minds?"

"We didn't change our minds and we didn't call for a reunion or any other meeting on the same subject. How can I make that any clearer? Are you listening at all?" Her tone was huffy and red spots were appearing on her cheeks.

"Did you call for a meeting on another subject?"

"No. No. No. Listen to me. We haven't seen any of them since that first meeting."

"Where was the first meeting?"

"In the company boardroom where they're always held."

Lisa looked at Frank as if to ask if there were any more questions. He spoke gently, not wanting to antagonize the twins any further. "How do you explain a hotel registration and a car rental in your names in Jackson Hole?"

The twins looked at each other briefly, some unspoken message flashing between the two. "We've stated several times that we haven't left the city. There are plenty of witnesses who've seen us here. We haven't the faintest clue why. Obviously, someone is trying to frame us."

Lisa jumped in. "Since you say that, do you know anyone who wants to harm the two of you?"

Again came the secret look. The air in the room felt electric. "We have no enemies that we know of." The twins stood. Obviously, the interview had run its course.

Frank and Lisa had no choice but to leave. They settled in a noisy coffee shop on Columbus Avenue to discuss the next steps, but Frank had something different on his mind. "I feel like I have plenty of material for my next novel, but the truth is I'd be stuck at this point in the story. The twins never left New York, yet they were in Wyoming. Can you figure this one out? I'm stumped." His shoulders sagged and he leaned back in his plastic chair like an elderly man.

Lisa put her hand over his. "You're not leaving me to do this on my own, are you? I'd be devastated." Lines formed on her forehead and Frank could feel anxiety pouring into him from the contact of her hand.

He gave her a tentative but heartfelt smile. "My dear Lisa, I'm not leaving you. It's the first time in my life that such an emotion has overtaken me. I'm not used to it. Even though I'm 28 years old, I find myself totally confused. I don't know what to do next."

"Oh, Frank, you do love me. That is so wonderful. Do you believe in love at first sight? Well... now I do. It happened to me when I first saw you. I've read about it in books but it always seemed to me to be an outlandish idea. Now I know better. Love at first sight does exist." She leaned over their coffee cups to kiss his lips while other customers avidly watched their own private soap opera.

"Lisa, if we do get together I don't think I'll be able to live in Wyoming. I'm a city boy."

She shook her head at him. "I'll go wherever. I want you to continue to write and be happy. I'll help you as much as I can. I don't care where we end up."

Frank felt he had said enough. He changed the subject. "Lisa, let's call the witnesses. We need to see all of them."

"Let's call from your apartment." She took his hand as they left the coffee shop, completely oblivious of the stares of the other patrons.

Walking back to his apartment Frank's mind was spinning, trying to compare Julia and Lisa. Each one was special in her own way. He came to the conclusion that in the two years he'd been with Julia, in reality it meant nothing to him. He felt no sense of unhappiness or loss away from her and over the past few days there were times when he'd forgotten her existence. Lisa was different. She had aroused his emotions. Her love for him seemed genuine. Frank's silence indicated to Lisa that his mind was working, either on his future book or the current case. Wisely, she remained silent, thinking her own happy thoughts.

She made appointments with all the witnesses, then said, "Frank, once the extradition papers have been served, the twins will be arrested. I have a feeling the witnesses will verify their presence in the city. This case is bound to be very complex."

"It certainly will be. I'm not a lawyer but even I can't predict the outcome. It's not like writing a novel when I'm in control of every situation."

9.

The following morning, over lattes and fresh cornmeal muffins, Frank said, "Lisa, since we have several days to wait for the appointments, I'm going to start on my novel."

She smiled at him in delight, never having been this close to a real author about to begin a piece of work. "Great. I'll do some sightseeing. I've never been to New York before. I've heard it's an incredible city."

Frank spent the day at his computer with only a short break for lunch. Lisa returned a little after five, collapsing on the sofa. "Wow, what a great city. I took a double decker bus. The weather cooperated so I was able to sit up top and ooh and aah just like a tourist. Then I took the Circle Line boat tour around Manhattan. I didn't realize that the East River and the Hudson were so enormous, and so dark. It made me wonder what lurked beneath the surface. I'm sure there are lots of stories for both rivers." She chattered on and on, over stimulated by all the sights, sounds and smells of her two trips. She shared with Frank how she got goose bumps when they passed the Statue of Liberty.

Frank ordered dinner for the two of them from a nearby Chinese restaurant. Lisa wasn't used to the concept of delivery boys on bicycles. They sat down to eat as soon as the meal arrived. Lisa turned on the television for the 6:30 news while Frank filled their glasses with a fine Merlot. "Well... here's to a great novel," Lisa toasted Frank, the two of them clicking Waterford glasses together, as the NBC newscaster said, "A terrible tragedy took place early today. New York's favorite Assemblyman, Hugh Desnick, was found dead this afternoon in a secluded men's room of the government building where he maintained his Manhattan office. It appears he was shot. Details are unavailable until police finish their investigation."

Lisa leapt from her seat. "What? That's awful. We needed to talk to him."

Frank couldn't believe what he just heard. "You just made an appointment with him this morning, for God's sake!" He took a long sip of wine. "What is the world coming to?"

"How awful for his family. Was he Republican or Democrat?"

That comment rated a curious glance. "Lisa, what difference does that make? A good man has been murdered. I'm sure all of New York will miss him. He's done a lot for us."

"I don't know anything about him. I'd never even heard of him before we made the appointment."

Frank remained silent for several moments. "I wonder if he was involved with the Swansen family in any way. I must say the killing of Assemblyman Desnick is perplexing. If the twins named him as part of their alibi, why would they kill him? It couldn't possibly have been them." He was perplexed, paying no attention to Lisa's own curiosity filled glance.

"Why connect his murder with the Swansens? He probably had enemies for reasons we know nothing about. I assume he's been in politics a long time."

"I don't know. It was a gut reaction."

They dismissed the topic, going on to discuss more of Lisa's perspective of the city. They talked so long that Lisa ended up spending the night, too tired even to grab a cab back to her hotel.

As Frank retired to his bed, a thought flashed through his mind. Could Lisa have killed Desnick? He dismissed the thought as quickly as it had come up. What would that have to do with Lisa? Would she benefit in any way from his death? Rubbish! He laughed at himself. Sheer stupidity. Finally, he fell asleep. Both of them had a little too much wine.

Lisa settled down in Frank's guest room. She had hoped Frank would ask her to sleep with him but that hadn't happened. His speech about his confusion came back to her. She realized she had to give him some time. She was still emotionally wound up, even though she was tired on a physical level. She turned on the television, leaning back against several pillows. She decided to watch something mindless, falling asleep in the middle of a night show.

The eleven o'clock news came on with the sounds of screaming police sirens. Lisa awoke in time to catch the announcer say, "A well known New York socialite, P.J. Thomson, known as a sponsor for young artists and authors, has been found dead in her brownstone. Her husband discovered the body and notified the police. It appears she'd been strangled."

Lisa jumped out of bed to run to Frank's bedroom. She shook him with vehemence. "Frank, P.J. Thomson has been murdered. I just heard it on the news."

Frank thought he was dreaming, deep in a nightmare. Lisa shook him again. "Frank, wake up, P.J. Thomson is dead." Her voice was loud and urgent but she couldn't make him understand.

"What? Who? What? Who's dead?"

"P.J. Thomson, another one of the Swansen twins' witnesses."

"Have you been dreaming too?"

"Frank, for God's sake, wake up."

Frank sat up in bed, staring at Lisa. A huge smile appeared on his face. He said nothing, simply pulling Lisa over so he could hug her warmly.

"Frank, you do love me. That makes me feel so good." She kissed him passionately. Frank didn't resist, but he didn't really respond. Lisa paid no attention to his lack of spontaneity, just went ahead to kiss and caress him. She felt confident she would make him care, given her success in the past with other men.

Finally, Frank spoke, "Did you say P.J. Thomson was dead?"

"Yes, darling. It's insane. First Desnick, now Thomson. I don't know what to make of it."

"I think we should go and see the twins before they're arrested."

"What good will that do?"

"I don't know, but obviously something is very wrong. In fact, if these murders are related, we should also warn Weiserman."

"Sounds right. Let's go to his office first thing tomorrow morning."

Frank tucked Lisa into bed right next to him, arms around her. She put her head on his chest. She was in heaven. This was where she had dreamed of being. Lisa finally fell asleep but Frank's mind continued to race with thoughts about the latest events. The killing of the witnesses made no sense, unless someone was trying hard to frame the twins. What could the motive be? He wondered what the twins had been doing in the afternoon and evening.

Despite all his efforts, sleep shunned him. He extricated himself from Lisa, who had entwined him with her arms and legs. He got up early, showered, dressed, then prepared breakfast. Lisa slept on soundly. He didn't want to wake her, so he left her a hurried note saying he'd gone on ahead to Weiserman's office.

Frank arrived at the Swansen Metal Company office building by eight. He had no idea what time Weiserman started his day. By nine o'clock most of the staff had arrived, but there was no sign of Weiserman. He checked with the secretary who said her boss should be arriving momentarily.

An hour passed -- no show. Frank paced the hallway next to the elevator. People came and went but still no sign of Weiserman. He tried the secretary again. She hadn't heard from him. Frank continued his nervous pacing. Suddenly, the secretary ran out. "Mr. Weiserman was in a car accident on the Bronx River Parkway. He's been taken to Lawrence Hospital in Bronxville."

Frank tried to say something, but she was gone. At that moment Lisa showed up. "What a mess. Weiserman's been taken to Lawrence Hospital. Let's go." They raced to the parking lot to retrieve Frank's car.

As they drove to Bronxville, Frank's mind was going in circles. "I don't pretend to understand any of this. Did we stir things up by trying to find proof that the twins hadn't left New York? If so, why would the twins kill the people who could alibi them? If someone else is doing the killing it points to a masterful plan to frame the twins. Who could that be? I'm so confused by this case, I can't even think straight."

Frank and Lisa became silent, each in a sphere of their own. It seemed there were no answers to the situation. They arrived at the hospital and rushed to the information desk. Against all hospital policy the assistant shared with them that Mr. Weiserman had died from his wounds several minutes before they got there.

Frank propelled Lisa away from the building. "We must get to the twins right away before they're arrested." Despite his desire to rush back to Manhattan, Frank maintained all speed limits. The thought of ending up in jail again reminded him of his recent stupid behavior.

Lisa finally spoke, voice as neutral as she could make it. "I think it's a waste of time."

"Why? We need to find out where they were and what they did yesterday and this morning." Frank kept his eyes on the road but Lisa saw his fingers tighten on the steering wheel.

Frank was really unaccustomed to being questioned. "Eliminating their witnesses is totally illogical." He thought about Lisa's comment, then about his own previous questionable analysis. "Think about it for a moment; by killing them, they can show that someone is out to frame them."

As Central Park West was on the western side of Manhattan, Frank decided to drive south on the Henry Hudson Parkway. A collision between a truck and an airport van at the end of the ramp to the Washington Bridge had caused a pileup, completely blocking traffic going south. Frank looked but there was no way to leave the parkway, short of jumping into the Hudson. It took the police and an ambulance over two hours to get to the scene of the accident because the streets were so congested with stalled traffic. There was a cacophony of horns from frustrated motorists.

They did not reach the apartment building where the twins lived until well after 1:00 p.m. Two police cars were double parked in front of the entrance. The twins, handcuffed, loudly protesting their arrest, shouting and struggling, were being shoved into one of the cars. A moment later, sirens blaring, the police cars drove away. Frank exploded. "Damn it, we're too late. I must call Joe Caputo. Let's go back home."

Before leaving, however, Frank parked where the police cars had been. He signaled to the doorman to come over. "Did the Swansen sisters leave the building this morning?"

The doorman hesitated, then recognized Frank from his prior visits. "One of them left around seven and returned at ten."

"Was she carrying anything?"

"Yes, a large carry-on... you know, the type with a long shoulder strap."

"Had you seen that carry-on before?"

"I don't think so."

"Which of the two left?"

The doorman smiled. "Sorry, as many times as I've seen them, I still can't tell one from the other."

Frank nodded. "I know what you mean. Thanks for your help." A folded bill passed into the waiting hand of the doorman.

"My God," Lisa blurted out, "do you think one of them killed Weiserman?"

"Somehow we have to get in and search their apartment."

"I'm sure the police will do that."

"I know that but I want to see for myself. I'm sure Joe can help."

Frank changed the TV channel to the local news station. It didn't take long before the news anchor reported that Weiserman had been shot, causing him to lose control of his car and collide with two others in the left lane before overturning. The car behind Weiserman was too close to maneuver, smashing into the overturned car. The pictures on the screen were horrendous.

"I'm absolutely convinced that the murder of the three witnesses is connected to the Swansen estate, but I can't figure out who's responsible. All the evidence points to the Swansen twins, but this last killing throws a wrench into my thinking. It doesn't seem to fit the picture."

Frank spoke at length to Joe Caputo, but there was little he could do to help. The Swansen case was in the hands of the Lower Manhattan precinct headquarters located next to the courthouse. The twins would be placed in a basement cell. The Wyoming extradition request would be brought to court the following morning. A prosecutor from the State of Wyoming

Attorney General's office would have to make their case, but the Manhattan issues would likely take precedence.

Frank became impatient. "Let's go to the courthouse. I have to talk to the twins."

"I'm going to stay here, if you don't mind. I'm tired and I want some quiet time to analyze the entire situation."

"Ok... I'll see you later." He planted a kiss on her forehead, then left.

Frank took a taxi downtown. Driving at this time of day would be a nightmare. As expected, his request to see the twins was denied. He was told they were with their lawyer, the only one who would be permitted to see them until their case was heard by the court.

The extradition petition was set for the coming Friday to give the Wyoming prosecutor time to travel.

Frank and Lisa sat in the section reserved for spectators. The room was small, wood paneled and cold, the floor underneath a much abused carpet of indeterminate color. Once the case began, the prosecutor presented his evidence, including the handbags, drivers' licenses, hotel and car rental registrations, the marina boat rental, and the check for $10,000. He went on to state that the twins, trustees of the Julius and Adela Trust, had killed their sisters and brother to gain complete control over the assets of the trust. He also added that the twins had presented a plan to their brother and sisters to sell the Swansen company, but they had been turned down. He concluded, "Your Honor, this is a clear case of murder for financial gain. I request the court's approval of my petition to extradite these two to Wyoming." He seemed quite sure of himself, presenting a façade of self control that secretly he was not feeling.

The defense attorney, John Cavanti, talked at length about the twins being in New York at the time of the murders. He produced the doorman as witness, but he became completely confused during cross-examination. The judge had to warn him against perjuring himself. He couldn't remember if he'd seen the twins together, alone, whether it was morning or evening. What about change of shift? He became totally lost. Sweat was visible under his arms. It was all the defense attorney could do to keep from shouting at his witness. Frank whispered to Lisa, "The defense attorney hasn't mentioned the witnesses who were killed. It seems the twins and their attorney know nothing about it."

The judge didn't have to think too much. In a matter of mere minutes he started to describe the case, and was leading up to his judgment when Frank leapt from his seat, pushed open the small gate between the spectator section and the court, and said, "Your Honor, I have evidence about this case that hasn't been addressed. It is crucial for this case."

The judge, incensed, ordered the officers of the court to remove Frank from the room, shouting, "If you don't leave quietly, I'll have you arrested."

Frank struggled between two armed men, speaking loudly and addressing himself only to the judge. "Your Honor, I was in Yellowstone when the murders took place. The ranger who conducted the investigation is right here in this court. Please, let me talk to you and the defense attorney before you pass judgment."

"Who are you? What's your name?"

"Frank Galitson. I'm the author of several novels. I can tell you more about this case than these two lawyers together."

A smile appeared on the weathered face of the judge. "Oh, I've read a couple of your books. What do you know about this case that's so important?"

The prosecutor from Wyoming objected to such unusual procedures, but the judge shut him up. Frank explained about his visits with the twins and gave him the names of the witnesses they had produced. "Your Honor, the Swansen twins met with these witnesses during the two days of the murders. I had appointments with them to verify their statements, but they have all been murdered. Someone killed these witnesses in order to frame the twins. There's something critically wrong with this case."

The defense attorney surged to his feet, white with rage. "Your Honor, all of this is news to me. If it's true, I demand a thorough police investigation before you rule on the extradition petition."

100

The judge ordered the prosecutor, who had jumped out of his seat, to remain silent. "This case will adjourn until tomorrow at ten." He summoned the bailiff, "Get the police commissioner on the line." He retreated to his chambers, leaving a courtroom filled with stunned participants.

Frank returned to Lisa, who was dumbfounded by Frank's outburst. "Why did you interfere with the proceedings? We..." Lisa stopped, correcting herself, "I prefer that they'd be brought to court in Wyoming."

Frank was taken aback. "Look, I know how you feel about this case, but justice must take precedence over everything else. There's something extremely bizarre about these murders. If you had witnesses, you'd want them to testify in your behalf, wouldn't you? Why would you kill them? I'm convinced there's a third party involved."

Lisa didn't respond. She was trying hard to hide her resentment. Frank couldn't figure her out. He dismissed her response as egotistical, not realizing how like his own response this was. "Let's go to the Swansen Metal offices. I'm curious about who will replace Weiserman."

Weiserman's secretary was surrounded by reporters, photographers, and two TV men, all asking questions at once. "There's nothing new to tell you. Go away. I'm very busy." She was yelling at them but no one was listening. No one moved, several men were loudly demanding answers to their questions, while others were jostling her for the best picture.

Frank, trying to help move the media away from her, shouted at the top of his lungs, "Ladies and gentlemen, I have news from the courtroom." The crowd turned as one. "Who are you? Do you work for the company? Are you Weiserman's replacement? What's your name? Who shot him? Did the police find the assassin?" Questions were being thrown at him from every side.

Frank didn't respond to any of the questions. He said to the group as a whole, "If you want news, go to court tomorrow at ten. Leave the secretary alone. She knows nothing."

"Who are you?"

"It doesn't matter. Get out. You'll get nothing here."

They all looked at each other, then one asked, "What did happen in court today?" There was a ring of curious faces around Frank. He reveled in the limelight. "The three defense witnesses are now known to have been murdered. Don't waste your time here. Out...out... out." He shoved them away as if they were a flock of pigeons.

The men and women of the media paraded out like children on their way to a show. The secretary approached Frank, thanking him profusely. She was tittering with relief. "You were here the other day, weren't you? Do you know who killed Mr. Weiserman?"

"I'm afraid I don't, but I'd appreciate any help you can give me."

"I don't know much." She spoke with shyness, but she felt she owed Frank something for his help. "I'll tell you what I do know." She waited patiently for Frank to formulate his questions. She was used to waiting for others.

"In a company this size, the chief usually grooms somebody to replace him in case of need. Who would this man or woman be?"

She thought before responding with care. "Mr. Weiserman never confided such information to me. I know he liked both Ruth Stewart and Christopher Bolt. He often consulted with them about important issues."

"Have either of them taken any action regarding the future of the company?"

"Well yes, they've both called in security analysts. They want the public to understand the strength of the company. I guess that's to try and avoid a slide in share price."

"Have they been successful?"

"I think so. They acted speedily enough that our shares have only declined by a hair."

"Did Mr. Weiserman have any enemies that you know of? Has he ever been threatened?"

She stared at Frank with a hint of dismay on her face. "Not that I know of. He was highly respected by our management team. Everyone seemed to like him. He was fair and he always showed interest in the welfare of the employees. He was a true gentleman. I can't believe someone would want him dead." She had tears in her eyes by the end of the statement.

"Please, will you make appointments for me with Ms. Stewart and Mr. Bolt? Any time, at their convenience. I would greatly appreciate that. Here's my number." He passed his business card to her while she dried her eyes on a crumpled tissue she'd found in a skirt pocket.

"Why do you want to meet with these people," Lisa asked, as Frank pushed her out the front door. "What can they possibly know?"

"Has it occurred to you that one of them may have been the killer?"

She stopped dead in her tracks, forcing pedestrians to plow around them like water around an iceberg. "You must be kidding."

"It wouldn't be the first time a CEO has been killed to make room for someone else. Usually the killer is more circumspect and makes it look more like an actual accident."

An odd smile showed up on Lisa's face. "Yeah... I suppose that's possible."

Frank wasn't sure what the smile was about and he really didn't want to know. He didn't want Lisa to attend those meetings. He had a gut feeling he couldn't even explain to himself. "I'm still curious about who will take Weiserman's job."

They spent the rest of the day in the apartment, Frank busy with his novel and Lisa watching the local news station.

By ten the following morning the court was crowded to capacity. The back seats reserved for reporters were crammed. The judge emerged from his chambers precisely at ten. Immediately after the opening procedures he voiced his opinion. "I've spoken twice with the police commissioner. He has verified that Assembly Legislator Desnick was murdered, as well as Ms. P.J. Thomson and Joseph Weiserman, CEO of the Swansen Enterprises Company. I am of the opinion that the defendants couldn't have been in two places at the same time. Mr. Prosecutor, the New York police will conduct, jointly with your office, a complete investigation of this case and report back to me. Meanwhile, the defendants are required to post bail in the amount of one million dollars. Their passports will be retained by the court and any travel out of the city is strictly forbidden. Court will reconvene on this matter in thirty days."

His gavel came down like a crack of thunder in the silent courtroom. Reporters fled while the Swansen twins were quickly ushered away by two court guards. They looked dazed.

In the afternoon Lisa heard from the Wyoming prosecutor that she was to return immediately to Yellowstone. She was devastated. "Frank, I feel so torn. I don't want to leave you, yet I must return to Yellowstone. I love you. I want to be with you." She held him to her closely, tears leaking from her eyes.

Frank kissed Lisa passionately. "I think I love you too. You don't have to go back to Wyoming. Come, live with me here. I'm sure you can find a job in New York." Immediately after having said these words, he wondered if he was really ready for a relationship that might lead to marriage. He was amazed at what he'd said, but even more amazed that Lisa might really consider it.

"I'd love to, but I can't. I must return. You could write your books in Wyoming, couldn't you?" Her voice was hoarse with emotion.

"Likely, but not until this case is over. I've got material now for the best mystery I'll ever write. I'm interested in this case because it's so bizarre."

Lisa reiterated, "So you could move to Wyoming." Excitement was evident in her face. She was anxious for Frank to make a commitment, to show her that he was just as excited about their relationship as she was.

Frank couldn't do it. "It's possible, but I can't make any promises. I'm sure I'll be coming back as this case warrants. We can keep in touch until we see each other again."

Lisa left the following morning. Frank drove her to the airport. While his earlier sense of confusion about whether he could love Lisa seemed to have disappeared, he was still afraid to get involved in too close of a relationship. He thought that being away from Lisa for a while would either cure his doubts or bring him to his senses. They parted with a passionate kiss.

****

Christopher Bolt, at 30, was a tall, slim but well muscled man. His lightly tanned face was warmed further by a small smile. He looked quite charming. He seemed to be the kind of guy you'd quickly want as a friend. Frank liked him immediately. They shook hands with warmth.

"What can I do for you, Mr. Galitson?" His smile widened. "Janet mentioned your kind help when she was under siege by the reporters."

Frank returned his smile. "Please, don't think that my intention is to pry into the affairs of this company. I got thrown into the Swansen case by accident." Frank went on to explain in detail how he had become involved while in Yellowstone. "As a writer of mysteries, the bizarreness of this case caught my attention. I was seeking a subject for my next novel. The most disturbing fact about this case is that all three witnesses who could have verified the presence of the Swansen twins in New York at the time of the Yellowstone murders have also been murdered. I've met with the twins twice and I truly think that they are telling the truth. The real mystery seems to be that all of the circumstantial evidence, including their personal identification, points to their presence in Yellowstone. Do you see my dilemma?"

Bolt had listened as if fascinated. After a short delay he finally spoke. "Frankly, I don't know how I can help. I don't know much about the Swansen girls, and I know even less about crime investigations. I'm not even a mystery buff."

"How long have you worked with Mr. Swansen?"

"About six years. He recruited me straight out of Yale after my doctorate in business and finance. He told me at the time that the company needed an injection of younger talent."

"Did you ever have any doubts about the plane crash that killed Julius and Adela Swansen?"

Bolt sat forward, attention fully engaged. "What an odd question. I only know what I read in the paper and what Mr. Weiserman told us at the time."

"What did he say?"

Bolt began to show irritation. "I don't know where this conversation is leading. Why do you ask such questions?"

Frank realized the meeting was just about over. He decided to use pity as a tool to keep it going. "Mr. Bolt, would you like to see the Swansen twins charged for murders they didn't commit?"

"Of course not. What do you take me for?"

"Then please, let me go on… If the twins are indicted and sentenced to death, or life imprisonment, there'll no longer be a family continuance in this company. The twins are trustees of their parents' estate. The court will have to appoint an outside trustee. Who knows what will happen to the company then. Do you follow me?"

"My God, I hadn't even begun to think about that."

"Then, please, will you answer my question about the plane crash?"

Bolt's irritation had been superceded by concern for himself and his cushy position. "I honestly don't know. Newspapers mentioned the crash, saying the plane had run out of fuel. My guess is that Mr. Swansen's pilot forgot to fill the tank."

"Do you know where they were headed?"

"Sure. Mr. Swansen was scheduled to attend an industrial convention in Chicago."

"Did Mrs. Swansen always travel with her husband?"

"Not always. I heard him talk with Adela about his upcoming trip to Chicago. He spoke about how nice it would be if she renewed her relationship with her sister."

"Do you know her sister's name?"

"I don't, but Janet might."

"Janet? Julius' secretary?"

"Yes."

"Who will decide on Weiserman's replacement?"

"The Board of Directors."

"Would you like the job?"

"Who wouldn't?" He grinned widely.

Frank's quick style of interrogation had lulled him enough to respond honestly. He got up, smiling. "Please call me if you find out anything that might be important to this case. Thank you very much." They shook hands. Bolt seemed a bit relieved to see the back of Frank going out the door.

Before leaving the building, Frank stopped at Janet's desk. "Thanks for arranging the meeting with Bolt. He's a fine man. He mentioned that Mrs. Swansen had a sister in Chicago. Do you happen to have her name and address?"

She flipped through her rolodex. "Here it is. Ilene Samps, 37 Lakeshore Drive. Telephone: (815) 326 5555."

"Thanks. What do you know about her?"

Janet took a moment, as if to draw something from deep in her memory bank. "Mr. Weiserman said once that Mr. Swansen had been engaged to Ilene, but then he ended up marrying Adela."

"Hmmm... did he say why the change?"

"No. He didn't elaborate at all. I never felt it was my place to ask for more details."

"Thanks. I'll see Ms. Stewart tomorrow. Have a great afternoon, Janet."

Frank went to the New York Library on Fifth Avenue. He perused old, brittle microfiche so he could review former issues of The New York Times. It was a lengthy process but finally he came across the article he was looking for.

The industrialist Julius Swansen, 52, and his wife Adela, 50, were killed yesterday in a small engine plane crash. They were en route to Chicago to attend a convention. The pilot, Andrew Commer, is presumed dead, although police were unable to identify the third body which had been completely burned in the fire. Initial investigations have revealed that the plane may have run out of fuel. Mr. Commer had 15 years experience as a pilot.

Mr. Swansen was Chairman and CEO of the Swansen Metal Company listed on the New York Stock Exchange. He and his wife are survived by five children, Sheila, Margaret, Elizabeth, Sandra and Paul.

Frank read the article several times. How could a plane have run out of fuel when the pilot had so many years of experience? One of the many checks a pilot is obliged to undertake before take-off is the level of fuel in the tank. If there was a leak it would have shown up on the tarmac. Frank's mind turned in a completely different direction. Since most of the children had been murdered, was it possible that he had also been targeted? After spending a great deal of time thinking through all of the events, including the possible framing of the twins, Frank became more than ever convinced that someone wished the entire Swansen family out of the way. He sat, lost in thought, oblivious of other patrons who wanted access to the microfiche reader.

The biggest problem Frank had was identifying a motive. He couldn't figure out anything remotely close to a reason for all the killings. He needed to find out who would inherit the enormous Swansen wealth if the entire family was wiped out.

Frank went home, had a quick meal of leftovers and went to bed early. His racing mind wouldn't let him settle. New questions continued to spring up. Did Julius have brothers or sisters? Nephews or nieces? What about Adela? He knew of the one sister. What about all of the parents? Were any of them still alive? Any one of them could be after the money. He was restless all night and eventually dragged himself out of bed at 6:00 a.m.

Frank returned to the Swansen building to meet Ruth Stewart. Before going into the meeting he stopped at Janet's desk. She was pleased to see him. "Mr. Bolt bought a couple of your books last night," she told him with a smile.

Frank smiled back. "Did either Julius or his wife have any brothers or sisters?" Frank had received some information about Adela before, but he wanted to be sure.

"Mr. Swansen had a brother who lived in Brazil. He died years ago. As I told you yesterday, his wife has a sister. I understand she's never been married." She seemed comfortable with a bit of gossip.

"How old is the sister?"

"I don't know."

"Do you know if the sister is in need of financial help?"

"Yes. Every month I mailed her an envelope Mr. Swansen gave me. On two occasions I saw him write checks from his personal account, but I don't know the amount."

"Have you ever seen her?"

"No... she's never been here."

"Thanks. I better go visit Ms. Stewart. I appreciate your help."

Ruth Stewart, a woman in her mid 40's, welcomed Frank with a friendly smile and an extended hand which Frank shook warmly. Her blue eyes shone against smooth, pale skin. Her face was rounded and her nose perfectly proportioned, almost too perfect. She was a pretty woman, the kind of woman that men looked at twice. "Please, take a seat," she said, her voice a pleasant cadence. She picked up a pencil and tapped it gently on her desk. "What can I do for you?" There was no hint of curiosity in her question.

"First, let me thank you for seeing me so promptly. I'm sure you must be extremely busy these days. Secondly, I have several questions to ask." Frank went on to explain how he had become involved in the Swansen case. "Normally I don't get involved in police investigations. I just write mysteries. But this case is so bizarre, I find I can't stay away. Actually, I've already begun to write my next novel, using this mystery as part of my plot."

"Will it be all about the Swansen case?"

"Not exactly. I'll use some of the scenarios, but the story will be a complete work of fiction."

She nodded as if his answer had satisfied some of her concerns. "I see. Well... what do you want to know? Keep in mind that I won't divulge any company business."

"How long have you worked for Mr. Swansen?"

"About twenty years."

"What is your position in the company?"

Ms. Stewart hesitated for a moment. "I'm an executive vice president. I oversee the managers of production, marketing, sales, and accounting." There was a slight tinge of pride in her answer.

"Would you say Mr. Swansen considered you a very valuable employee?"

"I always hoped he did. There was no indication he felt otherwise."

"Did Mr. Swansen have brothers or sisters?"

Ms. Stewart's face changed, mirroring some confusion. "What has that got to do with anything?"

Frank felt she was trying to avoid the subject. He persisted. "I'm trying to determine what the motive might have been. Please, don't worry about telling me anything. Remember, I'm not the police. This is just for my information, in a way, to satisfy my curious streak."

She hesitated. "He had a brother who was quite wild during his youth. He died several years ago in Brazil." The pencil was being tapped furiously, making Frank wonder what she was trying to hide.

"Are Julius' parents still alive?"

"No. They died mysteriously about a year after the plane crash."

"Mrs. Swansen?"

"Her mother died years ago from leukemia. Her father lives in a nursing home, suffering from Alzheimer's."

"How well do you know Margaret and Elizabeth?"

"I see them from time to time, usually when they come here."

"Do they come here often?"

"Quite often, especially during the past year."

"Do you know why?"

"They were interested in selling shares in the company held by the trust."

"How many shares do they own?"

"Around 80%."

Frank shifted the topic. "What's your thinking about why Mr. Weiserman was killed?"

"If anyone wanted him dead, it would have to be our competitors. He was loved by everyone in our company."

"It's come to my attention that he had dinner with the Swansen twins at the time of the Yellowstone murder. Were you aware of that dinner?"

She became aware of the rapid tempo of the pencil and laid it gently on the desk, perfectly aligned with the edge of the desk. "Yes. In fact, he brought it up with me."

"Why?"

"He thought I could help him. He didn't want the company sold. He thought it was a stupid idea, but he couldn't convince them of the mistake they were making."

"How did the twins behave? Were they aggressive, impolite?"

"Very aggressive. Fortunately, the trust requires a majority vote to sell the company and the twins couldn't get it. I believe they tried to influence Mr. Weiserman to push the others to vote their way."

Frank couldn't think of any more questions to ask. He thanked her, then left, not noticing the sag in her shoulders and the sigh of relief as he left the room.

10.

At his invitation, Joe Caputo met Frank for lunch. They settled into a booth in the ever busy Carnegie Deli on 7th Street, where the ambient noise level meant they could speak with impunity. They ordered corned beef on rye sandwiches, slathered with hot mustard. The first bite made both of them sigh. "This case is driving me crazy. Every day I find out something new. The problem is, I don't have an organization to help me work out all the angles."

"What's new?"

"The New York Times article stated that the Swansen plane crashed because it ran out of fuel. The same article indicated that the body of the pilot could not be identified due to fire. If the plane had run out of fuel, why was there a fire?"

"Hmmm...you're right. It seems no one considered that. The case was immediately closed."

They each took another huge bite of sandwich, followed by a long swig of malt beer. "Julius Swansen had a brother who supposedly died in Brazil. I wonder if he is really dead. If so, was he also killed? Julius' parents died mysteriously within twelve months of the crash. It looks as though the entire Swansen family might have been targeted for elimination. I'm convinced someone is after their money. The question is, who? It seems as if it must be a living relative. I say that because a stranger wouldn't be entitled to inherit the fortune."

"Anything else?"

"It's a minor issue, but Mr. Bolt, a key Swansen executive, spoke about Mrs. Swansen using her first name. Normally, you wouldn't refer to the chief's wife by her first name."

Joe nodded. "You're right, this case is mind boggling." He was silent for several moments, then slapped his hand on the table. He said, "I'm going to talk to my supervisor. I'll tell him the whole story and ask to be responsible for the investigation. I'll tell him I know you personally, and that together, we might get to the bottom of this case."

Frank couldn't hold back his smile. This was exactly what he had hoped for. "That would be wonderful. I was hoping we could work together, but I didn't want to be too forward."

Joe snorted at that. He knew Frank for what he was, an opinionated man full of self-importance.

****

Frank's deeply hidden emotions were beginning to surface. He missed Lisa. In fact, his desire to have her back by his side was growing rapidly. He called her several times, telling her of his feelings. Lisa seemed delighted, responding to his words with affection of her own.

Frank wanted to be able to talk to the Swansen twins again but he had to wait until bail had been put up for their release. He also had to wait for Joe to get authorization to investigate the Swansen murders. Since he didn't want to waste any time, along with missing Lisa, he decided to fly to Jackson Hole. He took a charter plane to avoid having to wait, the expense being unimportant to him.

Lisa was waiting anxiously at the airport. They hugged and kissed, Lisa jumping for joy. Frank, too, felt overwhelmingly happy. The confusion and uncertainty that had gripped him had disappeared without a trace. They finally separated from their embrace but Frank held firmly to her hand.

"Since we're at the airport, I'd like to check on the car rental that the Swansen twins made, as well as reviewing their flights in and out of Jackson Hole."

Lisa pouted. "Can't you forget this case for a few days? Let's just have a good time together. I've missed you so much." She laughingly pulled Frank to her, kissing him with great enthusiasm.

"Darling, I missed you too." Frank wondered how the word 'darling' had sprung out of his mouth, quickly realizing how dear she had become to him. "Maybe this will sound selfish to you, but I'm really interested in this case because it is helping me build the scenario for my next mystery."

Employees at the three car rental agencies at the airport all knew Lisa. They willingly checked their records, starting several days before the first murder. Elizabeth Swansen had rented a compact car from one company, and Margaret Swansen had rented an SUV from another. The compact car was returned one day before the murder of Paul Swansen, while the SUV was returned two days later.

Airline employees reported to them that details regarding the twins' flights had already been given to staff members for the District Attorney's office, and they weren't going to duplicate their efforts. They left somewhat disappointed, but hopeful the DA's office would share the information with them.

Frank updated Lisa about his visits with Bolt and Stewart, and reviewed court proceedings while they traveled to Jackson. "I want to interview the twins again. I want to learn as much as possible about the Swansen family. I have a strong feeling someone is trying to eliminate the entire family."

Lisa didn't respond. She drove in complete silence. As they entered the city, she finally spoke, "Frank, I've rented an apartment in Jackson. It'll be much more comfortable for you than a cabin in Yellowstone, particularly with winter coming." She spoke to the windshield, afraid of his response.

"That's great. I'll share expenses with you."

Her shoulders retreated from her ears and a smile wreathed her face. She took a moment to smile at him before getting back to driving. "Don't worry about it."

"We have time to stop at the District Attorney's office."

She shook her head. "Tomorrow. You're tired from all the traveling. I want you to rest before dinner. Tonight we're eating in. You'll get a taste of my cooking."

Frank was surprised, both by her renting an apartment for them and offering to cook for him. Their relationship was moving in a good direction. He felt strongly that she cared for him and it left him with a warm glow.

The apartment was on Millward Street, two blocks from Broadway. It consisted of a sizable bedroom and a large living room with an outdoor terrace facing the ski slopes. It was modest but comfortably furnished, nothing to write home about but livable. There was also a small room which Lisa had equipped with a computer-desk and two filing cabinets. A late model laser printer was ready on a bottom shelf, all set to be connected to Frank's laptop. Ten reams of copying paper stood on a corner table.

Frank smiled. "You've thought of everything, haven't you?" He grabbed Lisa to him, kissing her warmly. She returned his kiss with passion. Dinner was even better than Frank had expected and Lisa was thrilled by his reaction.

The following morning they went to the DA's office. Passenger lists for all airlines that had flown in and out of Jackson Hole during the week of the murders were made available. Elizabeth and Margaret had arrived on a Delta Airlines jet two days before the first murder. Elizabeth left on a Delta flight a day before Paul's murder. There was no record of Margaret flying out of Jackson. Frank went over the names of the passengers several times, to no avail. "How did she leave Jackson? Or did she?"

Lisa's response was immediate. "She might have left on someone's private plane. It's not unusual around here."

"But why didn't they leave together? That's one more inconvenient twist in this case. Why didn't the prosecutor bring this up in court?" He tapped his fingers together before shuffling the pages over and over.

"He showed evidence of their arrival. Their departure was probably irrelevant in his mind." She took the pages out of Frank's hands before he ruined them.

Frank's mind raced as they strolled down Broadway toward their apartment. Sidewalks were crammed with tourists going in and out of the many art galleries and Western themed shops along the street. Many had elaborate displays of hunting and fishing equipment, things Frank had no knowledge of having not being an outdoor type of a guy.

A large display window at the Tradeside Galleries drew Frank's attention. A magnificent iron sculpture depicting a fly fisherman caught his eye. He stood as if mesmerized by the work.

As he turned his head he caught a glimpse of two well-dressed sales women standing behind a square wooden counter. One of them reminded him of Julia, but it couldn't be. This woman had glossy black hair and wore glasses.

"What's wrong?" Lisa noticed a queer look on Frank's face.

He was immobilized, staring intently at something she couldn't see. "Nothing. This is an incredible piece of work."

"Would you like me to buy it for you? I would love to give you anything you want." Her tone was that of an eager to please schoolgirl.

"No... no... thanks. Maybe I'll buy it before we return to New York."

"New York? I was hoping we'd settle here."

"I don't mind us living here for a while, but I miss New York. The book publishing business is in New York. I must stay close to it." Frank missed the look of dismay which flitted across her face.

She was terribly disappointed but said nothing more. During the next several days, while waiting to hear from Joe Caputo, Frank spent most of his time at his laptop, writing at a furious pace. His story was moving along quickly. In reality, his work looked more like a journal record of events rather than a story. He stopped several times to review his progress. He concluded that due to the complexity of the case he would complete his mystery once all the facts were in and the killer, or killers, had been found.

Lisa went to work every day, providing Frank with the solitude he needed while busy developing his story. Lisa's passionate behavior toward him began to bother Frank as it reminded him of Julia. However, his love for Lisa was growing and he felt comfortable with her. The thought of being loved by someone began playing a completely different role in his mind. He could feel himself loving her in return.

Despite his burgeoning emotion there was something amiss in his gut that Frank couldn't begin to decipher. He found himself keeping certain information away from Lisa although outwardly he was very demonstrative.

Joe finally called on the fourth day. He hadn't been able to get the sole investigator status he'd requested because of the judge's conversations with the police commissioner. However, he was told to join the three detective team that had been authorized to work on the Swansen case. Joe knew the other two officers well and felt they'd be able to work together without a problem.

Frank asked Joe to investigate the passenger lists for flights leaving New York to Jackson Hole, as well as the return flights. The fact that the twins hadn't left Jackson together bothered him a great deal.

Frank called the Cody Airport manager to find out whether they offered flights to or from New York, but there were none. His mind raced. If Margaret returned her rental car two days after Paul's murder and after Elizabeth's departure, she must have left via one of the airports he'd already been to. The question was, how had she managed it?

Frank sat in front of his laptop, trying to continue work on his story. Words would not come. Suddenly, he leapt from his chair as if galvanized by an electric current. What if Margaret had flown somewhere else? Passenger lists were arranged by final destination. The airlines' computer systems could provide him with such information. Immediately he called the DA's office, requesting an amendment to their passenger lists. They told him it might take them a few hours to get him that information.

Frank returned to his desk but he had writer's block. His mind was elsewhere and he found he couldn't concentrate on his book. By late afternoon, he'd received the phone call he was waiting for. Three airlines had found nothing. Delta reported that there was no passenger by the name of Margaret Swansen, but they had found a passenger by the name of Margaret Jones. Despite his disappointment, Frank inquired what her destination had been. Minneapolis was the answer.

Lisa brought in dinner she'd picked up at a take-out restaurant. She was in good spirits, but Frank ate in complete silence. He was busy trying to figure out how the Swansen twins could have left Jackson Hole.

"Darling, what's on your mind? You've been so quiet this evening." She reached across the table to tap the back of his hand.

Frank flinched but didn't respond immediately. He took a long sip of his wine, a fine Merlot, then spoke. "There was no mention of Margaret Swansen's name on any of the passenger lists. How the hell did she leave Jackson?" He wasn't even looking at Lisa, eyes downward to his plate where he pushed food around with no interest in eating.

"Darling," Lisa spoke lovingly, "why are you so worried about this? Obviously, she left somehow. Maybe a friend gave her a ride. Plenty of people drive to Yellowstone, some even come on their motorcycles."

Frank paid no attention. "Margaret returned her rental car two days after Paul was murdered. She must have still been here when we discovered his body. What was she doing in those two days?"

"So what?" She said, still smiling, but a bit grim. "Did it occur to you that she might have had someone else return the car? By the way, how are you doing with your book?"

Frank finally looked up. "Not too good. I can't concentrate. My mind is constantly on the Swansen investigation."

Frank's cell phone rang, his broker at Smith Barney. "Sorry for the delay, Frank. I've been busy as hell. The markets are fluctuating like a yoyo. The Swansen estate is valued at around six hundred million. I called Jack at Forbes to double check. He agreed with me."

"Is there a way to find out who might have made inquiries about the Swansen company, say sometime during the past year?"

"That would be very difficult. A variety of investors, including hedge funds, explore all stocks every single day, looking for potential investments. However, you could check with the company's transfer agent to see if he had any inquiries that stood out in his mind."

Frank hung up, frowning. He turned to Lisa. "I'll have to explore this with Christopher Bolt and Ruth Stewart."

"Explore what?"

"Who made inquiries about the strength and value of the company? I'll call in the morning."

Lisa shook her head. "I don't think that's a good idea. I think you'd get better information by talking with them face-to-face."

"You're right. I'll call on them when I return to New York." Frank finally started to pay attention to Lisa, giving up the Swansen issue for the night.

When Frank woke the following morning Lisa was already gone. Her morning shift began at six. He shaved, showered and cooked a serving of thick oatmeal for breakfast, along with a strong cup of black coffee. His mind was clear. He wished he could get The New York Times every morning. In Jackson, delivery was not till late afternoon.

He sat at his laptop where this time ideas turned into words. He typed enthusiastically, pleased at progress. A little after eleven his thinking was disturbed by the phone. Lisa was on the line, speaking with urgency, her tone one of worry. "Frank, you need to come immediately to Teton Village. There's been another murder." She hung up before he could say a word.

"That's all I need," Frank said to himself. "It can't possibly be connected to the Swansen family, they're already all dead." He rushed out to his rental car.

Teton Village, located about fifteen miles from Jackson, consisted of only three buildings; a hotel with a street front gift and souvenir store, a structure housing the air-tram that lifted people to the heights of Rendevous Mountain, with a restaurant at the back, and a combination theater/museum building.

Lisa was waiting for Frank on the sidewalk in front of the air-tram entrance. Frank rushed to her from his parking spot across the street. "What's the matter? You sounded really upset."

"A woman was found dead early this morning. She was hidden under the stairway that leads to the air-tram. She'd been strangled. The Jackson police were called in and they found your business card in her purse. What's going on, Frank?"

Frank was dumbfounded. He searched his wallet where he kept a supply of cards. They were all gone. "Who is she?"

"Her driver's license is in the name of Gertrude Miller of 1022 Second Avenue, apartment 1608, New York. She looks like she's in her mid sixties, with a wrinkled face and silvery white hair. A pair of prescription glasses was found with the body."

"I don't know who she is. I've never heard of her."

"Chief Crawley wants to see you. He's in the back."

Frank exploded. "How in God's name did my business card get into her hands? I don't have a clue as to who she is."

"Frank, are you telling me the truth?" Lisa looked straight into his eyes.

He blew out an exasperated sigh. "Of course I'm telling you the truth. I don't know this woman from a hole in the ground. I've never even heard of her. I haven't a clue who she is, period."

Lisa's face mirrored her uncertainty. She pushed Frank to get him moving. "You'll have to answer Crawley's questions." She spoke authoritatively, no love in her voice. Frank felt a jolt of fear.

Crawley stared at Frank's bewildered face. "Where were you between midnight and six this morning?" He was gruff, unsmiling.

"Sleeping."

"Any witnesses?"

Frank looked at Lisa. She shook her head slightly. "Do you have a witness when you sleep?"

"I'm the one who asks the questions around here."

Frank became angry. "What do you want me to tell you? I went to bed around eleven and got up at seven." Frank had got the message from Lisa that she didn't want Crawley to know about their relationship.

Crawley pressed on. "Explain to me how your business card got into this woman's purse."

Frank laughed. "Sure... I killed a woman I don't know, then put my card in her purse. How stupid do you think I am?" His tone was full of sarcasm. Crawley was not impressed.

Frank was surprised by Lisa's silence. He turned angrily to her. "Don't you have anything to say?"

"This is not my jurisdiction." No smile, no evidence she knew Frank intimately.

Frank couldn't believe his ears. "Not your jurisdiction? Then what are you doing here?"

"Chief Crawley called me."

"Lisa, your station is seventy-five miles from here. Tell Crawley where you were last night."

Crawley interfered before Lisa could respond. "Answer my question." His tone was unpleasant and he moved in closer to Frank, an intimidating presence.

"Look… I don't have a clue who she is, nor do I have the faintest idea how my card came into her possession. I've been helping in the investigation of the Swansen murders. I'm a writer, not a killer." He could feel sweat stains spreading under his arms.

Crawley paused for a moment. "The murdered woman is Gertrude Miller, from your neck of the woods. I don't know a damn thing about New York, nor do I care to. I suggest you tell me the truth."

Frank's face reddened. He stared at Lisa, his neck vein pulsing. "If you don't tell him where you were last night, I will."

Crawley looked toward Lisa with a frown. "What has she to do with you?"

Lisa maintained her silence. Frank shouted, "She was in bed with me last night. She's my witness."

Lisa's face paled. "That's true. I went to bed with Frank around eleven but I left as soon as he fell asleep."

Frank thought he was in the middle of a nightmare. "Why are you lying? We made love, or have you forgotten? You fell asleep in my arms." Lisa had blotches on her face and neck, her humiliation evident.

Crawley was puzzled. "What's going on between you two? Lisa, is Frank telling the truth?"

"Yes, but I didn't stay the night. I left around one."

Frank grabbed Lisa by the arm. "Why are you lying? What's the matter with you?" Suddenly he turned to Crawley. "If she left at one when I was asleep, she's the only one who had access to my wallet. She's the one who took my card and placed it in the dead woman's purse. She's the one who killed that poor woman." Frank took a deep breath, thinking he had turned the tables. He realized Lisa's silence was intentional even though he didn't know why. He needed to implicate her to free himself.

Lisa looked like she was ready to throw up. She screamed at Frank, tearing her arm away from his clutching hand. "I've given you my love. Is this how you treat me? All you New Yorkers are the same."

Frank made a huge effort to calm himself. "All New Yorkers... what do you know about New Yorkers. You'd never even set foot there till recently. There are more than five million honest, decent, hard working people in New York. You could both learn a thing or two from them."

Crawley quickly came to the conclusion that Frank was telling him the truth. He chuckled, interested in the lovers' dispute. A small smile appeared on his face. He pulled Lisa away from Frank. "Why did you leave at one? Did you go to Jim?"

Frank stared at her, open mouthed. "Jim?"

Lisa was mad. "That's none of your business." She spat the words at Crawley.

Frank couldn't help himself. "Lisa, you said a few minutes ago that Chief Crawley called you. Didn't you?" She didn't answer. Frank turned to Crawley. "Did you call her at Jim's place?"

Crawley was openly enjoying the scene in front of him. His smile broadened. He was curious how this lover's war was going to play out. "That's where I called her."

Frank was fed up with the whole affair. "Can I go? I don't think I can contribute anything further to this investigation."

Crawley's smile vanished. "Both of you need to come to the station. I want your written statements." He signaled to a nearby police officer to accompany them.

Frank got into his car. Lisa sat next to him while the officer sat in the back, hand on his gun. Frank spoke. "Lisa, don't you think you owe me an explanation? You behaved like a total stranger. You know damn well you were with me most of the night. You say you love me. Ha! I'll tell you something... my love for you has evaporated into thin air." He was spitting his words out, more angry and upset than he had ever felt before.

Lisa didn't respond. She remained silent all the way to the police station, face forward, chin outthrust.

Frank wrote out his statement in great detail, then left the station. He wondered how his real first love could have ended in deceit. Questions raced through his mind. Had Lisa ever been honest with him? Had his sudden appearance in Yellowstone provided Lisa an opportunity to play her game? What was her game? Did the three murders in New York have anything to do with Lisa? If she really did love me she would have told Crawley immediately that she was with me. Why did she lie? What was she hiding? Who was Jim?

Frank remembered that he'd had a queer feeling in his gut about Lisa that he couldn't reason out. Her beautiful, honest face had distracted his attention from some of the things she'd said. She'd manipulated him into loving her. He decided he needed to find out who Jim was. Why had Lisa kept him secret when Crawley seemed to know about him? Perhaps he could supply some answers. Frank paced as he worried through his problems.

He called Joe Caputo to tell him about the murder of Gertrude Miller. "Please, find out who she is, what might have brought her to Wyoming, who her family is, and if she has any connections to the Swansens. I'll be back in New York in a couple of days."

Next, he went to the leasing office. The rental manager, a woman in her mid forties, was pleasant looking even though her smile was thin lipped. Her smile doubled when she saw Frank walk in, thinking he was a candidate for an apartment. "Sorry to bother you, but I'm interested in knowing who rented apartment 307 for me."

The woman stared at Frank for a moment. "Ah... yes... you're the author..." She shuffled some papers around as if trying to kill some time. "It was a ranger from Yellowstone. She said you were helping in an investigation and needed an apartment for a month."

"What was her name? Did she sign a lease?"

"She said it was a police matter and it had to be kept hush hush."

"Did she give you a name?"

"No. She said this was an order from Chief Crawley." She frowned at Frank, thinking he should already have all this information.

"Who paid the rent?"

"She did, in cash."

"Have you ever seen her before?"

"Sure… I've seen her going into Jim Jones' apartment."

Frank swallowed hard. He was shocked. How convenient. Lisa was hopping from one apartment to the other. "What's his apartment number?"

She hesitated, thinking maybe she had said too much. "I suppose I can tell you since you're involved with them. It's 601."

"How long has Jim lived here?"

"A little over six months."

"Did you check him out before leasing the apartment?"

"I didn't have to. His apartment was also an order from Chief Crawley."

Frank and she stared at each other for a few moments. He didn't know what else to ask and she was already regretting that she had spoken with him.

"Thank you. I'll be leaving by the end of the week."

Frank walked out of the office, flabbergasted, but determined to find out who this Jim Jones was. He called Chief Crawley, asking to see him as soon as possible. At first Crawley told him he was too busy but after Frank made a strongly worded demand he agreed to see him at six.

"Jim Jones… what's your interest in him? I don't need you starting some sort of a lover's quarrel. Jackson is a peaceful city." He was leaning back in his chair, hands clasped across his chest, a smirk on his face.

Frank laughed. "Peaceful… this whole area has been inundated with murders lately."

Crawley leaned back even further. "As you know, the murders have all been of strangers."

"I know. The word 'peaceful' got to me. No, I'm not about to start a quarrel. I don't want to leave any stones unturned. Did Lisa bring Jim Jones here?" Frank was tamping down his hostility so he could get some answers.

"As a matter of fact, she did. She said he was a wild one back home and she was helping in his rehabilitation."

"Where did Lisa actually come from? How did she become a ranger?"

"Lisa's from Minneapolis. She was a police officer there. I must tell you that Jim Jones has given us no trouble at all since his arrival."

"I assume you checked Lisa out with the Minneapolis police."

"I didn't. I thought the park authority would do that."

"Is Jim working?"

"As far as I know he's still working at George's Garage. I've heard he's an outstanding car mechanic."

"Please, would you do me a great favor? Talk with the park authority about Lisa's background. I have a feeling she's here for some hidden reason." Just as Frank spoke, he leapt from his seat, smacking himself in the forehead. "My God, I was told that a Margaret Jones had flown from Jackson to Minneapolis. I'm willing to bet you there's some connection between Lisa and Jim and the Swansen murders."

"You must be out of your mind. Lisa is a sweetheart," was Chief Crawley's emphatic response. "Don't go getting any crazy ideas in your head."

"Yea… I thought she was a sweetheart too. However, as a police officer, I know you will look into every nook and cranny. Please check and let me know. If I'm right, you'll have these murders solved."

Crawley hesitated, then gave Frank a nod. Frank left the police station to find George's Garage. It was located on William Street, the garage empty except for one lone car up on a hydraulic lift. The owner sat behind a small desk, head down, adding up receipts for the day. "I hear you have a super mechanic here. What time could I bring my Chevy in?"

Frank's request was duly considered before the owner replied laconically. No extra energy was wasted by this guy. "We open at seven."

"Thanks, I'll be in tomorrow."

Frank was up early the following morning, stationing himself next to an oak tree so he could observe Jim's apartment door. Jim came out at 6:45, carrying a blue nylon case. Frank followed him from a distance until Jim arrived at the garage, emerging from a restroom minutes later dressed in a stained overall. He immediately began to work on the car still up on the lift.

Frank walked back to the apartment building, waiting impatiently for the office to open up. The rental manager arrived a little before eight. "Could you open 601 for me? I'd like to leave Jim some papers he asked for, but I missed him this morning. He must have left for work before I got there."

The manager agreed. "I'll meet you up there in a minute. Let me get the coffee on and check the answering machine." She let the door slam behind Frank, who quickly ran upstairs to the apartment he and Lisa had been sharing.

He placed several blank sheets of paper in a legal sized envelope, sealing it tightly. He unfolded four sticks of chewing gum and crammed them all in his mouth at once. The manager opened the door with her master key, watching with interest as Frank placed the envelope on a table, then both of them turned to leave. At the door Frank began to cough, making sure the manager was paying attention. Surreptitiously he spit the wad of gum into his hand, then jammed it into the latch receptacle and pulled the door close behind him. He apologized to her for his coughing fit, then thanked her for her help. She hadn't noticed a thing, intent on her own concerns.

Frank waited until a family of four entered her office. He quickly ran back upstairs to let himself into Jim's apartment. He removed the wad of gum and closed the door firmly.

601 was a two bedroom apartment, the living room furnished with cheap furniture and two plants that looked like they hadn't been watered in weeks. Both beds showed signs of use. Soiled clothes had been left on the floor in what appeared to be Jim's room. Frank checked through the chest of drawers and the closet. A carry-on briefcase, like those used by business travelers, sat on the hat shelf in the closet. Frank was lifting down the briefcase when he heard a rattle from the front door. Someone

was coming in. He quickly returned the briefcase to its place, pulling the closet door shut, hiding himself inside.

Through a crack in the closet doors Frank could see Lisa placing a green manila folder underneath the mattress. She left the room without a look around. Frank waited several anxious minutes before he cautiously left the closet. He peered out the door – Lisa was gone.

The folder was a slender police file containing investigative forms used for hiring new officers. The name on the file was James Jones, address: 75 Riverdale Circle, Minneapolis. Frank was shocked. Why had Lisa smuggled Jim's file from the Jackson police? Why had Jim been investigated if he wasn't employed by the police? Was he an undercover officer? The application form was dated six months ago. Was Chief Crawley involved in the Swansen case? Why? How?

Frank removed the papers from the folder, replacing them with blank sheets he took from the envelope he'd dropped off earlier. Then he went back to the briefcase. It contained statements of a securities account Jim maintained at Amtrade Brokerage. Frank quickly perused the statements – all had the same name on shares and bonds. He pulled a monthly statement out from the middle of the pile, hiding it, along with the other papers, tucked under his shirt. He returned everything, then searched the drawers in the chest.

In the bottom drawer he found a handgun and two boxes of bullets. He carefully picked the gun up so any fingerprints on it would not be ruined, then placed it in his pocket. There was nothing of interest in the kitchen, so he left the apartment. Frank checked around every corner to make sure no one saw him. He was very nervous, his hands slick with sweat.

He entered his apartment, shocked to see Lisa rising from the sofa. After his harsh words he had thought he wouldn't see her again.

She spoke calmly, a smile on her face. "Frank, I owe you an explanation."

Frank wouldn't let her go on. He snapped his words out. "I don't need any explanation from you. Our relationship is done. It's over."

Lisa grabbed his arm. "Please, Frank, listen to me. I can't bear this. The truth is that I do love you. I fell in love with you the moment I saw you. I know I behaved badly. It was Crawley. He forced me to keep my mouth shut. He believes that you killed Gertrude Miller so he forced me to deny that I was with you. I don't know why he did that."

Frank pushed her away in disgust. "I don't believe a word you say. I don't want to have anything to do with you. Get out." He pointed toward the door. If he hadn't been so wrought up in the moment he would have laughed at the melodrama of it all.

Lisa gave him a piteous look, her voice pleading. "Frank, please, give me another chance. I love you with all my heart, and I know you love me too." She began to weep, her nose runny, her hands trembling.

"No, you messed up. If you loved me you would have stood up for me, no matter what. You failed the first test of love. Go. You and I are finished." Frank entered his bedroom and slammed the door. He immediately took the papers out from under his shirt, hiding them and the gun in his suitcase. He could feel his blood pressure rising. He undressed and hopped into bed, laying flat on his back, his mind spinning.

What was Lisa up to? Was there any truth in her statements about Crawley? She'd cast a huge doubt on Crawley for Frank. Why had she stolen Jim's file from the police department? Did Crawley know about it? Why had Jim applied for a police job? Had he got it and was he secretly with the police? What about the gun? Had it been used recently?

Heavy knocking at the door cut into Frank's line of thinking. Lisa entered without waiting for his response. "Please, Frank, can't you believe that I love you? I've never loved anyone else. I can't stand this." Her cheeks were wet, eyes puffy and rimmed in red.

Frank said, "Who is Jim Jones?"

Lisa took a shaky breath. "You have no reason to be jealous of Jim. He's an old school friend I've been helping to rehab." She was avoiding eye contact with these words so Frank immediately assumed she was lying. He decided not to make an issue of it. Let her build her own trap. "I see. I'm not concerned about him, just curious."

"I'll do anything you want, Frank. Please don't throw me out."

Frank was still lying on his back. As Lisa approached the bed, he sat up. "That's as far as you go. Our relationship is over. Get out."

Lisa's sobs increased. She wiped at the river of tears with her hands. "Oh, Frank, I love you so. I've made a terrible mistake. Please, won't you forgive me?"

"Sorry, Lisa, it's over." He turned on his side to face the wall. Lisa left without another word. Only her sobs could be heard as she left the apartment.

Frank sat up as soon as he heard the door close. His mind began to race, his thoughts revolving around Crawley's method of investigating him. Frank believed Lisa had told him the truth about being ordered to remain silent, yet, there was something illogical about the whole thing that had taken place at the murder scene in Teton Village. Was there something more than just police work between Crawley and Lisa? If so, he better be careful. Frank knew he looked like a hard hearted bastard but he was used to being self-protective.

Frank wanted to put Crawley to the test, but he couldn't figure out how to do it. The more he thought about his encounter with Crawley the more he felt there was some sort of an arrangement between him and Lisa. How had Lisa been able to get hold of Jim's file? Surely the police kept personnel files under lock and key. Who was Jim? What was he really doing in Jackson? He seemed to have an excellent reputation as auto mechanic and he was fully employed in a well known garage. What's his connection to the police? Was Jim related to the woman listed as Margaret Jones who had flow out of Salt Lake City? Frank knew he needed to look into every angle if he planned to use the Swansen mystery as the basis for his next novel.

Frank fixed himself a snack to go with the oversized glass of wine he poured for himself. He continued to ruminate over Lisa, Crawley and Jim until he fell asleep on the sofa.

Before calling on Charles Dickson, the District Attorney, Frank packaged the gun along with the boxes of bullets and mailed it to his New York Address.

Charles Dickson, a man in his mid forties stood over six feet tall. He looked more like an athlete than an attorney. His broad football player shoulders were evident even in his tailored suit. His face was large and round, presenting an aura of strength and authority.

Frank walked in without an appointment. How busy could a district attorney be in such a peaceful city? He was right. Dickson was leaning back in a black leather swivel chair, eyes closed, smoking a thin cigar. Smoke wafted lazily to the ceiling tiles.

"Good morning, Mr. District Attorney," Frank said cheerfully, "I hope you have a few minutes for me." Frank didn't think much of the man's professionalism after having watched him bungle the Swansen case in New York. Perhaps the size of the New York court had traumatized him.

Dickson showed no emotion, his face blank. "What can I do for you?" He sounded bored.

"As you know, I'm helping in the investigation of the Swansen case. Certain issues have come up that lead me to suspect a member of the local authorities. I don't have any proof, and as a result, I have to be extremely careful how I handle this matter." Frank was beating around the bush to try and determine whether the district attorney could be trusted. In a small town like this there were always hidden connections between people that an outsider would know nothing about.

Dickson turned out to be much sharper than Frank had anticipated. "There's no love lost between me and the police chief. When I went to New York to file the extradition papers the police withheld vital information from me. I felt like an idiot when you spoke up." His voice had lost its tone of boredom and Frank could sense his bitterness over being made to look like a fool.

Frank seized the moment. "Oh... I knew it wasn't your fault. I assumed as much. In such bizarre cases police officers tend to seek notoriety. It helps them with their re-election campaigns."

The DA sat up straight, cigar forgotten in an overfull ashtray. "I'm glad you agree."

"I have written a number of successful mysteries. My books have sold in the hundreds of thousands. I've been on the New York Times bestseller list for months. I'm good at analyzing people." Frank paused for a brief moment in his preening, thinking how he had misread Lisa. "I need your word of honor and a confirmation of confidentiality before I go any further."

Dickson stood up, extending his hand. "You have my word," he said, his face serious.

"Very well. May I close the door to your office?"

Dickson immediately circled his desk, dashing to close the door himself. "Go ahead. I'll do what I can for you."

"The investigation of the Yellowstone murders of members of the Swansen family, and the framing of the Swansen twins, has led me to believe that someone is after Julius Swansen's wealth. In several instances I noticed that Lisa Warrenton, the park ranger, was trying to put me off track. Crawley seems to have done the same thing. Then, there's this fellow, Jim Jones, brought to Jackson from Minneapolis by Lisa, who's also from Minneapolis. Apparently, Jim applied for a police position, but works as a mechanic in a garage. I found out that his folder has been removed from the police personnel files. To top all this off, a Margaret Jones left Jackson on a flight to Minneapolis about the time of the murders. I can't help but think that Lisa is somehow connected to the Jones family. Yesterday, a woman was found strangled in Teton Village. One of my business cards was found in her purse. That led Crawley to investigate me. His way of asking questions was bizarre. Lisa stood by, obviously completely in cahoots with him. I feel deceit lurking all over this picture."

While Frank was speaking Dickson's face was hard to read. "What can I do? I need hard evidence and you can't give that to me. Feeling and intuition aren't worth a damn in court."

"Let's start by making some discreet inquiries about Crawley; where he came from, his past, etc. I don't believe he's a native of Wyoming. His accent is different."

"Anything else?"

"Yes. Crawley said that Lisa had been hired by the park management. He claims not to have any knowledge of her. How about checking her out with the Department of the Interior?"

"You really think that Crawley came from somewhere else?"

"I'm absolutely sure."

"It'll take a while but I'll get back to you."

Frank gave Dickson his cell phone number, then left. He felt there was some progress, even though he was going to have to rely on someone else to make it happen.

11.

Frank spent nearly all of the next two days feverishly writing. If he wasn't at his laptop, his mind was grinding, going over and over every detail since the day he'd got caught up in the Swansen affair. He was anxious to get news from Dickson but nothing came. He felt stale, reviewing the same details over and over until he felt like screaming. He drank endless cups of coffee and rarely ate. The apartment smelled musty as he neglected to bathe or shave and no fresh air was admitted.

On the third day Frank was totally fed up. He packed his suitcases, drove to the airport, returned his car, and booked a flight to New York via Chicago. He decided it was time to visit Ilene Samps, Adela Swansen's sister. He felt better, having a plan of action, even if he didn't know where it would lead.

Fortunately, he didn't have to wait long. An American Airlines plane arrived and was made ready for departure within the hour. The flight to Chicago was uneventful. The two seats next to him were unoccupied so he stretched himself out and relaxed. He didn't think about the Swansens, just kept his mind clear. Frank checked into the Statler Hilton Hotel in the city's downtown. He showered, shaved and treated himself to a gourmet dinner at a nearby Italian themed restaurant.

The following day, after a restful sleep, completely relaxed, Frank went down to the hotel restaurant. He consumed a huge breakfast of eggs, sausages, toasted English muffins with cream cheese, and a fruit salad. He downed three cups of coffee. When he finished, he rubbed his belly just like a happy child would have done.

Rejuvenated, and ready to get going on his quest, Frank took a cab to 37 Lakeshore Drive. He didn't want to call ahead for fear she'd refuse to see him. The trip was pleasant, particularly when the road left the city and began circling around

Lake Michigan. Skies were clear, it was sunny, and the leaves and grass were competing with the lake for best in show.

Ilene Samps' house, like all the other houses on the drive, was built on the south facing the lake. Her house was small, ranch style, an old vintage with wood planks as the exterior. The paint had long ago cracked and was peeling everywhere. Her house stood like an ill kept antique among other beautiful, modern houses. Frank was surprised the city hadn't stepped in to demand restoration to maintain equilibrium in the area.

Not sure if she was home, or whether she would receive him, Frank asked the cab driver to wait in the empty driveway. He noticed that the house had no garage, an anomaly for the area. How did anyone live out here without access to a vehicle?

Frank knocked at the front door which was slightly open to let in fresh air. A woman he assumed to be Ilene Samps opened the door immediately. Frank thought she must have come to stand watch when she heard a car pull in. "Forgive me for dropping in unannounced. My name is Frank Galitson. I've recently met with several members of the Swansen family. I don't know whether you're aware of the latest news concerning the family. May I come in?" He tried to look harmless and above suspicion.

Ilene Samps reminded Frank of the wicked witch of the north from the film The Wizard of Oz. He couldn't tell her age. Her salt-and-pepper hair was ragged and unkempt, her face sagged, and she wore a pair of eye glasses not seen since the early part of the last century. She stared at Frank for a long moment, before curtly giving him a signal to enter.

Frank's first shock at seeing her doubled when he entered the small living room, furnished with furniture that had seen better days. He couldn't even consider any of the pieces of furniture as antiques, just rubbish to be disposed of. He sank into a sofa like a rock dropped into a pail of water. He wondered how he'd extricate himself. He stared at bare walls which hadn't seen fresh paint since the house was built. Curtains covered two windows. Once they had been off-white, now they were black. There was a strong odor of decay in the room.

"Are you aware of the latest tragedy to befall the Swansen family?"

She snorted, then spoke in a husky voice that sounded unused. "Tragedy? Ha! Those people are stuffed with money. How could anything bad happen to them?"

"Are you aware that your sister was killed in a plane crash?" Frank asked that question since it seemed his hostess was living in some other time.

It seemed to Frank that she had no interest in her sister's well-being, or in responding to his question. "Why didn't I get a check this month? Do you know why?" She scratched at an open sore on her right arm, other ugly marks and bruises evident on her papery skin.

Frank thought that the only reason she had let him in was to do with money. "I don't know why, but I can check it out for you. I'll be in New York in a couple of days."

Frank decided to leave family issues until later. He wanted to get as much information as he could before she made him leave. "Do you own any Swansen shares?"

She hissed at him, spittle dotting her lips. "I wouldn't touch anything Swansen if my life depended on it."

It was clear to Frank how much Ilene Samps despised the Swansens. Should he pressure her for more information? "I understand they send you money every month. It's good of them to support you."

"Right... good of them to support me... the bastards couldn't begin to repay me for the damages they've inflicted on me. My life was ruined from the first day I laid eyes on the Swansen family." She spoke with disgust, hands clutching each other as if to stop her from hurting herself.

"What did they do to you?"

"It's been too long, too many years. I don't want to open old wounds. I've lived a miserable life and I hope it ends soon. I'm ready to die."

"You do know that Julius and Adela are dead, don't you?"

"God has punished them."

He realized no more useful data would come from this line of questioning. "I'm curious, where were you born?"

"Minneapolis. I had such a wonderful childhood. My world turned upside down when I met Julius, may he rot in hell."

"What about Adela?

"She was just as rotten as Julius. I wish them both eternity in the everlasting fires of hell." By now she was up and pacing, her anger rising.

Frank thought it best to bring the discussion to an end. He realized he'd have to do a lot of research in Minneapolis. He struggled to get up. Before leaving he renewed his promise to look into why her monthly payments had been stopped. "I'll let you know as soon as I return to New York." He didn't wait for a response, dashing to the door, anxious to get away as quickly as he could.

12.

Frank couldn't get Ilene Samps off his mind during the short flight to New York. She was the oddest old woman he'd met in a long, long time. Minneapolis surfaced in his mind once more. Jim Jones, Margaret Jones, Lisa, and now Adela's sister. Was Julius also from Minneapolis? Why had Ilene's payments suddenly stopped? When did they begin? What did the Minneapolis connection have to do with the Swansen murders?

Frank was bothered by Ilene Samps' open hatred for the Swansens. What had they done to her? Were they paying her to cover up for pain they'd caused? Was it blackmail? He wasn't sure how to get such information but he was anxious to do something. He was a fretful passenger and the flight attendants were glad to see the back of him.

Frank took a taxi, anxious to get home. The Swansen case interested him as the basis for his current novel, but it seemed everything he touched was becoming even more complicated than he could ever have dreamed.

As Frank's taxi approached the apartment building he noticed two police cars double-parked in front of the entrance, lights flashing, sirens silent. The first thing that came to his mind was the murder of Ms. Smith. Had Julia finally been found out?

The doorman greeted Frank warmly. "I'll have your luggage brought right up."

Abnormally for Frank, he felt a rush of warmth for this well known face. "Has Ms. Rendel returned?"

"No sir, I haven't seen her since she left with you."

As he left the elevator Frank was shocked to see the door to his penthouse apartment wide open. He heard voices within. He hurried his steps, wondering who was there and by whose authority. His belongings were in disarray. Every cupboard door stood open, piles of manuscript paper were mixed with bills on the table.

"Ah! You're back."

Frank heard a familiar voice from his left. It was Joe Caputo. "What are you doing here?" Frank was incredulous, his mouth agape, eyes wary.

"Executing a search warrant."

"Joe, what the hell are you talking about?"

"We received word from the District Attorney for Jackson Hole. He told us you're wanted for the murder of Gertrude Miller. Papers have been served electronically. You're to be held in jail until extradition papers have been filed."

Frank groped for the right words and the right demeanor. He'd learned his lesson about antagonizing the police. There was no upside to it. "Joe, this is insane and you know it. We spoke on the phone only two days ago. What evidence do they have? My business card? I've given out cards to hundreds of people over the years. I don't know her from a hole in the wall. I'd never heard her name before I saw her dead."

"They claim to have new evidence."

"Joe, sit down for a minute. You've known me for a long time." Frank told him about his conversation with the district attorney, his suspicions of some of the players in the drama and the help he'd solicited to obtain additional information. "It's obvious they're trying to get me out of the way. I've just come from Chicago where I met with Adela Swansen's sister. Something sinister must have happened in the past that's driving someone now to kill off all of the Swansen family."

Joe nodded but responded with a weary sigh. He dry scrubbed his face as if he'd been up too long. "The problem, Frank, is that legal papers have been filed. There's no way around it. When your time comes in court, you'll have a chance to fight the extradition process. Basically, you'll need to prove your innocence."

At that moment a female officer emerged from Frank's bedroom. "Joe, there's nothing here."

Joe turned to face his colleague, but before he could utter a word, Frank pulled Joe's gun from his holster. He pointed the gun at both officers, shouting, "Back up, get in the bedroom."

They stood their ground but Frank waved the pistol with menace. "Frank, you're making a huge mistake."

"I'm not going back to jail, not for a second. You know me better than anyone. I've kept you informed about the Swansen case from the very beginning. You know I'm innocent. I don't want to be a fugitive. I want you to demand to see the evidence. It's obvious the folks in Jackson Hole have conspired against me. I don't know the reason yet, but by God, I'm going to find out."

Joe thought a moment about Frank's statement, then said, "I don't doubt you for a minute. The problem is, I have to keep to the legalities."

"Joe, I'll leave quietly. You haven't seen me. You don't know where I am. I give you my word of honor. I'll call you every day to keep you posted on my findings. As long as I'm not here, the Jackson folks can do nothing."

"They may report you to the FBI."

"I'll take that chance."

Joe remained silent for several moments, reflecting on Frank's proposal. The other officer stayed quiet, hand hovering near her gun. Finally, he said, "I'll be taking a hell of a risk. I may end up losing my job."

"Joe, you won't lose a thing because I haven't committed murder. On the other hand, I can and will provide you with the goods so you can get all the credit for solving this case."

"Alright, Frank. Get out of here. Call me at home tonight."

Frank laid the gun on the floor with care, then rushed out. Fortunately, his luggage was still downstairs. The doorman hailed a taxi. "Milford Plaza Hotel, hurry." Frank chose a hotel near the Broadway theaters, mostly occupied by tourists, and completely unlike the pretentious places he usually frequented.

****

Immediately after checking in, Frank went to the Swansen office building. Janet, Weiserman's former secretary, had been promoted to Executive Assistant for the company's new CEO, Christopher Bolt. She was pleased to see Frank but her words were somber. "Mr. Bolt has been taken to the Cornell-Presbyterian Hospital. I was told it was food poisoning."

Frank felt a shock hit him. "When did this happen?"

"Sometime after dinner last night."

"Who's in charge now?"

"Ruth Stewart. The Board of Directors promoted Christopher to Chairman and Ruth to President. The market has taken these promotions well. We've seen only positive changes in our position."

"I must see her right away. It's damn urgent."

She was taken aback by the profanity but stayed with the conversation. "What about? I have to tell her secretary something."

"I met Adela's sister in Chicago. Something sinister has taken place which may seriously affect the company. The murders in Yellowstone may have been just the beginning." Frank sounded melodramatic and Janet took a step back.

"Let me see what I can do."

She returned a few minutes later. "Follow me. She'll see you right away. Her secretary and I are good friends."

Ruth walked around her huge desk to extend her hand. She looked different. Her hair was now a burnished auburn with strategic highlights, with a shorter, more current cut. She looked much younger. Her tailored blue business suit gave her the aura of a polished executive. "Janet told me you have some worrisome news."

"I'm afraid I do." Frank said, sitting himself at Ruth's invitation in a comfortable leather armchair across from her desk.

Ruth sat down, a worried look on her face. "I knew something must have gone amok when the security analysts seemed concerned. I know Janet thinks all is well but I have some doubts."

"It's really a Swansen family matter, but it may affect the company. I'd appreciate it if you would tell me everything you know about the Swansen family, before the death of Julius and Adela, particularly about Julius' parents, brothers, sisters, and their children."

"I'll tell you what I know, but first you said you had worrisome news." She stared at him, waiting, a woman used to being in charge.

Frank realized Ruth wanted to know the reason for his visit before she would open up. "I will tell you everything I know, that's why I'm here. However, a few pieces are missing in my investigation. Hopefully, by talking with you, I'll be able to tie some loose issues together."

"Where do you want me to begin?"

"From whatever you know, or heard about the past of Julius and Adela."

"Julius was in his early twenties when he came to New York after graduating from MIT. I don't know why he didn't return to his hometown of Minneapolis. He was proud of his personal history, telling us many stories about his success in the world of business. He started as a clerk in a scrap metal company and moved up quickly. The owner of the company was an immigrant from Poland who'd lost his family during the war. There were no survivors. He willed his entire business to Julius whom he considered a son. Julius was a self-educated man with a lot of street smarts. He invented the fabrication of certain metals used for aircraft and NASA. He changed the name of the company, building it up, mostly by buying scrapped navy vessels. The business mushroomed. He took the company public, then ventured into every related metal and alloy business. Since going public the company's shares have soared. Sales grew each year by hefty percentages and the company paid better than average dividends. The shares always sold well and the people hung on to what they were able to get."

"Do you know anything about his family in Minneapolis?"

"Not a thing. Julius never spoke about Minneapolis. In fact, I recall a reporter asking him a question once about his hometown. Julius changed the subject before you could bat an eyelash. At the time I felt he was hiding something, but I didn't think it was any of my business. His personal life was his." She was watching Frank closely to see his reaction to her story.

"Did you know Adela?"

"I met her several times. She was a tough woman, always wanting to be in control. She was particularly concerned when Julius was traveling on business. I always felt that she wanted him by her side every single moment of the day. The telephone operator gossiped about the frequency of her calls, sometimes three or four of them a day."

"I understand Julius' parents are dead. Did their death result from illness? Where did they live?"

"They lived in Minneapolis. He never went to visit them and they never came to New York. I believe they were estranged. They died from food poisoning some time after the plane crash."

"What about Adela's parents?"

"Also from Minneapolis. She had no relationship with them either."

"I'm told Julius' brother died in Brazil. What do you know about him?"

"I know nothing about………"

At that moment Janet rushed into Ruth's office, hysterical, screaming, "I called the hospital to find out how Christopher was… he died several minutes ago." She was sobbing loudly. Frank got up, put his arms around her and sat her in the armchair next to his. "Can I get you anything?" He looked up at Ruth, saying, "I strongly believe that your life is in danger too. We'll have to talk about that in a moment." She looked on in disbelief as Janet was consoled by Frank.

Ruth's secretary took charge of Janet, speaking to her quietly and calmly while slowly easing her out of the office. Ruth dropped heavily into her chair. Frank had nothing to say for a few minutes but he was thinking feverishly. The picture was getting uglier by the minute. Food poisoning had reportedly killed Julius' parents, now Christopher Bolt. There had been some poison in Sheila's system. The killings of Joseph Weiserman, Gertrude Miller and Christopher Bolt, none of them members of the Swansen family, were a total mystery. Except for Gertrude, who Frank believed had been killed solely to incriminate him, the others must have had some connection with the family, but what?

Ruth sat immobilized, face blank. Frank finally spoke. "We must keep going. What was the brother's name?"

"I don't know," she whispered. "Why would anyone want to kill Christopher?" Her eyes welled. "This is getting out of hand. We have to call the police." She picked up the phone, hands trembling so much she needed both of them to lift the receiver.

Frank leapt from his seat, slamming her hands down. "Let's talk about your safety first. The police aren't going to watch out for you. They don't provide the kind of service you're going to need."

"What do you mean?"

"I suggest you stay put in the office, day and night if necessary, until this investigation is over and the culprits are found. Hire private bodyguards to literally live here in the building with you. Have someone bring you clothes and anything else you might need. There must be someone you can trust to bring you things. Don't set a foot outside of the building. Order food from different restaurants every day, never from the same place. Are you following me?"

Ruth nodded attentively. Tears still ran down her cheeks, but they flowed unnoticed.

Frank reverted to their previous conversation. "What do you know about Adela's parents?"

"They died years ago."

"Adela has a sister, Ilene Samps. I spoke to her two days ago. She lives a miserable life. It seems she hates the Swansens with passion, but she refused to talk about the past. What do you know about her? Why is she so angry?"

Ruth wiped the tears from her face. Her makeup was a mess. "I can't think straight." She began to sob again, then exploded, "I could kill the person who started all this with my bare hands. We were such a peaceful company." She slammed her hands on the desk, knocking the telephone to the floor.

"Ruth, you have to pay attention. Time is of the essence."

Ruth pulled out several tissues and scrubbed at her face. Mascara was streaked under her eyes. "Christopher told me that a check in the amount of $2,000 was delivered to her every month. He didn't know why. Julius refused to talk about her. Her expenses were charged to a miscellaneous account."

"Who wrote the checks?"

"Christopher's secretary."

"Who signed those checks?"

"Christopher. Sometimes I did if he was away."

"Have his secretary come here."

A young woman in her late twenties rushed in, obviously shocked, her face wet with tears. Ruth introduced her to Frank, then asked her to sit down. "Allison, pull yourself together for a minute. Christopher's death is a great tragedy but we have to think about the hundreds of men and women who work for Swansen Metals." Both Ruth and Frank watched with compassion as she tried to take control. She sat up straight, pushing her disheveled hair back into place and said she was ready.

Frank took the lead. "Allison, I'm investigating the Swansen murders. Please tell us whatever you know about the family, including any gossip you may have heard. We believe that Christopher's death is directly related to all the other killings. Anything you can tell us may help solve the case. Leave nothing out."

"Oh my God… oh my God…" Allison fell back in her chair, unconscious. Ruth ran out to get help.

Allison's right hand had fallen to the side of her chair. Frank could see a large, square cut diamond ring on her finger. Frank wondered whether Allison had been engaged to Christopher, given the depth of her emotional outburst.

Two women came into the office with Ruth, one carrying a first aid kit and the other a bottle of water. Gently they moved Allison to a sofa on the other side of the office, an area usually used for informal conferences. They placed a damp cloth on her forehead, then brought a small bottle of smelling salts to her nose. Allison stirred, slowly opening her eyes. She was very pale, her face blank. It seemed as if she were recovering from a coma rather than a faint. She looked completely at sea.

Allison was helped into a sitting position and a heavily sweetened cup of tea was placed in her hands. She sat with her hands wrapped around the cup for warmth. It took a couple of minutes before she whispered, "Did I pass out?"

"You'll be ok," Ruth said. "You've had a shock."

"We were supposed to get married next month." She spoke, hysteria evident in her voice. The cup of tea sat beside her, but she couldn't bring herself to drink it.

Ruth tried to say something but Frank shushed her, leading her to the other side of the room. "Let her calm down. This is not the time to pressure her."

"I had no idea those two were in love."

"How long has Allison worked here?"

"Three, maybe four years."

"Ok... I'll be back tomorrow. Make sure to engage bodyguards. Don't you dare leave this office until the investigation is over. Your life depends on it. Don't meet with any strangers. Speak only to people you know personally." Frank was so authoritative that Ruth could only nod her agreement.

"I'll be hounded by security analysts and the media. We've gained too much notoriety already for this to pass unnoticed."

"Call the Board to an urgent meeting. Explain the circumstances. Let them handle the press and the market. Stay out of sight."

Frank left a bewildered Ruth trying hard to remain calm. She was afraid for both herself and the company. Someone was after the Swansens and the company. Why? Who? What was the motive? Her head spun as she returned to her desk, sinking heavily into her chair. She held her head in both hands, completely dazed.

13.

Frank took himself off to the Swansen twins' apartment on Central Park West. He hoped to find them at home. They were and surprisingly they agreed to see him with alacrity.

Both Margaret and Elizabeth hugged and kissed him. "You saved us from being jailed. We don't know how to thank you." What a change from their recent encounter.

Frank could hardly hide his disbelief. "You can help by giving me some information. I have a lot of questions and I'm concerned about the two of you."

"What do you want to know?"

"Everything about your family from the very beginning."

Both Margaret and Elizabeth took a brief look at each other. Margaret sighed, then started a story they both knew all too well. "We know nothing about our parents' history. They never talked about their past. Whenever we asked questions, and we had many, in particular about our grandparents whom we hardly knew, they would change the subject. Our curiosity only got worse because of their denials, but there was no way to find out anything."

Frank looked at them in amazement before going on to his next topic. Both of them sat facing him, looking innocent and calm. "Why did your father choose the two of you to represent his trust when there were older children?"

"We don't know. We only found out about it when the wills were read after their death. We were more surprised than anyone."

"Who was the attorney for your parents?"

"David Ramsey of Ramsey & Stern. They're still at 117 Madison Avenue. Our parents never used anyone else."

"You told me that you were having dinner with Mr. Weiserman the night your sister was killed. What was that get together about? Did you see him often?"

They shook their heads in unison. Frank was momentarily sidetracked by the twin behavior, unnoticed by them because they were so used to it. "We've met with him several times since our parents died. Naming us as trustees was the main reason we saw him. We didn't know a thing about business and felt a need to educate ourselves. At the time, there was a lot of talk about whether or not to sell the company."

"Did you trust Mr. Weiserman?"

"Absolutely. It seemed to us that he always wanted the best for the company. He adored our father."

"Was he for, or against, selling the company?"

"He was against. He said the company was doing well, that every year it grew more profitable. Bank debt was declining accordingly, which helped elevate our share value in the market. He believed the value of the company would more than double in ten years. We talked with him often about this, sometimes in meetings, but more often over the phone." The twins were taking turns to answer, so Frank was swiveling his head back and forth.

"How well did you know your mother's sister, Ilene?"

"We only know her by name. We've never seen her."

"Yet she claims you came to her to talk about selling the shares she owned." Frank deliberately lied, wanting to check their reaction.

They looked at each other in amazement. "Frank, we give you our word. We've never seen her. We don't even know where she lives."

"Why do you think your brother and sisters were murdered?"

"It's quite obvious, isn't it? Someone is after our wealth."

"Who do you suspect?" Frank knew this was a stupid question, but he couldn't leave any stone unturned.

"We don't know. It seems to be too big of an enterprise for one person."

"Are you afraid the killer, or killers, will come after you?"

At his question the twins each gave an involuntary shudder and grasped each others hand. "We are. That's why you had to go through all the security checks in our lobby. We're afraid to set foot outside the building. We feel like unjustly accused prisoners."

"You're doing the right thing. If I were you, I'd also find a reputable company and post an armed guard at the apartment door."

Frank left behind two badly frightened women. He returned to his hotel, ordering dinner from room service. He settled down in a comfortable chair to watch the local six o'clock news. Minutes later a breathless news anchor announced the mysterious death of Christopher Bolt, recently elevated to the position of CEO after the death of Joseph Weiserman, head of the Swansen Metal Company. Deaths of two CEOs in a very short period of time will raise many questions was the finale of the two minute blurb.

Frank got on the phone right away to Ruth Stewart. "Christopher's death was just announced on the evening news. The anchor said the death of two CEOs, one right after the other, is highly suspicious. Has the Board met?"

"It's set for tomorrow morning at 8:30. Two directors were out of town, flying back in tonight."

"Did you get Allison to talk?"

"Yes. She said they had fallen in love almost as soon as she began to work for him. They had to keep it secret because Christopher was in the process of divorcing his wife. The divorce finally came through about three months ago."

"Good work. What were you able to find out about the checks to Ilene Samps?"

"Allison found a letter in Christopher's safe, signed by Julius, which authorized a payment of $2,000 a month to Ilene Samps. It expired upon her death, or two years after his death, whichever came first. That's why she isn't getting any more checks."

Frank thanked her for her help, reminded her to exert caution in all her movements then said, "Please let me know the outcome of the Board meeting. I'll wait for your call."

****

Julia's disappearance began to haunt Frank. The following morning he stopped to chat with the doorman in his building, inquiring whether Julia had returned. He was surprised to hear that she had come in late the day before and had left early in the morning. Had there been anything unusual about her? His reply was that she had been carrying a large carry-on bag with an airline tag attached, but he hadn't been able to read it.

In the late afternoon he decided to call on Julia's father at his office in the charity foundation. Surely he hadn't left yet, being dedicated to his work as he was. Frank hailed a taxi, asking the driver, a swarthy ill kempt man, to drive as quickly as he could through the heavy traffic.

Julia's father was pleased to see Frank. Before he could say a word her father asked, "Have you any idea where Julia is? I've been trying to connect with her for weeks."

"I'm afraid not. We had an argument and she disappeared."

"What were you two arguing about? That's not like you." He seemed quite interested in what might have caused her departure. He knew his daughter well and was surprised at such impetuous behavior.

Frank shook his head. "If I knew what was on her mind, I'd be happy to tell you. The argument was about her jealousy. While we were in Yellowstone a ranger recognized me and corralled me into helping with a murder investigation. Julia became jealous of her. Her anger and her incessant questions drove me crazy. There was no reason for her to behave the way she did. I came here in the hope of you telling me where I might find her."

"I wish I knew. I can't do the work of two anymore. I'm tired. I badly need her help."

"Can you think of any place she may have gone?"

Julia's father became quiet and pensive. His hand rubbed his chin as he leaned back in his chair. Frank remained silent. Finally, "She must be paying her rent. Check with building management. They may know something."

"Excellent idea. I hadn't thought of that."

Frank ordered dinner sent in from a nearby Thai restaurant. His mind was racing. He wondered why he was so interested in Julia's whereabouts. Had his sudden surge of love for Lisa been real, or was his unhappy estrangement from Julia the reason for his emotions? Frank suddenly sat up as an image of Lisa surfaced in his mind. There was something in her smile that reminded him of Elizabeth's smile. He quickly dismissed this line of thinking since many people have similar facial expressions.

Dinner was delivered, but before he could relax enough to eat, he had to call Joe Caputo. First, he reported the results of his meetings. He asked Joe to check recent airline passenger lists to determine where Julia had been. Joe told him that was an impossible task. There was no way he could possibly check every airport across the country. Frank felt a surge of disappointment that he quickly checked. He understood Joe's time was not his own.

The next morning Frank went to the management office to speak with the clerk who looked after rent payments. The clerk laughed at Frank's request, saying he could care less where the envelopes came from so long as they brought in the money. Frank returned to his hotel unsatisfied. He began calling every friend of Julia's that he knew. No one had heard from her. Everyone expressed their concerns. It was completely unlike Julia to be out of touch.

Frank wondered if Julia had taken her life. She had been so distraught when she left. His conscience was nagging him. He fought this off in his mind. While he had liked Julia a lot, he believed subconsciously he had rejected her because of the aggressiveness of her love.

In the middle of his sad thoughts about Julia, a picture of Gertrude Miller sprung up. Who was she? Why had she been strangled? Had she been related to the Swansens? Her death seemed so similar to the murder of Ms. Smith. Had Julia killed her, leaving Frank's business card in her purse to incriminate him? Frank decided he needed to find out who she had been. It was another tangle of knots to unravel.

Later that evening something occurred to Frank. He got on line to look up Genie.com, a service that helped build family trees. He plugged in Julius Swansen's name. There were a number of Swansens in the Minnesota area, but only one Julius Svansen, a typical Swedish name. Had Julius Americanized his last name? If so, for what purpose?

Frank was sure that all the murders were related to someone in the family seeking access to all the wealth. There must be something in Julius' background. The fact that the twins had repeatedly said their parents would never talk about their roots served to strengthen this conviction.

As soon as he'd started an investigation of Gertrude Miller, and got word from Ruth Stewart, he'd be on his way to Minneapolis. He was finally able to go to sleep once he had a plan of action.

****

1022 Second Avenue was a four story brick apartment building. There were three small stores on the ground floor; a cigarette and newspaper shop, a shoe repair shop, and a pet grooming facility. A locked entry door stood between the pet and the shoe repair shops. An electronic entry system was located on the right side. Frank scrolled down the names. There were six in all, among them 'Miller'.

He pressed the button with no response. He turned to leave, but pressed it one more time. Frank was shocked to hear a deep, tremulous voice. "Gertrude, did you forget your keys again?"

Frank decided to try and imitate a woman's voice, whispering, "Yes."

The buzzer went off. Frank pushed the door open. He was in. He climbed to the third floor. The door to Gertrude's apartment was open. He entered, quietly closing the door behind him. The air was musty and there were worn spots on the carpet.

A very old man sat on the sofa, his wrinkled face a blank mask. He was still in his pajamas. Frank couldn't determine his age. He hadn't seen anyone this old before. "Are you Gertrude's father?" The old man didn't move or respond. Frank raised his voice, repeating his question.

The loud voice made the old man turn his head slightly. He stared at Frank with glassy eyes. Finally, he said, "Hello, you look good." His voice was so low pitched Frank could barely understand him.

Frank realized the old man must be suffering from Alzheimer's or some form of dementia, yet he tried to get some sort of information out of him. "I saw Gertrude a few days ago."

The name 'Gertrude' brought a change to the man's demeanor. He looked more closely at Frank, saying in a whisper, "Is Gertrude here?"

Frank continued with his questions, fearing the old man would lose his momentary lucidity. "Do you know Julius Swansen?"

"Julius... Julius," he repeated to himself several times. "I miss him so much."

"Are you related to Julius?"

"Julius... are you hiding behind the tree? I'll find you." The old man spoke the words of a child in his husky voice.

Frank caught on quickly. "Here I am," he said joyfully, despite the fact he had no interest in playing games. He wanted answers and fast.

"Help me find Ilene. Where is she?" The old man turned his head as if looking for someone. It was painful to watch his movements.

Just then the front door creaked open. A heavy set Afro-American woman, wearing green scrubs, entered the room. She looked at Frank with obvious suspicion. "Who are you?" The high pitch of her voice came through like a shrill to Frank's ears.

.   He put on a fake smile. "I have news about Gertrude. Are you taking care of this old man?"

She reached over to pat the old man on the cheek. He was obviously special to her. "What news? We haven't heard from her in days."

"The news is bad. She was found dead in Wyoming."

"What? How? What happened?" She held her hands to her cheeks, trying to take in this awful news.

"I'm investigating her death. I'm here to try and find out what I can about her."

Like everyone else she assumed Frank to be a detective. "Was she murdered?"

"Yes. Please be seated. I need some answers. Who is this old man?"

"Gertrude's father. He lost his mind several years ago. We're trying to keep him in his own home as long as we can."

"How long have you worked here?"

"About two years."

"Does the name 'Julius Swansen' mean anything to you? Have you heard that name?"

"Yes, he mumbles the name Julius sometimes in his delusions, but it all sounds like when they were children. That's quite a common experience with people suffering from Alzheimer's."

"What about 'Ilene'?"

"Yes... yes... he's been saying that name a lot lately."

"In conjunction with what?"

"It's always about children's' games."

"Has he ever said anything outlandish or completely out of place?"

She remained silent for several moments. Finally, "I don't know if this means anything, but twice now I've heard him say something about twin dolls. Men this age usually never played with dolls."

"Did Gertrude work?"

"Not that I know of."

"What do they live on?"

"I saw checks coming in regularly from a bank."

"Could you show me?"

Frank followed her into a small bedroom. A narrow desk stood in the corner, cluttered with papers and unopened mail. He found an envelope with the Chase Trust logo addressed to Simon Miller. He found a check inside made out to Simon Miller in the amount of $2,500. The check was dated the first of the month.

Frank turned to the nurse. "Do the Millers have any relatives?"

"I've never seen any."

"How do you get paid?"

She seemed unsurprised by his questions. "Every other Friday. I should have gotten a check last Friday but Gertrude wasn't here. What should I do now?"

"Stay put for a few days. I'll be back." He thanked her and spoke gently to the old man as he left the apartment.

Frank's mind was going in circles. The old man had talked about Julius and mentioned Ilene's name. Was this Ilene the same Ilene Samps he'd met? He rushed to the Chase Bank offices on Broad Street in downtown Manhattan.

Using his well known name and with persistence Frank finally bullied his way into the administrative area. Hugh Templeton, Vice President in charge of the trust division, sat behind a large mahogany desk reading his computer when Frank was shown in. He rose promptly, extending a welcoming hand. "How can I help you, Mr. Galitson. Are you Frank Galitson the author?"

"Yes, in the flesh."

"I love your stories. Keep on writing." His response was quite cheerful.

"Actually, I'm in the middle of a real mystery which I believe may become my best novel ever."

"Sounds terrific. I love mysteries."

"I'll send you my first copy, signed."

"I'll cherish it."

"Well... speaking of mysteries, I know the information I'm looking for is confidential. Let me give you some background." Frank went on to tell him about the Swansen murders as well as the killings inside the company. "I'm helping the police with the investigation. If you can't give me the information, they'll have to come with a search warrant. I think I can save you the trouble."

His listener looked on with great interest. "What do you need to know?"

"Simon Miller gets a monthly check from your trust division. I want to know who established the trust and the terms of it."

Mr. Templeton remained silent for several moments before speaking. "Trusts are absolutely confidential. If I break confidentiality I may lose my job."

"Then don't concern yourself. I'll have the police here in minutes." Frank pulled his cell phone from his jacket pocket and dialed. "Detective Joe Caputo, please, its Frank Galitson."

"Hang up."

The detective came on. "Joe, I've discovered something about the Miller murder. I'll call you tonight." Frank hung up before Caputo could say a word.

Templeton was already on the intercom. "Get me the Simon Miller Trust, please."

A green folder was delivered in minutes. The young man carrying the folder studiously avoided looking at Frank. He entered and left without a word. The door hushed shut. Templeton read through some papers before saying, "The Simon Miller Trust was set up by Julius Swansen twenty-five years ago, with five million dollars. From the income we were to pay Simon Miller $2,500 a month until his death. Upon his death the balance of the fund is to be given to Ilene Samps. In the event that Mr. Miller survives Ilene, the money will go to Julius' twin daughters."

Frank let out a big gust of air. Finally some actual facts. "Thank you very much. I'll make sure the police don't bother you."

"Don't forget to send me your book."

"I won't."

The few words that had been uttered by Gertrude's father, along with the information Frank had received from the bank was drawing him in a new direction. He was amazed by the continuing twists and turns of the Swansen mystery. He took a taxi back to the Miller residence. The nurse let him in. "I'm sorry to bother you, but I have one more question. Do you know where the old man came from before he moved to New York?"

"No idea."

"I'll need to go through his papers in greater detail."

She gestured him back into the bedroom, returning to something on the stove in the kitchen. She seemed completely unconcerned, no curiosity. He searched the drawers in the chest, went through the closet, then went through a metal filing cabinet standing next to the desk. He checked through endless files until he found one containing old documents; a marriage license, birth certificates, outdated driver's licenses, insurance policies, high school diplomas, and clips of old newspapers. It looked like the old man had been a pack rat, which was certainly in Frank's favor.

The old man had been born in Minneapolis as had his wife and daughter Gertrude. There were no other birth certificates, leading Frank to assume that Gertrude had been an only child. Simon Miller's high school diploma had been issued by Lincoln High School in Minneapolis.

There were three yellowed newspaper clips. All three had an identical date scribbled by hand at the top. Frank read through them quickly. He was able to determine that the articles had been cut from three different newspapers.

Julius Svansen and Simon Miller, eleventh grade students at Lincoln High School, were arrested yesterday by the police, charged with breaking into the YWCA pool area. They were discovered in the women's locker room peering at the girls in the shower. Judge Hamilton locked them up for a week before ordering them to community service for a month cleaning the public restrooms in the courthouse. The boys' parents were also reprimanded, being told quite sternly to keep a better eye on their children.

The articles confirmed that Julius was a native of Minneapolis, and that there had been a connection between him and Simon Miller from an early age. Why a trust had been set up for Simon was something Frank hoped to discover while continuing to investigate Gertrude's murder.

Frank's cell phone rang, Ruth Stewart on the line. "The Board of Directors is looking for an outside chairman. They have decided to look for a man with great prestige, to properly maintain the company's image." She sounded sad and tired and hung up quickly.

Frank returned to his hotel where he called Joe Caputo. After filling him in on the latest details he told him, "I've booked a seat on United to Minneapolis. I'm leaving early in the morning. This mystery keeps getting more convoluted. There have to be some answers somewhere."

14.

Frank left LaGuardia airport on a Delta Airways plane which delivered him to Minneapolis at 1:30 p.m. He flew first class as usual, reveling in the luxury of space to stretch out his legs. A short taxi ride to the Hilton Garden Hotel in downtown Minneapolis pleased him. He was in no mood for long rides. The Swansen mystery, with all of its twists and turns, was turning into a heavy burden. The only thing keeping him going, though, was that his findings would help him write a great novel.

As soon as he checked in, he canvassed the local telephone directory, finding a Lincoln High School on 44th Street, in the northeastern part of town. He called there to find out that the school's principal was now a Ms. Deborah Farrell who agreed to see him at 3:00 p.m. There was not much time for him to fill in so he contented himself with a cappuccino in the lobby restaurant.

Ms. Farrell, a gray haired woman in her early sixties, had as her most prominent characteristic a pair of multi colored framed glasses. Her face was pale, and the glasses served to accent dark brown eyes. To Frank she looked like a typical librarian. Her office was small, a wooden desk taking up most of the space. Two simple wooden chairs stood against a wall. Pictures of past presidents, all men, decorated the wall behind her desk. There was barely room to move. The floor was a utilitarian tile, much scuffed. This did not have the appearance of an affluent school district.

Frank explained who he was and filled her in on his latest adventure. "I've come to believe that something occurred in this city that had a long standing effect on the life of Julius Swansen. I've obtained some old newspaper clips connecting Julius and a friend of his, Simon Miller, to this school. I wonder if you have records dating back forty years."

She shook her head at him, wondering what kind of idiot would think any organization would keep records for so long. "We don't keep anything beyond twenty-five years. Our Board of Education set that as a time frame many years ago."

"What a shame. Do you know if there is anyone in the area who might have worked or taught here at that time?"

She took a moment or two, searching her mind. "There are two or three. A teacher named Peter Fodor... and a Jennifer Roberts."

"Do you know where I can find them?"

"The school secretary might know. He's been here a long time. Please wait." She left the room, returning a few moments later. "Here you are," handing Frank a sheet of paper with two names and addresses on it.

He almost grabbed at it in his hurry to unravel the next piece of this puzzle. "Thanks. Please, call me if you find out anything... anything at all about these two men. I would really appreciate it."

She watched him go with some understandable concern. No one had ever wanted to know things like this before.

Frank decided to make good use of the remaining hours of the afternoon. He hailed a passing cab. "Minneapolis Home for the Aged on Park Avenue." This was the address of the first person on his list.

Peter Fodor was more than happy to see Frank. He was a lonely man in his 80's and there were no family members in the area. He welcomed anyone who wished to talk to him. He missed having an active social life, and the activities at the nursing home bored him to tears. He loved children but could not develop a liking for the old men and women in his present home. Frank's appearance was a godsend for him and he really didn't care what they talked about. Having a visitor at all was a coup for him as some of the residents had no one to come and visit them.

Frank's questions about Julius Swansen brought back many old memories. "Who could forget Julius. He stood out among thousands of students. He was a clever boy, one of the best math and physics students I ever had. He was my prize student. I was glad when he told me he had taken my advice and enrolled at MIT. I knew he would make something of his life. He was a genius with numbers." The old man spoke with pride, as if he was personally responsible for Julius' success.

Frank wasn't looking for a report on a triple A student. He felt Julius must have had a dark side given what he'd already found out about the man. "Do you know anything about him apart from his school talents? Was his behavior that of a normal child? Was he eccentric in any way? Did he mix well with other children?"

"Every genius throughout history has been an eccentric. Look at Einstein, Teller, Oppenheim, Bloch or Serber, they were all half crazy." He was reverting to his former position, an educator who expected others to be interested in his views.

"Did Julius commit any criminal acts that you can recall?"

The old man remained silent for a while, then shook his head. "I really don't know much about his private life. I never got involved in any of my students' personal affairs and I wasn't one for gossiping or listening to gossip."

"Did you hear from or see Julius after he left Lincoln High?"

"He called me once after he graduated from MIT. That was the last time I heard from him. I've wondered what became of him."

"Does the name Ilene Samps mean anything to you?"

"Ilene Samps... Ilene Samps... no. It doesn't ring a bell."

"Does the name Simon Miller mean anything to you?"

"No, I don't recall that name either." The old man was becoming upset because his memory was being called into question.

"If anything comes to mind I'd appreciate your calling me." Frank left his card, hoping for more. Maybe Jennifer Roberts would have some answers but it was late and he didn't want to call on her at night. He returned to his hotel where he ordered dinner from room service. He didn't feel like eating alone in a restaurant. He couldn't get his mind off the Swansen case. The reason why Julius had set up a fund to pay Simon Miller $2,500 and $2,000 a month to Ilene Samps was eluding him. After all, neither recipient was a family member. Frank tried to think of a set of circumstances that might have led to such payments, but quickly realized that speculating would produce nothing. It took him a while to settle his mind so he could finally get some sleep.

Jennifer Roberts lived in an assisted living complex provided by the State of Minnesota. There was no response to his repeated ringing of her doorbell. Eventually he found her in a recreation room in the lobby, sitting at a round table with several other elderly women, playing cards. They were intent on their game, but chatting all the time they made their moves.

Frank's sudden appearance caused some commotion among the players. They weren't used to visitors at that hour of the day. Frank apologized, then asked for Jennifer, who introduced herself. She joined him for a brief chat, glad for any change in her routine. The other ladies eyed the pair speculatively, whispering to each other.

Frank explained the reason for his visit without going into all the sordid details. "I know it isn't easy to remember events from forty years past, particularly since thousands of pupils passed through your classroom, but several people have been killed and the investigation is far from over."

Jennifer Roberts was in her late seventies. Her upright body was slim and she had excellent posture, her shoulders squared. There wasn't a single wrinkle to be seen, either a testament to a great genetic background or a gifted plastic surgeon. She smiled at Frank's remarks. "You're underestimating me, young man," pointing her finger at him, "I can remember every one of my students. I never forget a name or a face."

Frank returned her smile. "That'll make my life much easier. I'm interested in several people: Julius Swansen, Adela, his wife, Simon Miller, and Ilene Samps. They're all part of the puzzle."

Jennifer stared at Frank over reading glasses perched low on her nose. "You've come to the right place. I can tell you everything you want to know about them. Shoot."

Frank felt like a rock had been removed from his shoulders. Finally, someone who remembered the past. "I want to know everything about Julius Swansen. He's at the very center of my investigation."

"First, you must know that his name was Svansen, not Swansen, and second, Julius and Simon were like two peas in a pod. Those two boys were inseparable." Her tone was tutorial but her face was full of interest in their conversation.

Frank had to smile at the tone but didn't comment. "I read a clipping taken from an old newspaper that stated both Julius and Simon had spent some time in jail, then did community work as punishment. What can you tell me about their behavior?"

"I always had a feeling that Julius was far wilder than Simon. We overlooked his behavior because he was such an outstanding student, perhaps even a genius." Her smile broadened as she recalled this wonderfully gifted young man.

"What did you overlook?"

"He was always chasing after girls. He was suspected of impregnating two girls, one in the tenth grade and the other in the eleventh, but somehow the affairs were hushed up. The girls were wild about him. They all wanted to be with him and there were plenty of fights and tears over him."

"Was one of the girls Ilene Samps?"

"How did you know?" She was astonished by his question.

"Frankly, I wasn't sure. What happened with the pregnancies?"

"They both had abortions. The school principal did his best to keep the matter out of the press and away from the school population, but I got wind of it." She spoke with pride, as if to show her superiority in her awareness of gossip.

"Did Julius or Simon have a relationship with Ilene?"

"They both did. Those three always hung out together. They used to be the talk of the class. There was a lot of whispering whenever they came into a room together."

"Did you know that Julius and Adela died in a plane crash?"

"Of course, I read newspapers." She was affronted that Frank would think her so out of touch. Just because she lived in an assisted living facility didn't make her old and useless and she

162

wasted no time telling Frank so. He offered profuse apologies to placate her.

"Anything about Ilene and Adela?"

"It seems you're unaware that they were twins."

Frank straightened up, staring blankly at Jennifer. The word 'twins' hit a nerve. "Who was the other pregnant girl?"

"Adela. Who else?"

"Julius was an active bastard."

"Actually, it was Simon who admitted to impregnating Ilene."

Frank's head was going in circles. "When did Julius marry Adela?"

"A year after he married Ilene."

Frank's mind was now in a complete whirl. "Did Julius and Ilene have a child?"

"I don't know. They left town. They moved to Chicago or New York."

"Did you follow Julius' career?"

"The financial papers were always full of information about his company. His success didn't surprise me one bit. I knew this genius of a boy would make something of himself. I even bought shares when his company went public. I made a fortune. I didn't care about his earlier problems with girls. By the time he left high school all anyone cared about was what his next move would be."

"I was told Julius had a brother. Was he also a student in your school?"

"Sure. He was eight years behind Julius, and a very difficult boy he was. He had a terrible attitude, a chip on his shoulder that he couldn't seem to shake off."

"Do you recall his name?"

"Of course, Matthew." Anticipating Frank's next question, she continued, "He left the country soon after graduating. I heard he went to South America."

"Is there anything else you can tell me about the Swansens?"

"Julius' parents were a queer couple. I always doubted their parental abilities. I don't think they had any interest in controlling their sons."

"You've been very helpful. I thank you very much. Should anything related to this family come to mind, I'd appreciate your calling me." Frank gave her his card, making sure she knew how grateful he was for her information.

Frank couldn't get over the fact that Simon Miller had first married Ilene. It was obvious both Julius and Simon had some deep attachment to Ilene. Adela and Ilene were twins. Something had gone on between this foursome. How could he find out the details of those relationships? Frank became even more convinced that the murderous events of the last few weeks were all related to the past.

Frank began to think about Julius' brother Matthew. He couldn't remember who told him Matthew had died in Brazil. Since he was certain, beyond any doubt, that a member of the family was after the Swansen wealth, he decided he needed to investigate Matthew. Has he really died, or was this just a smoke screen?

15.

Frank booked a first class seat, as always, on an American Airlines flight to Rio de Janeiro, Brazil. The nine p.m. flight left Kennedy Airport on time. The plane was completely full. After a gourmet meal of filet mignon and steamed vegetables, along with a small bottle of red wine, Frank slept for several hours. He was able to recline almost full length and he was warmed by a light blanket. Even the pillow was soft, like his down filled ones at home. Frank certainly enjoyed the little luxuries his success allowed him.

The seven and a half hour flight was uneventful. As scheduled, the plane landed at seven-thirty. A town car and driver awaited his arrival. The new Marriott Hotel where he had booked himself was located on Copacabana Beach Avenue, facing Guanabara Bay and Sugar Loaf Mountain. The view was exquisite, the beach crowded with well oiled and well muscled bodies.

Immediately after settling in his room, Frank called the U.S. Consul in Rio, requesting an appointment. The consul, Jerry Cox, wasn't busy. He accepted Frank's invitation for dinner in the restaurant at the Copacabana Palace Hotel. Frank spent the next several hours making notes to avoid forgetting any details. As he wrote, the complexity of the Swansen case became more vivid in his mind. Most murder cases were simple, but this one, he concluded, had been well planned and well executed. Chances were the last murder hadn't happened yet.

Frank was convinced that the present tragedy had taken root after Julius and Simon graduated from high school. He made a mental note to visit Ilene once more to pry out more information, even if he had to use force.

Jerry Cox, a young man in his 30's, wore a dove gray business suit with a tie to match. He arrived at the restaurant precisely on the dot. Frank recognized him immediately; he had the look of a sleek, well fed diplomat. Cox's light hazel hair bordered on blonde and he wore a pair of gold rimmed bi-focals. Frank's first thought when seeing Cox was that anyone with him would gain in prestige.

They shook hands with warmth. Cox had a grip that represented confidence and authority. He wasn't a man to bother with small talk, getting right to the point. "Mr. Frank Galitson, the author, I presume. Are you seeking a mystery in Rio for your next novel?"

Frank was both amazed and deeply pleased by the acknowledgement of who he was. "The mystery is actually set in the U.S., but a tiny segment of it may be in Brazil."

"Ah!... How interesting. Shall we order first, then talk?"

Cox's precise way of talking amazed Frank. He had to bite his tongue to keep from smiling. "By all means. I'm actually quite hungry. The meal on American was ok but not satisfying, and it was a long time ago."

"Have you been to Brazil before?"

"This is my first visit."

"Then let me order. Do you prefer beef or fish?"

"Fish."

Frank read through the menu but left the decisions to his guest. He watched Cox with admiration as he discussed the finer points of the menu with the Maitre D'. Finally, they settled on the order. "You see, this is the best gourmet restaurant in Rio. I've ordered a rare bottle of Brazilian Chardonnay. It'll go well with the fish."

Frank decided to cut the bullshit short. "Do you know a man by the name of Matthew Swansen?"

"Matthew Swansen," he repeated. "The name rings a bell. Let me think. Ah... yes... He's in jail, sentenced to life for killing his girlfriend. It was a sensational story, even for Brazilian passion."

Frank was shocked. "I was informed that he'd died."

"Then why are you here? What's your interest in him?"

"I wanted to be absolutely sure. His being alive raises many questions. When did the murder take place?"

"About a year ago."

"Was his girlfriend Brazilian or American?"

"Brazilian."

"How long has he been in Rio? What was he doing here?"

"I don't know when he arrived, but I can find out. If I recall correctly, the prosecution described him as a vagabond, a good for nothing. There are quite a few Americans here, very much like him, chasing women and making a nuisance of themselves."

Frank became pensive, finally saying, "The odd thing about this is that the Matthew Swansen I'm interested in is not a kid anymore. He must be a man in his forties."

"He wouldn't be the first old drifter to get into trouble. Why is he so important to you?"

"His brother, a highly successful industrialist, perished, along with his wife, in a plane crash. Several members of the family, in fact, all those in line for an inheritance, have been murdered. It wouldn't surprise me if Matthew was being framed."

Cox recoiled in distaste. "I never heard of such a thing."

"Now you have. Do you recall how his girlfriend died?"

"She was stabbed. The knife had his fingerprints on it. Neighbors testified that a huge fight had taken place before all became suspiciously quiet. Police found him next to the body, holding a knife dripping blood. He swore he was innocent, of course."

"I'd like to see Matthew. Could you arrange a visit for me?"

"That's easy."

"Also, could you find out the address where he lived?"

"Give me a couple of days. I'll get my secretary on it."

"Thanks. I must admit the food here is exceptional. I've enjoyed every morsel, the wine, too, is outstanding. You've made this a memorable meal for me."

"Since this is your first visit here, I'd suggest you do some sightseeing. Rio is one of the most beautiful cities in the world. I'll call you at your hotel as soon as possible. In the meantime, enjoy your time here."

The following morning, after a breakfast buffet he'd never before experienced, Frank strolled along Copacabana Beach boardwalk all the way to the base of Sugar Loaf Mountain. He took the cable tram to the top, walking around the viewing circle, completely mesmerized by the view.

After descending the mountain, Frank took a taxi to Corcovado, where the famous statue of Christ stands 2,500 feet above sea level. From this location the entire city of Rio, with its several furrows across bays and rivers, laid in front of him, a picture he would remember for the rest of his life.

Frank had just returned to his hotel room when Cox's secretary called from the lobby. He rushed downstairs. The secretary, a good looking woman in her forties, was waiting for him next to the lobby telephones. Frank smiled at her. "You're Brazilian. I expected an American."

She grinned at him, white teeth shining. "My name is Susan Cross. I'm half American. My father works in Washington. He married my mother, a former Brazilian Ambassador to the U.S. Mr. Cox has asked me to accompany you tomorrow to the Ary Franco Prison and later to Avenida Lisboa where Matthew Swansen used to live. Shall we say ten o'clock?"

Frank asked Susan to join him for a drink but she declined, saying she had other obligations.

Frank couldn't wait for the night to be over. He tried to imagine what Matthew looked like. Was he really guilty or was he being framed. It wouldn't surprise him one bit if he was, considering everything else that had taken place. Then a picture of Susan Cross flashed through his mind; an articulate, efficient woman who didn't mince her words. He found himself wondering about her life and just what those obligations entailed.

Susan arrived precisely at ten. Frank was waiting at the walkway where passengers were let off in front of the hotel. "Our appointment at the prison is at eleven. We should get there in about forty-five minutes. The Ary Franco Prison is well known in Brazil, as it's the most violent prison we have. That's where major criminals are housed."

Frank was silent for the duration of the drive, his mind churning. Did he or didn't he? Finally, they arrived at the prison, which from the outside looked like a fortress. He found out later that it had originally been an old Portuguese fort that had been converted to a prison. It was grim looking, the outer walls dirty and stained with rows of razor wire overlaid on the bricks.

Frank and Susan waited several minutes before Matthew, wearing a baggy bright orange uniform, was brought in. The man looked like a ghost. His face was drawn, eyes deep in their sockets, hair mostly gray with patches of black. His eyebrows were like oversized caterpillars. His face, especially his forehead, was a mass of wrinkles. Frank wondered how he had been attractive to women. He must have suffered in prison.

As Matthew sat down across from him and Susan, Frank spoke up. "My name is Frank Galitson. This is Susan Cross." Frank kept her profession out of the conversation. "I'm here because a number of the Swansen family members have been murdered. I was told you were dead, but I felt a need to verify that information. Now that I've found you, I'd like you to tell me about your ordeal."

Matthew stared at Frank as if he was an alien from Mars. It took him a while to grasp Frank's message. Frank and Susan remained silent, letting him digest the situation.

He spoke in a low, broken voice. "I didn't kill anyone. I'm not guilty of killing Rosita. I loved her." His eyes welled with tears, their rims already reddened.

"Tell me what happened."

"Can you get me out of here? The prisoners in this jail are treated in the most inhumane manner. You wouldn't treat a dog like we're being treated." His voice was piteous to hear.

"How long have you been here?"

"Right after my sentencing, about a year."

"When did you come to Brazil?"

"About twenty some years ago."

"Why did you leave Minneapolis?"

"I wasn't good enough. I would never be good enough. My parents always compared me unfavorably to my brother. I felt it was the only way I could become my own person."

"You mean Julius? Is that who your brother was?"

"Yes."

"You look much younger than Julius."

"My mother always told me I was a mistake. Nice thing for a mother to tell her child." His voice took on an edge of sarcasm. Some life, some animation returned to his face as his emotions began to surface.

"So you left the country because of your parents and your brother."

"You said it. I had to get away, far away."

"I see. What did you do in Brazil when you arrived?"

"I became a teacher of English. At the time such teachers were in high demand. I got a job almost immediately."

"Did you kill your girlfriend?"

"How could I? I loved her. We lived together for years, but she didn't want to get married." His voice came even more ragged and the tears in his eyes threatened to spill over at the mention of his former lover.

"Is that what you were fighting about?"

"We never fought."

"Two neighbors testified that you had a huge fight with your girlfriend right before you killed her."

"If there was a fight, it wasn't with me. I never once raised my voice to her. We lived harmoniously. I worshipped her. Yes, I wanted to marry her, but her refusal didn't matter to me as long as we stayed together."

"Tell us what happened that night."

"I got home a little before seven. I'd stayed late at school to referee a soccer game. When I entered our apartment I was horrified by the scene that met me. Rosita was lying on her back, a knife sticking out of her chest. She was bleeding heavily. I panicked, not knowing if she was alive or dead. That thought that she might be dead pierced my heart like an arrow. I grabbed the knife, pulling it out. I was praying Rosita was alive. Just then the front door opened and a neighbor from across the hall came in with a policeman. I was in a complete daze. I tried to talk but not a word would come from my mouth. The next thing I knew I was being handcuffed and taken away in a police car. No one would listen to me. The trial was a sham." He was filled with righteous indignation, tears gone and hands fisted.

"Ok...ok... did you know Julius' children?" Frank wanted to change the subject in the hope of settling him down.

"Julius left town right after graduating high school. I had no interest in him. I really disliked him and my whole family. I haven't seen him or any of his children. I know nothing about them."

"Are you aware he was killed in a plane crash?"

"No. Even if I had known I wouldn't have mourned for him. In reality I don't care much about America. I used to be very happy here."

"Who knew you relocated to Brazil?"

"I said as much before I left. It wasn't a secret."

Frank remained silent for a long while. His mind was racing. He looked directly at Matthew and spoke to him in a very serious manner. "I'll be very frank with you. I can't promise you anything. However, should I come up with anything that might benefit you during the course of my investigation I'll be the first to fight for you."

Matthew's eyes filled once more. He was pathetically grateful for even a crumb of hope.

As Frank and Susan left the prison, he spoke. "A child of a bad family. What a shame. He sounded so sincere. What did you think?"

Susan had been shaken by the experience and had to regroup before she could answer him. "I agree, but what about the circumstantial evidence?"

"We'll get to that later. Let's visit the place where he used to live." They kept quiet, each busy with their own thoughts while they traveled to Matthew and Rosita's former home.

Avenida Lisboa was located in the Ipanema section of Rio, running parallel to the beach highway. It straddled Guanabara Bay north of Copacabana. The road leading to it provided an excellent vista of the bay and the mountains to the south.

The four story apartment building where they had lived consisted of eight apartments -- two to a floor. The most helpful neighbor to Frank was a middle-aged man who lived on the third floor. He proudly announced he had been the main witness in the case against Matthew. His chest puffed with pride.

Frank had no difficulty getting the man to talk. He gave his questions to Susan who translated them to Portuguese. "How long have you lived here?"

"This is my fifteenth year."

"What do you do for a living?"

"I'm a certified accountant."

"Did you know Matthew Swansen?"

"Sure. He lived across the hall from me. We talked many times. He was a nice young man, but he went crazy."

"Why do you say that?"

"Lovers do crazy things out of jealousy."

"Did Matthew have a reason to be jealous?"

"It's obvious, isn't it? Why else would he have killed her?"

"Did Matthew and Rosita have friends? Did they entertain?"

"They had many friends, mostly teachers."

"Tell me about the day of the murder."

"Well... I came home from work around six. I washed my hands, then sat on the balcony to read the evening newspaper. About half an hour later my wife asked me to run to the grocery store for a bottle of vinegar she needed for the salad dressing. As I came down the stairs a young woman was coming up. I almost collided with her. I returned with the vinegar about fifteen minutes later just when the noise from the fight began. I heard shouting and screaming. It got completely out of hand, so I called the police. By the time the police officer arrived it was quiet." He had told his story so often he didn't even need to think about it anymore. It poured from him.

"How long did it take the police to arrive?"

"About ten minutes."

"Where were you during those ten minutes?"

"I was in and out of my apartment. I was concerned about Rosita."

"Did you see anyone else in the building?"

The man paused for a moment. "Well, yes... the woman I'd almost collided with when I went out was coming down from the fourth floor."

"Can you describe her?"

"I only saw her briefly but I recall she was about my height, slim, a good looking blonde."

"Was she carrying anything?"

"Just a handbag... it looked like a Gucci or one of those expensive purses."

Frank remained silent for a moment, his eyes on the accountant. Suddenly, he jerked upright. He took an envelope from his pocket and extracted a picture of one of the twins. "Is this the woman?"

"Yes... yes... that's her. I'd swear to it. " He had excitement in his voice, once more feeling quite important.

Frank almost passed out. "How can you be so sure?"

He laughed. "You don't know Brazilian men, do you? When we see a beautiful woman, particularly a blonde, our eyes open really wide." He kept on laughing. "Blondes are a rare commodity in our country."

Frank grabbed Susan by the arm. "I have everything I need. Get the man's business card and let's go."

Susan thanked the man in their own language. Frank shook his hand with vigor and said his own thanks in English.

"My mission to Brazil is complete. I can tell you right now that Matthew Swansen didn't kill his girlfriend. The woman whom the accountant identified is Julius Swansen's daughter, one of the twin sisters."

"What are you going to do?"

"Once the murderer in the Swansen family case is discovered, I'll be able to tie it with the Rio killing. Till then, Matthew will have to remain in jail."

"Brazilian courts are very difficult to deal with."

"Leave it to me. I'm going to stake my reputation on this one. Matthew Swansen is innocent. I'll get him out no matter the cost. In fact, once the motive is established, and the murderer found, Matthew will be the sole heir to the Swansen fortune."

16.

Frank took another leisurely first class flight back to New York, then called Joe Caputo. Joe was furious because he hadn't heard from Frank in several days. "You're about to destroy my career. I trusted you," he shouted. "Where the hell have you been?"

"Joe, calm down and listen... listen carefully. I have incredible news." Frank went on to report on his trip to Rio.

"You bastard, you should have told me you were going to Rio." Joe was still so furious that Frank had to hold the phone away from his ear.

"Sure, like you would have let me go. Don't take me for a fool. Had I mentioned it, you'd have thought I was escaping the country. I've told you the story. I'm back in Manhattan. Goodbye." Frank hung up, not wanting to continue the conversation. He was sorry he had so enraged Joe because he sure needed his support.

Frank checked back into the Milford Plaza Hotel. He lay on his bed, hands behind his head, thinking. Those damn twins, how could they have manipulated this entire affair? His mind spun with different scenarios. Finally Frank came to the conclusion that one of the twins was the operator while the other stayed home, coming and going, pretending to be one or the other. He himself couldn't tell one from the other. He jumped up, cleaned himself up, then strolled up the street to Columbus Circle, then on to Central Park West.

The doorman at the entrance to the twin's building was helping a resident with her luggage. Frank waited, leaning against a tree, until the doorman was free. He approached him slowly, constantly checking around to make sure the twins weren't in the area. The doorman smiled at him. "How are you Mr. Galitson? Do you wish to go up?"

"Not really. I have a question. Can you tell who's Elizabeth and who's Margaret?"

"You must be kidding. I couldn't tell one from the other if my life depended on it. They look identical and they always wear identical clothing."

"Do they always go out together?"

"No. Many times just one leaves."

"Can you tell which one leaves?"

"No way. They never speak to me on the way out, just wave at me."

"When you do talk to either one of them do you know if she's Elizabeth or Margaret by her voice?"

"I've never been able to. In fact, I've often wondered about it but the residents don't encourage any personal questions."

"That's all I wanted to know. Thanks." Frank walked away as fast as he could, after slipping a bill into the doorman's hand.

Frank called the U.S. Consul's office in Rio. "Susan, I have a special request. I don't know how you can do it, but please try. It's vital to find out whether a Margaret Swansen or a Margaret Jones was on a passenger list of any of the three U.S. airlines flying to Rio the week prior to the murder of Rosita. If you find her, please also look up her departure."

"I think I can help. I know the guy who's the local manager of United Airlines. I'll call you."

Frank pondered whether he should approach the twins. He felt he had done the right thing leaving out of his report to Joe that the accountant had seen one of the twins. He didn't want to give the police more firepower before he solved the case. He also decided he wouldn't mention Matthew's existence to anyone else. Once more his mind went in circles, trying to figure out what his next step should be.

Suddenly, a picture of Julia surfaced. Where had she disappeared to? Why had she disappeared? Even her father and closest friends hadn't heard from her. It all began in Wyoming. She may have never left Jackson Hole. Should he look for her? Had he been too harsh? What made her so jealous when he felt he had clearly explained his interest in helping in the Swansen investigation? Frank began to question why he should bother with her. That thought got thrown out quickly. After all, he'd had a pleasant relationship with her for more than two years. She'd even committed a murder to help him find a subject for his writing. How could he explain such a depth of love and loyalty to a friend? Her actions certainly were beyond any normal human behavior. She must have done it as a result of pure love.

A moment later, Lisa's image appeared. 'I felt like I had fallen in love with her', his subconscious hinted to him. What's the matter with me? Am I too fast in making opinions and it's distorting my judgment? "I'm going to Jackson Hole," he announced loudly to himself.

The next morning Frank flew to Jackson Hole. The three hour flight turned out to be a torture for him. His mind couldn't stop questioning Lisa's behavior. Why had she acted the way she did? Was something going on between her and Chief Crawley? She seemed afraid of him. Had her love for Frank been real or had she faked it? If she did, what was the reason? He kept analyzing every word she'd said, every look, her entire attitude. He felt that something, somewhere, was wrong but he couldn't figure it out. He was extremely annoyed with himself. All this self questioning was distracting him. He was unused to ever wondering about either his own actions or those of someone else, having been so absorbed in his world of writing.

Then, a completely new thought crossed Frank's mind. Lisa reminded him of Elizabeth and Margaret, her smile incredibly similar to that of the twins. So what? It didn't mean a thing. It was the second time that thought had flashed through his mind and he wondered why.

Frank closed his eyes, trying to relax, but his mind went off in another direction. He started to question his love for Lisa. Indeed it was the first time in his life that he had become emotional. He thought of how his heart had pounded when they kissed. He'd never had that feeling with Julia. He knew he'd shut the door on Lisa, but he could finally admit to himself that he had loved her.

Frank was relieved when the plane landed. His mind eased since he was able to take action. He rented a car and drove to the famous Hotel Wort where he had booked himself a room. He knew he had to be careful as the DA was still after him.

Hotel Wort was located one block from the town square. Western themes prevailed everywhere, particularly in the Silver Dollar Grill and Bar. Walls were decorated with western art, the product of local artists. The restaurant was famous for entrees made with wild game and grass fed beef.

The morning after his arrival, Frank called Charles Dickson, Jackson DA. "I'd like to see you."

"Where are you?"

"Sorry, I can't tell you."

"Frank, I know our police chief wants to hang you. I don't know why, but I had no alternative since he filed a complaint against you. He claims he has evidence that will nail you."

"Rubbish. He has nothing more than my business card."

"Where do you want to meet?"

"There's a restaurant inside the Jackson Playhouse. Be there at six. If I see any officers, I'm gone."

"I'll be there."

Frank donned a fake mustache, a goatee, and plain glasses he'd purchased at the costume shop next door to the theater. He canvassed the area carefully before entering the restaurant. He didn't spot any member of the police force.

Dickson sat alone in a rear booth, facing the door. He didn't recognize the man who suddenly took a seat across from him. "I'm delighted to see you, Dickson." Frank extended his hand, which Dickson decided to accept after a brief hesitation.

"I'm happy to see you too."

"It's good to be back."

"My failure in New York resulted from Crawley's misinformation. I wish I knew how to get rid of him. He made me look like a fool and I sure don't appreciate that."

"Something is definitely wrong in Shangri-La. Did you make the inquiries I asked of you?"

"Yes. Chief Crawley recommended Lisa to the park authority. She was hired without any checking."

"Where did Crawley come from?" Frank was convinced he wasn't native to the area.

"He arrived twenty-five years ago from Minneapolis after working several years for the police department in Minnesota. He worked his way up to chief fairly quickly."

"Interesting. I sort of thought that might be the case." Frank didn't want to elaborate. "You've been a great help. I'll keep you posted." He left in a hurry using the rear door of the restaurant.

Frank entered his hotel room to be shocked at the sight in front of him. Lisa sat in the only armchair, eyes closed. She had fallen asleep waiting for him. Frank was so surprised he didn't really know what to do. Finally, he spoke loudly to wake her up. "What are you doing here? How did you know where to find me?"

Lisa yawned, ran her hands through her hair and sat up, completely unconcerned. "I had my friends at the airlines watch the passenger lists. I expected you to come back."

"You seem very sure of yourself."

"I knew the Swansen mystery would bring you back.

"Actually, I'd like to talk to you."

A small grin showed on her face. "You look good in your disguise. Have you had dinner?"

"No. That's a good idea. Let's go to the Chinese restaurant across from the fire house."

They took a leisurely stroll to the nearby restaurant. Frank hadn't been sure whether he wanted to talk to Lisa, but her sudden appearance had forced his hand. Lisa had similar thoughts about him, but her objective was entirely different.

Lisa's first question as they sat down was, "Did you miss me?"

Frank stared at her for a moment, not sure how to respond. His feelings for her were mixed. His loathing for her had dissipated somewhat. He didn't respond directly to her question, saying instead, "I'm mixed up about our relationship. I admit that I was shocked by your behavior. I felt alienated. I've tried hard to figure out your change in attitude, but I've failed miserably."

"In everyone's life there are issues that cannot immediately be brought out into the open. The day will come when I'll share all my thoughts with you, but right now I can't. That doesn't mean I don't love you. The truth of the matter is that I do love you. I've loved you since I first saw you." She reached across the table, hands outstretched, but Frank refused to touch her.

"Wouldn't it have been simpler if you'd told me this ahead of time instead of behaving so strangely?"

"Frank, please forgive me. I won't do it again. I do love you with all my heart. I've had a difficult time since you left." She laid her hand over his and this time he let her.

"I'm still confused. I felt as if my heart had been torn apart."

"Let's turn over a new leaf. I won't keep anything from you. I want to be absolutely honest. I just need more time before I can tell you everything."

Frank felt the ice in his heart begin to melt at the sight of her pleading face. "What can be so terrible that you can't speak of it now?"

"It's a family matter."

"Ok... let's give it another try. When you're ready to tell me I promise to listen."

A huge smile made Lisa's face glow. "What brought you back to Jackson Hole? I hope it was me."

"You're part of it. I'm also curious about what happened to Julia. She seems to have vanished. Even her father hasn't heard from her since we first left New York. I have a feeling she's somewhere in this area."

Lisa felt shattered that Frank was looking for Julia but kept her game face on. He was a difficult man to understand, as he seemed unaware of how easily he could wound someone. "Is there a reason why you can't get her off your mind?"

"We've been good friends... actually more than good friends, for over two years. I suppose she thought eventually we would get married. Suddenly, you show up, and she became extremely jealous. Maybe it was the way I looked at you. Jealousy is not something I'd ever seen in her. With every passing day she became more irrational. Then she disappeared. I assumed she'd gone back to New York, but she hadn't. Her father needs her. He hasn't heard from her nor have her friends. I'm curious and somewhat concerned."

"I can understand being jealous. I'd be jealous too if I saw you with another woman, but I wouldn't hound you the way she did. The fact is, I never stopped loving you. I hope to God our relationship will continue without another interruption."

"I feel awkward about your inability to be totally frank with me. It makes me feel you're hiding something."

"Please don't. It's purely a family matter. It's embarrassing to talk about." Lisa stroked his cheek, admiring the softness of his skin. She took a moment to outline his lips with her fingertip. Frank felt a strong sensation within him but couldn't determine if it was love or lust.

"Have you been married before?"

"Thank heaven, no."

"Well… let's see what develops between us."

"Why did you come back to Jackson? Was it because of me?" She was repeating herself, hoping the answer would be different this time.

"Partly. I'm still working on the Swansen case."

"I'm interested in the 'partly'. It appears the Swansen case is on hold. I don't know who's doing what. Have you discovered anything new?"

"I've made a great deal of progress. I've had several meetings with the twins and met with certain officers of the Swansen company. Most importantly, I found out that Julius's brother is alive." Frank cursed. Had he not sworn he would keep that to himself? After castigating himself he happened to look up, only to discover that Lisa's face had turned white. The look on her face made Frank wonder why his last words had caused her such shock. His comments about the investigative activities he'd undertaken hadn't included his trip to Minneapolis. Something he couldn't explain was bothering him, but he decided to keep his reservations out of the conversation. "He's been jailed for life. Apparently he murdered his girlfriend."

Lisa said nothing, maintaining a silence for several long minutes. Their meal remained untouched. Frank could sense her mind racing. Again, he tried to figure out what was going on with her, and with them, but decided not to share his doubts. Finally, she spoke, completely changing the subject. "You said I was part of the reason you returned. I'd like to better understand your feelings and thoughts."

He grimaced, then took a deep breath – better to be honest with her. "Lisa, let's not discuss this in such depth. I'm willing to try again if you are but this time we'll move ahead very slowly. Ok?"

"I'll drink to that." They touched glasses, then turned to their lukewarm meal. Neither had much appetite.

Frank spent the rest of the night hammering away on his laptop. The story moved on. He was satisfied. He was extremely unsure about renewing a relationship with Lisa, but he was willing to give it a chance. He was doing his best to ignore the inner doubts for which he had no valid explanation.

17.

The following morning turned out to be the beginning of a beautiful day. Warm sun rays caressed the Grand Tetons. Clouds that had blocked the sky the day before had disappeared and flocks of dark gray sparrows zigzagged above.

Frank, in his cheap disguise, strolled along Broadway, stopping to look into gallery display windows. He stood, pondering a taxidermy shop at Trailside Gallery. He questioned why anyone would take this on as a career. He thought about Lisa's birthday, coming up in two days, so he entered the gallery. A Siamese cat stood out among the other animals on a large display stand, its fur appearing to ripple.

He decided this would be a perfect gift. He turned toward the cashier's desk in the center of the store. As he approached the desk, he caught a glimpse of a woman rushing out through the rear door. She seemed familiar somehow but he couldn't place her. He paid for the cat and had it gift-wrapped. On the way to his hotel he suddenly stopped. Had that been Julia? He rushed back to the gallery to look around, then went to the cashier. "Do you have a woman working here by the name of Julia Rendel?"

"No sir, there's no one here by that name."

Frank returned to his hotel, looking back several times to see if anyone was following him, but he saw no one he recognized. He laughed at himself, wondering if he'd gone crazy. "Who'd follow me in Jackson Hole, except for Crawley?"

After a light lunch in the hotel deli Frank napped for an hour, then continued writing. At seven he took himself off to the Silver Dollar Grill, expecting Lisa to arrive immediately. He waited a full hour but there was no sign of her. Finally, he called her office. No one answered the phone. Even the answering machine was turned off.

Lisa still hadn't shown by 8:30 so Frank ordered dinner and ate alone. He wondered why Lisa hadn't come since she had seemed so anxious to renew their relationship, telling him how much she loved him just the day before. Why hadn't she called or left a message?

Frank decided to check up on her. He knew that driving at night in Yellowstone was prohibited, but he decided to go anyway. The main entrance was closed but he remembered a side trail Lisa had shown him. Even before he reached Lake, a vigilant ranger stopped him. Frank shoved his disguise between the seats before explaining the situation and his worries. The ranger told Frank to follow him.

It occurred to Frank that he'd never been to Lisa's cabin before. How could he possibly have identified her cabin at this hour of the night? He would have been totally lost without the help of a ranger. Frank once again questioned his impetuosity. Would it get him in trouble once again?

It was close to midnight when the ranger stopped at a cabin community outside Mammoth Hot Springs. He parked his car next to Lisa's cabin, knocking loudly on her door. There was no answer. Frank too began to knock, calling Lisa's name loudly. Still no answer. "Something isn't right. Can you open the door?" Frank's voice reflected his rising concerns. Lights began to come on in neighboring cabins. Folks were not used to night noise here. They were the early to bed and early to rise kind of people.

"I don't have a key. She may just be over at a friend's house."

"I doubt it. She told me she would meet me for dinner at seven." Frank was insistent, anger and fear starting to percolate.

"I'm sorry, sir. There's nothing I can do."

"Break down the door." Frank's voice now held an edge of hysteria.

The ranger swung his flashlight in Frank's direction, wanting to gauge his level of emotion. "Are you out of your mind? I can't do that."

Without another word Frank pushed the ranger aside, rushing at the door, kicking it with all his might. The door flew inward. He fumbled near the door for a light switch. The ranger started to shout at Frank. As the light blazed on he stopped short at the sight of Lisa's body on the floor, a rope tied tightly around her neck, her face red and eyes bloodshot "What the hell?" the ranger shouted, unnerved at the sight and smell of death.

Frank had been looking toward the bed when the light came on. The ranger's scream made him turn. He was shocked at what awaited him. He touched Lisa's body, ice cold and rigid.

Frank grabbed his head in both hands, shaking it in anguish. "Why don't they kill me too?" he shouted angrily. "What's the matter with these people?"

The stunned ranger stared at Frank, his face a mask of trauma. "Why would anyone want to kill Lisa? She was such a wonderful gal."

Frank and the ranger remained silent for a little while, each caught up in his own search to understand this awful event. Frank spoke first. "I think we should look around but we need to be careful not to touch anything. It looks like there's a note on the desk."

Blindly the ranger followed Frank, stepping around Lisa's corpse. On the center of the small desk lay a single sheet of paper, two lines of print vivid in dark ink.

Since I can't have my loved one, I have no reason to live. Please forgive me.
Lisa

Frank looked at an overturned stool next to Lisa's body. A large hook that had been set in the ceiling lay on the floor at the other end of the rope. "Lisa must have committed suicide. It looks like the weight of her body yanked the hook right out of the ceiling. I can't imagine why she wanted to kill herself. We had such a good time the day before and we were talking about a future together." Frank's eyes welled up.

Both men stood in complete silence, staring at Lisa's body. Several minutes passed before the ranger uttered in a broken voice, "I must call our chief ranger." His voice was as shaky as his hands but it served to wake Frank from his state of deep contemplation.

The ranger picked up the receiver of a wall phone next to the unmade bed. "The line is dead." He looked at Frank in dismay. "I'll have to drive to my station. Will you stay here with her?"

Frank nodded and the ranger left at full speed, anxious to get away from the body. He knew that cell phones didn't function in the park. Frank was pleased the ranger was gone. Immediately he began searching the cabin. There wasn't anything of interest to him in the desk or the small closet. He checked through every piece of clothing, turning out pockets and checking hems and seams, but found nothing. As he turned the mattress a slim, worn diary fell to the floor, making an exceptionally loud noise in the silent cabin.

Frank read through about a third of the diary before hearing sounds from a rapidly oncoming vehicle. He hid the diary inside his shirt, tucked into the waistband of his khakis. The part of the diary he was able to read described ordeals of Lisa's youth, a hateful mother, her wonderful relationship with her sister, her inspiration to become a ranger, and her move to Jackson Hole. The writing was precise but there were gaps of several months between some of the entries.

The chief was a man in his sixties, wearing a worn Stetson and glasses with heavy, dark rims. His face was wrinkled, his broad shoulders reminding Frank of a football player.

The Chief ignored Frank until he read the note, scanned the room and stared at Lisa's body. Suddenly he roared, "I've heard all about you. What brought you here? Why are you in this cabin?"

Frank explained that he'd had a date scheduled with Lisa and she hadn't shown up. His concern for her forced him to come and look for himself. He wondered why the other ranger hadn't already told the chief all of this but maybe he was trying to corroborate what he'd already heard.

"Are you the man she mentions in her note?"

"I think so, but I'm not absolutely sure."

"Were you in love with her?"

"I thought I was."

"Was she in love with you?"

"Very much so."

"Why did she state that she couldn't have you?"

"I don't know. Our relationship was in the early stages."

"Are you married?"

"No... I'm not, never have been." Frank thought about how odd that question was but said nothing. No sense in antagonizing this guy.

"Where are you staying?"

"Wort Hotel."

At that moment a police car arrived, Chief Crawley leaping out like a young deer. "You! What are you doing here?" He was surprised to see Frank. "It seems like you turn up at every killing in the park."

Frank burst out. "What is that supposed to mean? I came here on vacation and was asked to help. That's how I got involved. You should know that better than anyone else."

"Lisa said she loved you."

"So what... I admired her too, but I wasn't ready to commit to anything. Is that a crime?"

"Why did she write that she can't have you?"

"I wish we could ask her. I never said anything of the sort."

"You've never been able to explain how your business card got into Gertrude Miller's purse."

Frank's face turned red. He spoke angrily, without thinking. "I've written several mysteries and you wouldn't fit into any of them. You're nothing but a hick. Take a refresher course. There's no evidence to incriminate me. You went to the District Attorney with a false complaint. If you continue with this charade I'll sue you. If you want me, I'll be at the Wort Hotel."

Crawley tried to catch hold of Frank's arm, but stopped in his tracks. He knew he had no hard evidence to connect Frank to any of the murders. Frank drove away, upset and concerned at the same time.

His mind was restless. Why had Lisa written that she committed suicide because she couldn't have him? A disturbing thought flashed through his mind in the midst of these mental deliberations. Had there been someone else in her life? If so, who could that person be? Was it Jim Jones?

Frank reviewed Lisa's behavior during the start of the Gertrude Miller murder investigation. She had acted weirdly for someone who declared herself to be his lover. His unease grew as the uncertainties increased and the twists and turns became more and more numerous. Frank came to the conclusion that he needed to return to both Chicago and Minneapolis, to talk to Ilene Samps and to investigate both Lisa's and Crawley's backgrounds.

****

As it was early in the morning Frank was able to call the airport to find out which airline might be flying to Minneapolis. He booked a seat on United Airline, which had an early flight with a stop in Salt Lake City. As he entered the terminal to pick up his boarding pass Frank was stopped by a man wielding a police badge. "Please step aside," he said politely. "You may not leave Jackson Hole until the investigation of Lisa Warrenton's death is complete."

"No one told me that. I'll be back in two days." He was trying to stay calm. Didn't this officer understand he was an innocent bystander?

"Sorry, you may not leave."

"Then you'll have to arrest me." Frank pushed by him gently, continuing toward to the ticket counter.

"Ok... you're under arrest."

Frank barked out a laugh. "On what charge?"

The officer hesitated for a moment, uneasy, before he said, "For disturbing the peace."

A small group of women stood talking nearby. Three of them were facing Frank and the officer. Frank stepped toward them, calling out to the women. "This officer wants to arrest me for disturbing the peace. Did you see me creating a disturbance?"

They stared at the two men, not wanting to get involved. No one spoke.

The officer got mad, shouting at Frank, "What do you think you're doing?" He grabbed Frank's arm, pulling him away toward the exit.

Frank stopped, bracing himself against being tugged away. "You can't arrest anyone without cause. By law you're obliged to tell me what the charges are and read me my rights. You've done nothing of the sort." Frank pulled himself out of the officer's grip, walking away rapidly. The officer chased after Frank for a few steps then stopped. He realized he hadn't received enough instruction about what to do in a situation like this.

Frank picked up his boarding pass, went through security without incident, then settled on a bench close to the departure gate. He expected Chief Crawley to show up, so he readied himself for a fight, but there was no sign of him. Frank had to board at the cattle call as there had been no first class seats available.

He arrived in Minneapolis at 3:00 p.m., exhausted from the tension created by his encounter with the police and the long flight in coach. He had an early dinner, then went to bed. It took him a while to fall asleep, but then he slept soundly through the night.

Frank rose early the next morning, peeking out the window to discover the sun was out and the sky partly cloudy. He shaved, showered and dressed, then had breakfast in the hotel's restaurant. There were few people about, engrossed in laptop or newspaper.

Frank's first stop was at the central Minneapolis police station. He asked for an appointment with the Police Commissioner. The sergeant in reception looked at Frank's card, then left through a door behind him. He returned several moments later, asking Frank to follow him.

Police Commissioner Harry Fields, in his early sixties, sat erectly at his desk. His salt and pepper hair had a sheen as if it had been treated with Vitalis. His brown eyes had a kindly look, unusual in a man of his position. He welcomed Frank as if he'd known him for years. "Please come in Mr. Galitson. I'm delighted to meet you. I've read all of your books. I must tell you that your mysteries reflect a deep knowledge of detective work."

Frank shook his hand with warmth. "Thank you. I try to be as real as possible in my writing."

"Sit down. What brings you to Minneapolis?"

"It's a very long story. It has to do with the murders of several members of the Swansen family."

His listener sat up even straighter in his chair, his interest sharpened by Frank's opening comment. "Do you mean Julius Swansen, the industrialist?"

"Yes. I'm sure you're aware that he and his wife perished in a plane crash."

"Of course, about two years ago. The papers were full of stories about our local boy who made it big in New York."

Frank told him about the events of the past month. "It's vital you keep this inquiry confidential. Can I ask that of you?" Frank continued. Fields' nod was sufficient for him. "I have reason to believe that the police chief of Jackson Hole is involved in this mess. I'm interested in the man's background. I found out he graduated from the Minneapolis Police Academy."

"I understand." He flipped a switch on the intercom. "John, come in, please." A moment later an older, black officer entered. "Sir?"

"I need you to run a check on a Richard Crawley. He must have graduated twenty or so years ago from the academy. I want a complete report. On the double." The officer left quickly. He wasn't accustomed to the commissioner giving orders in this manner so it must be important.

"I also need information on a James Jones, last known address 75 Riverdale Circle. He's a native of this city. I was told he was brought to Jackson Hole for rehabilitation. He's now a car repairman, supposedly a man with a record."

Commissioner Fields turned to his computer. He stopped his search only a few minutes later, a smile on his face. "James Jones has been arrested several times for petty thievery. Altogether he's spent about two years in jail. He was accused of manslaughter once, but was exonerated by a jury."

"When was that?"

"About two years ago."

"I know my next request is unfair, but I'd appreciate any help you can give me."

"What's on your mind?"

"I'd like any information you can dig up about the Jones family. There's also a Margaret Jones involved, but I don't know if they're related."

"How long are you staying in Minneapolis?"

"I'll stay as long as need be. I'm at the Hilton Garden Hotel."

The officer who had been ordered to obtain information about Crawley, returned. "Sir, Richard Crawley joined our police force immediately after graduating from the academy. He worked for us for three years, then resigned. There's no record of his current whereabouts."

Frank interrupted. "What was his address in Minneapolis?"

The officer perused the papers he was holding. "75 Riverdale Circle."

"Bingo" A huge smile appeared on Frank's face. "The Crawleys and the Joneses were neighbors. Now I understand why Jim applied for a job with the Jackson police, and why his personnel file was removed."

The commissioner smiled. "I'm glad I could be of help. I've never met an author who was involved in real detective work."

Frank returned the smile. "When I started this case I had no idea where it would lead. This case is far more complex than anything I've ever written about in the past."

"Let me help you with the investigation. This case intrigues me."

Frank had found another ally. He left the police building, hailing a taxi. "75 Riverdale Circle." He settled back in the rear seat, happily thinking about another twist in the plot to round out his story.

Riverdale Circle was a large cul-de-sac surrounded by small, identical three story apartment buildings. Each building had six apartments, two to a floor. Frank asked the driver to wait. The front entry door to number 75 was unlocked. Cautiously, Frank walked into a narrow lobby. Six mail boxes, with names attached, hung on the wall to the left. Among them he found both 'Crawley' and 'Jones'.

He knocked on the door of the Crawley apartment. Minutes later he heard a rattling noise as the chain was unfastened. The door was opened by an elderly woman. "I thought you were my neighbor. What do you want?"

"I have a message for you from Richard," Frank lied, hoping his face wouldn't give him away. "May I come in?"

She didn't budge. Her face tightened in sudden anger. "Tell my son he can call me once in a while." She started to close the door, but Frank pushed it back open. "I have to talk to you."

"What do you want? I can't stand for too long. Make it quick"

Frank seized the moment. "Let's sit down. I can't stand long either."

She shrugged, unconcerned whether he stayed or went. Frank closed the door and followed her into a living room furnished with old, outdated furniture, probably all purchased at the time of her marriage. Once off-white curtains covering the windows were now blackened from years of cigarette smoke. The wall-to-wall carpet was stained, dirty and worn through in spots.

"What does Richard have to say?" She got right to the point, not one to waste time on pleasantries. She lit a cigarette from an open package on the table, coughing wetly as the smoke hit her throat.

Frank was pleased she hadn't asked for his name. Had she, he would have given her a false name. "When's the last time you heard from Richard?" Frank decided to bank on her complaining manner.

"Maybe seven months ago. What's he up to now?"

"He mentioned you to me. He seemed concerned about you, but he's too busy running police business in Jackson Hole."

"Liar. He's concerned about me? Ha! I gave up on him long ago. If not for my cousin I'd be dead now."

"Does your cousin live nearby?" Frank was pleased she wasn't paying attention to his interrogation. He hoped this would continue, that she'd be too pleased to have someone to listen to her that she'd answer anything.

As she plopped into an oversize chair Frank sat too without an invitation. "Yea... upstairs."

"You mean Mrs. Jones?"

The old woman looked at Frank quizzically. "How did you know?"

"Richard mentioned it."

"That bastard. He has no respect for his own mother."

"You shouldn't be so hard on Richard. He's extremely busy at work." Frank decided to try to sweeten the atmosphere. "It's not easy to run a police department."

She spat into a handkerchief, the sound causing Frank to gag. "Tell him to call me once in a while, if he can't come visit. After all, I've lived here alone ever since my husband died years ago. The social security check hardly covers my expenses."

"Is Richard your only son?"

"Yes."

"I'm curious... how are you related to Mrs. Jones?"

"Well... she isn't really my cousin. We just use the term to facilitate things. You see, Rebecca, Ilene and I have been close friends since elementary school. We are like family to each other."

"How interesting. Have you seen Ilene lately?"

"She's in Chicago. We talk on the phone. Poor woman. She's suffered so much."

Frank was feeling good that the conversation was becoming friendlier. He assumed the old woman didn't have any friends and that she was lonely, anxious to visit with anyone. "Does Rebecca have children?"

"A son and two daughters."

"I met Jim. He seems to be a nice guy."

"He's had his problems."

"You mentioned that Ilene has suffered a great deal. Why?"

"She made bad marriages."

"Did Ilene have children?"

"I don't know. She moved away years ago. She's never spoken about her family, no matter how many times I've asked. She just keeps talking about other stuff."

"I understand she dated both Simon Miller and Julius Swansen in high school."

As soon as Frank made that statement, the old woman became suspicious. She frowned, her face reddening. "Who are you? Why all these questions?" Her tone was rough. She stared at Frank, sitting in silence. "Are you a police officer?"

Frank's mind raced. He straightened his tie, trying to save time. "Well... yes. I'm investigating a murder" He didn't elaborate, nor did he want to have a scene. He got up, thanked her and left.

The old woman remained sitting, speechless, completely bewildered by what had just happened. Absently she stubbed out her cigarette, lighting the next one.

Frank ordered the taxi to take him back to his hotel. His mind was now on a new track. He felt he was nearing the end of his investigation. The picture had narrowed significantly, even though there was much more to be done. He settled at the bar, ordering a local artisan beer.

Sipping slowly, unaware of the flavor, Frank's mind became restless. Ilene appeared in his mind's eye. She must be at the center of the Swansen case. She had refused to talk about the past. She'd been married to Simon, then to Julius, who then married Adela, her twin sister. Mrs. Crawley, once a close friend, was in the dark about Ilene. What could have been so sinister that the past was so deeply buried? After all, people get married and divorced all the time – that was not the end of the world for most. Why the payments to Ilene and Simon? Was blackmail involved? It was hard to imagine blackmail among friends. He had to find a way to break through Ilene's reticence. He knew whatever had happened in the past must have a bearing on the present circumstances.

Frank ordered another beer. He stared at his reflection in a huge mirror behind a vast array of bottles. His face was impassive. Jones... they lived in the same apartment building with the Crawleys, and Mrs. Crawley was Ilene's close friend – there had to be a connection. Crawley had arranged for Lisa to be hired by the park authorities. What was the connection between them? The way in which Crawley had handled the Miller murder investigation and how Lisa had behaved in such a peculiar fashion made no sense. Lisa committed suicide when it appeared to Frank that they were reconciling. There had to be some other reason for her to take her life. What was it?

Frank left the bar in a great hurry, as if someone was chasing him. He jumped into a cab waiting curbside. "75 Riverdale Circle."

It was dark when Frank arrived. He was so busy thinking about his search for the truth that he hadn't even noticed the sun disappearing. He ordered the taxi to wait. He stood in front of the apartment building, head raised to look at the upper floors. The sky was dark but clear, a huge array of stars shining clearly. "They don't know what's going on down here," he murmured, observing their beauty. They were remote from all the human undertakings and frailties.

He leaped up the stairs, two at a time. In front of the Jones' apartment he took a deep breath before ringing the bell. A middle aged man in loose pajamas opened the door. He looked at Frank, still breathing heavily. "Can I help you?"

Frank hadn't thought about how to approach the Jones since he'd had no idea who would be home. He mumbled, "I'd like to talk to you about Jim."

The man took a step back, hand flying to his chest. "What's wrong? Is he in trouble again?"

"May I come in? I don't want to talk about it in the hall."

"Of course... of course. Please, come in. Forgive the way I'm dressed. I go to bed early."

"Who is that, dear?" A woman's husky voice could be heard from the back of the apartment.

"There's a gentleman here about Jim. I'll take care of him."

Frank was directed to a dining room table on the far side of the living room. They sat down across from each other. Frank felt a liking for the man right away. A ready smile on his face reflected a man happy with his life. "I'd like to talk to you about Jim. He's been very close with Lisa Warrenton." Frank paused to see if there was any reaction but there was nothing. "Unfortunately, Miss Warrenton has been found dead."

"I don't know who you're talking about. Was Jim involved in some way? Why are you here?"

194

"Mr. Jones, do you know where Jim is?"

The man stared at Frank, not sure what to do. His face showed some embarrassment. Frank sensed that his host was experiencing some kind of dilemma. He maintained his silence. Finally, Mr. Jones came out with a flurry of questions. "Sir, who are you? What do you want? Why have you come here? We've had enough trouble. My wife is sick."

"I've come to help you. I know you've had problems with Jim. I can only help if you cooperate with me."

"Who are you? What's your name? How did you find us?"

"I'll answer your questions in a minute, but first, I need to know whether you know Jim's whereabouts."

Mr. Jones hesitated for a moment. "He's in jail." Embarrassment and disappointment chased across his face.

A thought quickly flashed through Frank's mind. Jim had been taken out of, or sprung out of jail, then taken to Jackson Hole. His police file had been removed because Frank was getting too close in his investigation.

"Have you seen him lately?"

"We were told he's in an out-of-state prison."

"What is he in prison for?"

"He was caught with a gang stealing cars. He's always been an excellent mechanic, he just picked the wrong way to use his talents."

"Has he been jailed before?"

His eyes welled up. "Why have you come here? Why are you opening up these old wounds?" He started to cry, then said brokenly, wiping tears from his face, "We've been good parents. We don't know why or how he became so violent. He knows more about cars than anybody else. He could have made a good living using his skills more wisely."

Frank decided it was time to leave. Commissioner Fields would surely have a complete dossier on Jim. He felt bad that he had upset Mr. Jones. He took his leave, saying, "I'll do what I can for him." As Frank turned to go, another thought flashed through his mind. "Was Jim married?"

"His marriage didn't last. They divorced while he was in jail."

"Was her name Margaret?"

"Yes... how did you know?"

"It was just a guess."

"You never told me your name."

"It doesn't matter. Thank you." Frank left without another word, leaving behind a bewildered Mr. Jones.

Frank wished he had the twins' pictures with him. He regretted not having asked to see a picture of Jim's former wife. He was convinced that whoever had traveled under the name of Margaret Jones must have been one of the twins, but how was that possible?

A message was waiting for Frank at the front desk. Commissioner Fields had called but it was too late to return the call. He went to bed, but his mind, having all these new details to think about, kept him wide awake. Why had Jim's parents been kept in the dark about his location? Why hadn't they been informed that their son was out of jail? It was obvious that Crawley, as a police chief, had fabricated Jim's escape or removal from a Minnesota prison. Therefore, there must be some connection between him and Lisa, since she had harbored him, and Crawley knew where to call her when the Gertrude Miller murder was discovered.

A new question arose in Frank's mind. Why had Lisa been called? There was no reason for Crawley to call her, except for the discovery of Frank's business card. It might confirm that Crawley had been well aware of the relationship between Frank and Lisa.

Frank gave up. "I can't go on like this," he said to himself, downing two full glasses of merlot, hoping it would help him fall asleep. It did. He woke hours later with a splitting headache but decided it had all been worth it to get some rest. He popped two aspirins and drank two full glasses of ice cold water.

Frank ate breakfast in a rush, anxious to find out what Commissioner Fields had for him. He was sure Fields had found something of interest, otherwise, he wouldn't have called so late the night before.

Fields was pleased to see Frank. He spoke as soon as Frank entered his office. "James Jones is a fugitive. Apparently, he was spirited out of our prison by a fake court order. We've searched for him in Minnesota but we didn't bother to look for him elsewhere. He had been imprisoned for stealing cars and we don't have the manpower to hunt across the country for this type of thief. The FBI doesn't deal with such criminals either unless they operate across state lines. The case was finally dropped."

"Well... I know where he is, and I have his address if you want it. However, due to his possible involvement in the Swansen case, I'd appreciate it if you stay on the sidelines until the case is solved. It shouldn't take too much longer."

"Can he escape from his present location?"

"I have a strong feeling that Crawley is the man who spirited Jim Jones away from prison. That's why he's keeping him busy in Jackson Hole. The question on my mind right now is what Jim might do now that Lisa Warrenton is dead. If my theory is correct, Crawley will keep Jim under close watch since he can easily incriminate him, if he's caught."

Fields sighed. "It would be simple for a police chief to arrange release papers. I think you're on to something."

"I met Crawley's mother yesterday. She's a lonely, miserable woman, living alone and subsisting on only her social security check. Apparently, there's been little communication between mother and son. It didn't sound like she even knew where he was living."

"I'll alert the department chief about Jim Jones but will order no action taken until I hear from you."

"I appreciate that. I also met Jim's father. He didn't know who I was. I managed to keep my name out of the conversation. He seems to think Jim is jailed in an out-of-state prison. He told me that Jim had been married to a woman named Margaret. He never heard her last name and they are now divorced. I feel strongly that Margaret Jones is one of the Swansen twins. The problem is I can't prove it. There's too much conflicting evidence."

"You've accomplished a great deal already. I know it's frustrating when you can't find the answers you seek. We're used to it in our work. Diligence is vital."

"I don't know why, but I have a gut feeling that today's problem relates to an affair from yesteryears. I'll have to go to Chicago once more to interview Ilene Samps."

"Keep me posted."

"I will. Thanks for your help. Call me if you find out anything that might be of interest."

18.

Frank changed his mind about traveling to Chicago, instead, he returned to Jackson Hole. At the airport he went into the men's room and put on his disguise; a mustache, a goatee, the plain glasses, and then covered his head with an old baseball cap.

He decided not to return to Hotel Wort, checking into a brand new Motel 6 on East Broadway. It was a big step down for a man used to first class action.

The cause for his change of heart was the thought of Julia. Frank left Commissioner Fields' office, feeling guilty about his brash dismissal of Julia from his mind. Had he completely misunderstood the extent of her jealousy? Was it a crime for a woman who had shared her life with him, as he had with hers, to be so jealous? Why had he let his male ego take over his sense of rationality? She had definitely deserved better understanding from him. It was true he hadn't loved her, but he certainly admired her. He realized, painfully, that he had used her love for him to his own advantage. He resolved to find her.

It was already dark, the sky clear, a light breeze coming from the south, the temperature a pleasant 72 degrees. He walked down Broadway to dine at Bubba's restaurant. He hated eating alone in restaurants, but Motel 6 had no room service. He always thought that a man eating by himself was seen as a man who had failed in society.

The hostess sat him at a small table for two. After placing his order, not having anything to do but wait, Frank looked around. Two women sat on the other side of the room, eating and talking. One of the women seemed familiar. It dawned on him that she was the saleswoman he had noticed exiting from the rear door at the Tradeside Gallery.

Frank couldn't stop staring at her. There was something about her that reminded him of Julia. Was it Julia? No, Julia was blonde and didn't wear glasses. His thoughts kept nagging him throughout his meal.

Finally, the two women paid their check and left, pulling on light jackets, still chatting. Without a second thought Frank left enough money on his table and followed them from a distance. They were so engaged in their conversation that they paid no attention to their surroundings.

They crossed several blocks before one of the women turned to the left, waving goodbye. Frank hastened his step, getting ever closer. Julia paid no attention to the rapid footsteps behind her, feeling very safe in this town.

"Julia, is that you?" Frank almost whispered his question, unsure of what to do in the situation. He didn't want to frighten her.

The woman turned around, almost colliding with Frank. He looked straight into her eyes. "Julia... it is you. I've been looking for you everywhere."

"Frank?..." She stared at him, her eyes focusing on his face. "Is that you?" She had recognized his voice but not his face. "Since when did you grow a beard?"

Frank couldn't speak. He couldn't help himself. He grabbed Julia, hugging her close to him, feeling her soft curves against him. She didn't resist. "I felt terrible about the way I've treated you. I'm so sorry. Honestly, I had no understanding of your feelings. I was a selfish brute. Can you forgive me?" As Frank spoke to Julia, a memory of Lisa's apologies flitted across his mind. Had he believed in her, she may not have committed suicide.

Julia noticed Frank's momentary absence. "Frank, you seem to be lost. What's going on in your head right now?"

"No, Julia, I'm not lost. I was just thinking about what an egotistical ass I've been."

"Are you trying to tell me that you love me?" She sounded almost amused at his state of mind. This was a side of Frank she'd never seen before.

Frank was pleased that Julia hadn't rejected him at first sight. "Julia, love is a difficult subject for me. Can we talk somewhere else? My motel is around the corner." He took her hand, not wanting to lose a second of contact with her.

"Ok, Frank." Julia let him take the lead. They walked slowly to his motel room, both full of things to say but uncertain how to begin their conversation.

As they entered his room, Julia spoke first. "I want to be honest with you. I've had plenty of time to think. I, too, was out of place. My behavior toward you was atrocious. I was so afraid of losing you that I let my emotions control my thinking."

"Julia, it seems we're even. I admit I have a lot to learn about love. I've always looked at love from a selfish point of view. I didn't believe it was a necessity for me to be committed to you as long as you were committed to me and my needs. I feel now that I've come to know what real love is and why it's important in life."

Julia could not believe her ears. Frank was actually admitting he had been wrong. And not only that, but that he had real feelings for her. She had waited so long for this she didn't know what to say. After a minute, the only thing she could think of was, "What now Frank?"

"I think I'm heading down the right track. Don't force change on me, all at once. We'll be alright together. I believe this about us. I just need time."

Julia leapt up from her chair to grab Frank by the shoulders. "Those are the best words I've ever heard from you. I want you to know that I never stopped loving you. Deep in my heart I was hoping you would come around."

"Is that why you stayed in Jackson Hole?"

"Partly. I couldn't face going back to New York knowing what I'd done. I know I made a terrible mistake, blaming my behavior on love. To this day I believe I acted out of a momentary insanity, God forgive me. I can't release myself from guilt. I took a life."

"What's done is done. Let's turn over a new leaf. I'm willing, if you are."

Julia kept her hold on Frank. "Let's. I won't bring this up anymore. Let's start anew." They kissed with tenderness, not wanting anything more from the moment than a new beginning, a new chapter in their lives.

"I can't tell you how happy you've made me. I'll do the best I can, with your help, to treat you the way you deserve to be treated."

Julia sat back, face somber. "I read in the paper that Lisa Warrenton committed suicide. The article stated that you and a ranger found her body. What happened?"

Frank didn't respond to Julia's statement, not wanting to set off a rift so early. "I have a lot to tell you about the Swansen case. It's so complicated I don't even know where to begin."

Julia knew intuitively that he was avoiding any talk about Lisa. She didn't really care about the Swansen case as that had been the cause of so much unhappiness for her. "Not now. I'm emotionally exhausted."

Frank took her in his arms and they kissed each other with great depth of feeling. Finally, they drew apart. "I was planning to look for you at the Tradeside Gallery. I was in there buying something when I glimpsed you leaving through the rear door. I wasn't sure it was really you."

"I got a job there right away. It's kept me busy and I've rediscovered how much I like the world of art."

"I'm going to be very busy with this Swansen investigation. I feel I'm getting closer to solving the murders."

Julia felt a twinge of irritation that Frank kept returning to what interested him instead of listening to her, but decided to let it go for now. He couldn't be expected to give up his pattern of self interest right away. "Why were you disguising yourself?"

"Police Chief Crawley is trying to pin a murder on me. I believe he's involved in some way with the Swansen case. That's what I'm working on. It looks like the local DA is on my side."

"Does Crawley have any grounds to accuse you?"

"He found my business card in the purse of a dead woman."

"So what? You've given out cards to a lot of people."

"It's a long story."

"Do you have any work to do here in Jackson or did you come back for me?"

"Mostly it was to find you, but to be honest I also want to talk to a fellow by the name of James Jones. I know where he lives."

"Frank, I can't tell you how happy I am that we found each other. I hope you feel the same."

"I do. I feel so much better now. I was ridden with guilt. That was what brought me back here."

"Let's go to my apartment. There's more room there."

****

Julia prepared breakfast while Frank washed up. They ate, talking, smiling, happy, as if nothing had ever come between them. Julia went to work while Frank took a stroll toward George's garage. He took the sidewalk across from the garage, peering in, trying not to be obvious while doing so. Jim was nowhere to be seen. Frank returned a while later but still no sight of Jim.

Several cars pulled in, one leaving abruptly, the driver obviously pissed off about something. The garage owner ran from car to car, his hands waving, shouting, obviously upset. Frank sat on a convenient bus stop bench diagonally across from the garage, maintaining a watch. About an hour later, Jim slowly entered the garage, head and arm bandaged, his right eye black.

In several minutes Jim came out, walking away even more slowly. Frank followed him to his apartment. By the time Jim opened the door to his apartment, Frank was right behind him. Jim had been in so much pain, and in such an emotional turmoil that he hadn't noticed he was being followed. Frank pushed himself in right behind Jim, slamming the door shut.

Jim leapt away, fright evident on his face. "Who are you? What do you want?"

"I'm not going to hurt you. We need to talk."

"About what?" He continued to edge away from Frank, cradling his injured arm.

Frank stayed put, not wanting to spook the man even further. "Let's sit down. Take it easy. I'm on your side."

"Who are you?"

"I was a friend of Lisa. I was shocked by her death. Do you know why she killed herself?"

Jim stared at Frank, not knowing what to do. He had no idea who Frank was, or what he was after. Finally, he spoke, his voice hard. "I know nothing."

Frank put a smile on his face to try and reduce Jim's tension. "To prove to you that I'm on your side, let me tell you I know Chief Crawley arranged your so called transfer from the Minnesota jail. I could report you but I haven't." Frank waited for Jim's reaction, knowing he had taken a risk by lying.

Jim's face paled, his forehead suddenly wet with beads of sweat. He was at a loss for words. Frank remained silent, letting Jim digest his words and decide whether he would talk or not. After several minutes Jim opened up. "That bastard Crawley beat me up last night. What an asshole."

Frank held himself still, not wanting to react to Jim's shocking statement. "Why?"

"He said that I was the cause of all his problems. He told me I needed to keep my mouth shut and not to talk to the DA or anyone from the police department if I wanted to live." There was a shiver throughout his body to accompany his last words. He obviously believed Crawley would kill him.

Frank was pleased. His risk had paid off. "Did Crawley tell you his reason for helping you escape?"

"Yeah... it was about Lisa. I'm sure he killed her."

Frank realized he had missed a key point. Crawley had shown up less than thirty minutes after he had discovered Lisa's body. At the time he had assumed the ranger had called both his superior and Crawley. The trip from Jackson Hole to Mammoth Hot Springs took an hour and a half at good speed so Crawley had to have been nearby.

"Why did Lisa want to help you?"

Jim clammed up. He was confused, not sure whether to believe Frank, afraid of being returned to jail. Frank realized his dilemma. "Jim, I want to assure you that I won't do a thing to hurt you. All I want is the truth. It's really as simple as that." Frank's face radiated sympathy and understanding.

"It isn't as simple as you say," Jim mumbled.

Frank thought it possible Jim had been brought in to commit a crime. He remembered the gun he had taken from Jim's chest of drawers. He wondered how he could get him to talk. "Have you done something you're afraid to talk about?"

Jim stayed silent for a minute before suddenly bursting out. "I've been a thief and I've committed some minor felonies but I'd never killed anybody. She made me do it." He began to cry. "I'm not a killer. I told her that over and over." He rocked back and forth, lost in his fear and confusion.

Frank gaped at him. "Do you mean Lisa?" His voice was incredulous.

"Who else?"

"Jim, was it you who shot the couple at the Mammoth Terraces?"

"Yes... yes... she made me do it." Jim was now sobbing heavily, his nose running. What a sight. "She told me she'd make sure I went back to jail if I didn't cooperate."

Frank was shocked. His Lisa, the woman he had fallen in love with? What had she been up to? Why would she want another member of the Swansen family killed? It was mind boggling. "Did Lisa say anything to you about why she wanted that couple dead? Is there anything else you remember?"

"The only thing she told me was that I'd earned my freedom."

"Do you know why Crawley got you out of jail?"

"He never said a word to me."

"Did you apply for a position with the police in Jackson Hole?"

"Yes... I was told I could get a mechanic's job, taking care of state troopers' cars."

"Did you get that job?"

"No. George's garage was advertising for a car mechanic and I've been working for him since then. He didn't ask any questions. He was desperate to get somebody."

"Do you have the gun you used to kill that couple?"

"Lisa gave it to me. It's police standard issue."

Frank wanted to create a situation that would keep Jim in the apartment. "Do you have that gun?"

"It's in my bottom drawer."

Frank had hoped for that response. "Show it to me."

Jim slowly walked over to the chest, nursing his arm. He knelt clumsily to open the bottom drawer, but, of course there was no gun there. He rocked back on his heels, shouting. "It isn't here. I bet Crawley took it. It has my fingerprints all over it." He sank to the floor, shaking his head. "He's really got me now, hasn't he?" He looked to Frank, hoping he could help him out of this dilemma.

"Don't worry. I'm on your side. Crawley is the one who's in trouble."

"What are you going to do?"

"Finish investigating the case I'm on. Meanwhile, you need to go to work every day as soon as you can. Act as if nothing has happened. I don't think Crawley will come after you. He's got too many other things to worry about."

Jim sighed gustily, relieved someone else was going to help him. "Thank you, thank you, thank you."

"Don't tell anyone about our conversation, especially Crawley. Keep out of his way."

****

Frank felt sorry for Jim, a young man who somehow got caught up in a gang of thieves. He knew he had made promises to Jim that he wasn't sure if he could keep. Frank needed to know everything there was to know about Jim's release from prison, particularly whose hands had been involved. Jim's story about Lisa ordering him to kill Eric and Sandra Swansen Chandler had completely changed his line of thinking.

It occurred to Frank that Jim might have lied. Knowing that Lisa was dead might have created a sort of an alibi for him in his mind. However, Frank was convinced he now had proof Crawley and Lisa had worked together. It was obvious to him that Crawley had to get rid of both Lisa and Jim to save his own skin. He'd done away with Lisa and was biding his time about Jim, not wanting another unexplained death so soon.

As soon as Frank returned to Julia's apartment he looked up the number for DA Charles Dickson. "Charlie, it's Frank Galitson. I hate to bother you but I need to see you right away. I have evidence that will incriminate Chief Crawley."

Dickson crowed in delight. "Come right over. I'll wait for you. I can't wait to get that bastard."

Frank left Julia a note to tell her where he'd gone. Dickson was waiting anxiously for him, holding his office door open wide. "Come in... come in... what have you got?"

Frank closed the door, not wanting any strange ears listening in on their conversation. He extracted a promise from Dickson that he would go easy on Jim before telling him about his latest findings. "I'm convinced Crawley will get rid of Jim too, to save himself. There's no question that he killed Lisa. I don't know why Lisa wanted the Chandler couple killed, but I'll find out. I know I'm on the right trail in these Swansen murders. I suggest you arrange for someone to watch out for Jim, preferably one of your own men, not someone from the police force."

"Frank, let me commend you on your work. I'll take care of this. I have exactly the right guy. I'll call him right now."

Frank left, pleased at finally seeing some progress. He'd never been as convinced as he was right now that he was right. Julia was in the apartment when he arrived and he hugged her with warmth. This time he wasn't waiting for her to make all the moves.

"Tell me all about your day. You look like you made great progress."

"We'll find out soon. Let's have dinner. I'm starved. I also want to hear about your day, too."

Frank and Julia both wore a disguise, smiling at each other at the silliness of it all. After a meal at the Bunnery, a small family dining place, Frank cautiously directed them in a stroll toward Jim's apartment building. He stopped diagonally across from the building and sat them both down in that convenient bus stop bench.

"If you're that tired we should have gone right home."

"I want to see if Chief Crawley will come by."

They stayed there for an hour, chatting in low voices. Crawley didn't show up. Julia was impatient. "We can't stay here all night. Let's go." Frank realized he wouldn't be able to watch Jim's place on his own, day and night. "I hope Dickson lives up to his promise."

Frank couldn't rid himself from Jim's words about Lisa forcing him to kill the Chandler couple. He wished Lisa was alive so he could confront her. He recalled the scene when her body had been found. It had definitely looked like a suicide. However, a clever killer could easily have fabricated the scene. It made sense that Crawley would kill Lisa to eliminate witnesses to his fraudulent activities. Frank became even more concerned for Jim's safety -- sure he would be Crawley's next victim. Once they were back in her apartment he paced so much Julia became exasperated with him.

"Julia, what would you do if you knew someone was likely to be killed?"

"I'd call the police."

"But what if the chief of police is the killer, what then?"

She checked his face, in doubt about the sincerity of his question. "That's a tough one. Maybe hire someone to watch out for him or her."

"I can't rest. I'm convinced Crawley is planning to kill Jim Jones and that tonight is the night."

"What are you saying?"

"I'm going back to watch over the apartment."

"I'm coming with you." Julia didn't want Frank out of her sight. She wanted to trust him but their past forbade that.

They bundled up as the night air had cooled. Frank drove slowly, parking his car on a side street next to Jim's apartment building where they could watch the entrance. Julia leaned against Frank's shoulder, soon falling asleep.

Frank forced himself to stay awake. From time to time his eyes closed for brief seconds. His head would come up with a snap each time. By four in the morning Frank was ready to start the car and go back home. From the corner of his eye he saw a police car passing by, lights out, coming to a silent stop in front of the building. He gently woke Julia and whispered to her what was going on.

Frank could see Crawley getting out of the car. The street lights provided just enough light for Frank to identify him. At first, Frank thought about following Crawley upstairs, but quickly changed his mind. Crawley wouldn't be so stupid as to orchestrate a killing in an apartment building where the slightest commotion would wake neighboring residents. Surely Jim would resist him.

Frank was now totally on the alert. He signaled to Julia to remain still. Minutes later he saw Jim emerging from the building, Crawley behind him, a gun pointing at Jim's back. He pushed Jim into the back seat of his car, closing the door gently. He drove away, lights still off. There was no other movement in the street and Julia and Frank stayed still.

Frank let Crawley turn the corner, then started his car. With his own headlights off, Frank followed Crawley to Route 89, south to the airport. Was Crawley taking Jim back to Minnesota?

Frank's dilemma was soon over. Crawley turned left, driving up a narrow road toward the Wildlife Museum. Frank had visited the museum in the past and knew that the road would end in a circle in front of the museum. He stopped half way there, instructing Julia to stay inside the car, paying no attention to her voluble pleas to stay where he was and not put himself in danger. He walked briskly up the road, as quiet as he could be, trying to avoid any noise.

Several clouds passed overhead obscuring the full moon. By now Crawley had taken Jim out of the car and was directing him around the back of the museum, gun still at the ready. Frank began to run, shouting, "Crawley, don't do it. I've already notified the DA."

Crawley turned, firing several rapid shots in Frank's direction. Luckily for Frank every bullet missed as Crawley couldn't see clearly. Jim wanted to fight Crawley but with his arm in a sling all he could do was throw himself at Crawley's back, knocking him off balance. The gun went off again, unfortunately for Crawley, right into his midsection. Frank arrived, turning Crawley's limp form over to find him winded and wounded. He was barely able to lift the hand which still grasped the gun. Frank kicked his hand and the gun flew away. Jim stood, immobilized, traumatized by the events. "Sit down." Frank watched him sink like a puppet whose strings had been cut. He returned to the police car where he keyed the two-way receiver, shouting instructions into the mike. "Send an ambulance to the Wildlife Museum, Crawley has been injured. Repeat, officer down."

Julia, against Frank's wishes, appeared at that moment, breathless from fear and running. "Are you alright? I heard shooting. What's happened?"

Frank let loose a huge sigh. "The Crawley mystery is finally over. I hope his life will be saved so we can get to the truth."

"You were right on target. I'm so proud of you." Julia kissed him with love. Frank welcomed the accolades and returned Julia's caress with his own.

Jim spoke from his seat on the stony lawn. "You saved my life. I'll do anything you want." He couldn't believe someone was actually doing something to help him out. He'd been ill-treated ever since he'd made his stupid decision to join the gang to make some quick money.

The ambulance arrived. Paramedics checked Crawley, saying he'd require immediate surgery but his condition was serious, not critical. "He'll survive."

No other official cars had arrived so Frank drove Crawley's police car while Julia, accompanied by Jim, drove Frank's car. They stopped right behind the ambulance at the emergency entrance. Frank rushed to a phone booth to call Dickson. "I was right about Crawley. He just tried to kill Jim. Where was the man you promised? I saw no one." All Frank got was some mumbled response. He hung up, frustrated that it seemed he was all alone in trying to uncover the mystery behind Crawley's actions.

Dickson showed up at the hospital, wearing a coat over rumpled pajamas, feet in fleece lined slippers. "What's the word on Crawley?"

"He's in surgery right now. We need police to post a guard at his door. We need to get the truth out of Crawley, not only about his association with Lisa Warrenton but the Swansen business as well."

Frank and Julia sat alone in a stuffy waiting room. Frank wouldn't budge, despite Julia's pleas for him to go home and rest. He insisted on staying. He desperately wanted to know about Crawley's condition. It was a long wait. They spoke little, sitting with hands entwined for mutual support.

After five hours the surgeon emerged from the operating room. "Crawley is in bad shape. I managed to get the bullet out. It damaged his liver and the bile duct leading from his pancreas, as well as several feet of small intestine. Generally the liver can regenerate itself to some degree, but not always. If he's lucky, it will. I've inserted a stent to reconnect the bile duct. The loss of part of the small intestine might cause him problems in the future. That's something I can't control. Right now he's being transferred to the intensive care unit. He'll have to stay there for two days."

"When can I talk to him?"

"When he's out of the ICU, not before."

"Thank you, doctor."

Julia forced Frank to return to her apartment. She tucked him in, then left for work. Sleep wouldn't come. He wished the two days were already over so he could interrogate Crawley. Suddenly he sat up. "What's happened to Jim?" He'd been so preoccupied with Crawley he'd completely forgotten about him.

Frank showered in cold water to wake himself up. He got dressed and rushed out. He found Jim back in his apartment. "Are you ok?"

"I'm shook up from this whole affair. It took me a long while to stop shaking. I was able to hitch a ride home. Crawley would have killed me if you hadn't shown up. I owe you my life."

"Jim, the DA is surely going to hold you as a material witness. I'd like you to go with me to his office. Both of us have to make statements. Be sure to tell the whole truth. I've talked with the police commissioner in Minneapolis. He's promised to close the file on your escape. The problem is you may be charged with manslaughter for killing the Chandler couple. I can help you out by introducing the Swansen murders. As soon as I find the perpetrator your attorney will have plenty of ammunition to help your case."

Jim stared at Frank, despair on his face. "I'll be jailed again. I'd rather run away."

"Don't be stupid. If you do that you'll have both the Minneapolis and the Jackson Hole police looking for you, as well as the FBI. Eventually you'll be caught and your sentence will be doubled. If you come clean now the prosecutor and the court will likely consider leniency. You've made a lot of mistakes in the past. It's time to start over."

Jim mulled over Frank's words. Frank kept quiet, letting him think things through. Finally Jim stood up. "OK, you're right. Let's go."

Frank's mind had been busy too. He knew he'd taken Jim's gun, mailing it to his New York address. He decided to keep any mention of the gun out of his statement to facilitate Jim's defense. The fact that Crawley had beaten Jim up and tried to kill him might imply that he was responsible for stealing the gun.

Dickson was shouting orders to his staff when Frank and Jim arrived. It was obvious he was gung-ho to nail Crawley. Frank announced that Jim had decided to surrender himself to the DA's office and was willing to make a statement.

Dickson smiled broadly. He escorted Jim to a room next to his office, instructing a stenographer to take down his statement. Both he and Frank sat at the other end of the table, listening without interruption. When Jim completed his statement, Dickson picked up the phone, demanding the presence of a police officer. "You're under arrest for the murder of Eric and Sandra Chandler." Frank made his own report about the events of the previous night. They all remained in the room waiting for the statements to be typed. The air was somber, no one speaking.

When the stenographer returned with the statements, Jim looked at Frank, as if asking him if he should sign. Frank nodded.

After the signatures were complete Jim was removed by a waiting police officer, who read him his rights as they left the room. Dickson called in his secretary, instructing her to obtain the Chandler file from the police department.

Frank asked Dickson to wait a bit. "I'd appreciate it if you could go easy on Jim. I convinced him to come and tell the truth about the whole affair. As far as I know, he's told you everything. The point I'm trying to make is that this all connects somehow to the Swansen murders. I urge you not to prosecute Jim until the Swansen family murderer is found."

"I have a clear murder one case here. That man just confessed to killing two people."

Frank's mind raced. It was his belief that DA's were always in a rush when they saw a case with an easy conviction. "I'd like to point out that Jim made a statement, not a confession. Any half-assed defense attorney could ruin your case in two minutes."

Dickson stared at Frank before bursting out angrily. "You orchestrated this whole thing, didn't you?"

Frank snorted. "I brought him in to make a statement about the events of the last two days. Most of what he said about his past, his relationship with Lisa Warrenton and with Crawley, is all news to me. I came to you days ago to air my suspicions about Crawley. I had no proof of his involvement. Now both of us know the facts. If you prosecute Jim now, it will cause you grief in the future. I'll have to tell the truth when I'm called in. Apart from all that, Jim deserves some mercy."

Dickson remained silent for several moments. He stared at Frank with open hostility. "You're a sharp operator."

"I'm not a sharp operator, just an author who writes mysteries. Facts are facts. You can't avoid them or turn a blind eye to them."

"You're right." Dickson decided he would be wise to soften his stance if he wanted to keep Frank working with him rather than against him. "I'll wait till the Swansen case is solved." His manner was not gracious but he meant every word he said.

Frank went to Julia's gallery. He had to wait as she was busy with a customer. As it turned out, the woman bought the very sculpture he had been planning to buy. He cursed under his breath.

Frank told Julia about the events of the morning before taking himself off to the hospital to inquire about Crawley. He was told Crawley was still under the care of the ICU, not responding well to his surgery. The nurses would not give him any more information than that, seeing he was neither family nor next of kin.

Frank passed by the hospital several times during the next few days. Crawley remained in ICU until the afternoon of the fourth day when he was finally moved to a regular hospital bed. At the DA's request, Crawley was placed in a private room, where a police officer on guard sat outside the door, monitoring all who entered.

Frank called Dickson from the hospital. "Crawley has been moved to a private room. His doctor said we can talk to him for five minutes."

Dickson came right over. Crawley's face was gray and sunken. He was hooked up to several machines and an intravenous drip. Blearily he managed to open his eyes when he heard Frank and Dickson enter. He looked at them with no comprehension.

Frank rushed to talk to him before Dickson could even open his mouth. "Crawley, what was the connection between you and Lisa? Was Jim Jones part of some deal you'd made?"

Dickson pushed Frank aside. "We need the truth Crawley. Why did you want to kill Jim Jones?"

Crawley's blank eyes darted back and forth between the two men. He mumbled something they couldn't understand. Dickson was impatient, raising his voice. "Speak up man, you're in deep trouble."

Crawley closed his eyes, silent. Dickson began to shout at him to no avail. A nurse entered, fussing at them about the shouting. She pulled Dickson away from the bed. "What's the matter with you? Can't you see this man is incapable of talking? Out... get out." She pushed him toward the door.

"The doctor said…"

"Out… this man can't talk to you. He's just had a strong sedative."

They left, both of them completely disappointed. Frank went back to Julia's apartment. He was completely exhausted. He fell asleep on the sofa while watching the news.

Frank called the hospital several times a day. The report wasn't encouraging. On the third morning Frank was told Crawley had died in his sleep. "Damn… now we won't know how he got involved, who recruited him, or whether he killed Lisa." He stormed around the apartment, angry at how the situation had turned out.

Julia watched him, wisely keeping quiet until he stopped ranting. "What are you going to do?"

"I have to go back to Minneapolis."

"Do you want me to quit the gallery and come with you?"

Frank hugged her, grateful for the offer. "Not yet. Let me finish this case, then we'll decide what we want to do."

"When will you leave?"

"I'll book a flight for tomorrow."

19.

It was raining heavily, a cold rain driven by a strong wind, when Frank left the Minneapolis terminal. He checked into the Hilton Garden Hotel, mentally tired and ready for some down time. He rested the remainder of the day, diverting his mind by reading a paperback he'd bought at the Jackson airport. He went to bed early after a room service meal that included two glasses of their best house red.

The following day Frank called on Police Commissioner Fields. He briefed him about the events which had taken place in Jackson Hole, emphasizing his arrangement with Jim. "He'll have to be prosecuted in Wyoming since he admitted to killing the Chandlers there."

Fields agreed that the crime of murder was far more extenuating than Jim's escape from jail, something that had been perpetrated by others. He also considered the expense involved in preparing for trial. He decided to drop the case against Jim. Frank was really pleased. "I'd appreciate another great favor. Simon Miller, Julius Swansen's best friend as a teenager, must have had family here. The phone book is full of Millers. Could you find out who the right one is for me?"

"Not a problem. I'll be happy to help."

"I'll keep you informed." They shook hands, murmuring a few social niceties. Frank needed this man's cooperation.

Frank's next stop was at the apartment where Crawley's mother lived. She wasn't pleased to see Frank. "You again? What now?" She held the door open only a crack, the safety chain in place. All he could see was a sliver of her sour face and one beady eye.

"I'm truly sorry to disturb you, but I'm the bearer of bad news. Could I come in?" Frank tried his most ingratiating smile.

"Bad news? Do you mean about Richard?"

"Yes. Please, let me come in. I don't want your neighbors to hear all the sordid details."

She stared at him for a moment. "Make it quick. No more questions about the past." She signaled for Frank to enter, sliding the chain off so she could open the door fully.

They sat across from each other. Frank took a deep breath. He felt sorry for this unhappy old woman. It pained him to have to tell her about her son's death. "I feel badly about recent events which have brought your son to a devastating end. I deeply regret to tell you that Richard is dead." Frank paused, thinking she'd become hysterical, but she continued to sit calmly, face blank. If she was shocked there was no sign of it. "Richard was caught while trying to kill a man named Jim Jones. He fell and accidentally shot himself in the stomach. He died from his wounds."

The name Jim Jones brought her out of her momentary silence. "The son of the Jones' who live up here?"

"That's right."

"Why? Why would Richard want to kill Jim?"

"Apparently Richard falsified certain documents to spring Jim from a local jail. He conspired with a Yellowstone park ranger named Lisa Warrenton to have Jim kill a daughter of Julius Swansen and her husband. Lisa supposedly committed suicide, but I believe Richard killed her, then tried to kill Jim to save his own neck."

She was paying close attention to Frank now, drinking in the story. "Are you sure of your facts? It doesn't sound like the full story."

"I was there. Richard was firing at me to keep me away, but Jim threw himself at Richard and knocked him off balance. Richard fell, and that's when he accidentally shot himself."

She took a moment to digest his comments. There was no sign of emotion other than a continuation of her sour look. "I lost Richard many years ago. He never helped me a bit after his father died. He didn't even show up for his funeral. Should I mourn for him? I think not." It was as if she was washing her hands of her son.

Frank was leery about asking the questions he had in mind, but decided to plow ahead anyway. "I know it's difficult for you to talk about the past, particularly when it brings back so many bad memories, but, a number of murders have taken place, and they are clearly related to past events. Your son's death is likely related to this drama." Frank paused, trying to assess her reaction. There was none. "Please tell me about your younger days, especially anything you can remember about Ilene Samps, her twin sister, and Jim's mother."

Mrs. Crawley stared right through Frank, as if he weren't there. Suddenly her eyes filled with tears. "It's so painful. I told Ilene that Simon was no good, but she wouldn't listen. She claimed to be in love with him. You're only sixteen years old, I told her and you've already given him your virginity. Talking to her was like talking to a wall. She was convinced their's was a great romance."

"When did Julius enter the picture?"

She didn't respond to Frank's question. "Ilene and Adela looked so much alike even I couldn't tell them apart. Both Simon and Julius had sex with Ilene. One day Ilene told me, laughing, that she and Adela had changed places and the boys never even knew the difference. They thought that was hugely funny."

"I understand that Julius was first married to Ilene. When did he divorce her, and why?"

"He divorced her about eight months after marrying her. I don't know why. They moved to Chicago, and Ilene wouldn't talk about it."

"If Ilene was so in love with Simon, why did she marry Julius?"

"She was pretending to be Adela."

Frank exploded. "That's crazy. If they looked identical, what was the difference?"

"They must have had some way of knowing."

"Ok. So when Julius found out he had married the wrong twin, he divorced Ilene and married Adela. Is that it?"

"I suppose so."

"Did Julius and Ilene have children?"

"I don't know."

"Where was Simon in those days? What was his reaction to all of this?"

"Simon suddenly disappeared. I heard he'd been sent away by his parents. I don't know why. I haven't heard from him, or about him, since."

"What can you tell me about the Jones family?"

"I've been friends with Rebecca since my school days. We've always been close, like sisters."

"What about Jim?"

"Jim was a wild one, always getting in trouble. He made poor choices in friends. He belonged to a gang for a while. Rebecca and her husband suffered a great deal."

"I was told he was married, then divorced. Did they have children?"

"I don't think so."

"Did you meet his wife?"

"Sure, she was a lovely girl."

"Is there anything you can remember from the past that could have been a cause for the murders of Julius Swansen's family members?"

"Apart from their wild life when they were young, I don't know a thing." She had said all she was going to, telling Frank she was through and he needed to get out. She slammed the door behind him and Frank could hear the security chain slide into place.

Frank walked up one flight to the Jones' apartment. Mr. Jones opened the door to Frank. "I hope you have some good news." He took Frank into the living room. "How is Jimmy?"

Frank told him about the events that had occurred since Jim had been removed from the Minnesota jail. "It's obvious that Richard Crawley, in cahoots with a park ranger, conspired to use Jim, then framed him for murder. I managed to save Jim's life. However, he'll have to stand trial for manslaughter. I'm sure the judge will be lenient because of the evidence I can provide."

"Thank you so much. Poor Jimmy." He closed his eyes, holding his head, feeling the pain of a father for a wayward son.

At that moment Mrs. Jones entered the living room. "I'm sorry to disturb you. I didn't know you had company."

Frank was first to speak. "Please come in. I've brought news for you about Jimmy.

Mr. Jones spoke, his voice sad. "Jimmy is in trouble. I'll tell you all the details later."

Frank interrupted. "Mrs. Jones, please tell me about Jimmy's marriage."

"There isn't much to tell. One day Jimmy brought home a young woman, saying he'd been dating her for a while and that he planned to marry her. After the wedding we rarely saw them."

"Was her name Margaret?"

"Why, yes. How did you know?"

Frank took out pictures of the twins, showing her one of them. "Is this Margaret?"

"That's her."

Frank felt an electric current go up and down his spine. He had cracked the case. The twins had fooled him and everyone else, but no more. He would see them hang. He got up abruptly, promising them both that he would help Jim as much as he could.

Frank rushed back to Commissioner Fields' office to report his findings. He promised to call him from New York after he confronted the Swansen twins in the presence of the police.

****

Frank was excited. Finally, he had the goods on the twins. He called Joe Caputo with the details. "I'm on the next flight to New York. Please wait for me."

Frank's mind raced, trying to build a time frame around every aspect of the case. By the time the plane landed at La Guardia he was mentally exhausted. He rushed to Joe's precinct.

Joe and two uniformed police officers were waiting impatiently for Frank. As soon as he arrived they rushed to a police car waiting for them by the entrance. They drove away, siren blasting. It was busy, as always, on the streets. Miraculously the siren's effect was to clear a narrow lane for them.

Joe led the group. He pushed the doorman aside as they rushed into the building. The Swansen twins were at home. He didn't ask a single question. Instead he immediately launched into, "Elizabeth and Margaret Swansen, you're under arrest for the murder of Paul and Sheila Swansen, Eric and Sandra Chandler, Hugh Kisnick, P.J. Thompson, Joseph Weiserman, and Christopher Bolt. You have the right to remain silent. Anything you say can and will be used against you in a court of law. You have the right to an attorney during interrogation. If you cannot afford an attorney, one will be appointed to you."

The stunned twins were handcuffed and removed from their apartment. They glared at Frank on their way out, one of them shouting, "You know we're innocent." Their shouts continued as they were led out, but Frank couldn't make out what they were saying.

Caputo was pleased. He called his supervisor while they were being driven to the station to advise him the Swansen case had been cracked. Frank, sitting next to him in the police car, wondered if this really was the end.

The twins were placed in a small sealed room to await the arrival of their defense attorney, John Cavanti. As soon as he arrived, they were sequestered in a private room for almost an hour before moving into an interrogation room. Frank was allowed to watch the proceedings from an adjacent room via a two-way mirror.

Caputo presented his case. He was in full control, asking one question after the other with what seemed to be a complete knowledge of the case. The twins were incensed. They vehemently denied every accusation Caputo made. Margaret went completely wild when told that her marriage to Jim Jones had been discovered and Mrs. Jones had identified her picture. Cavanti was told to restrain her. Several times they verbally attacked Caputo, claiming they'd been framed. When asked by whom, they had no answer.

The twins' violent denials began to weigh heavily on Frank's mind. Despite Caputo's careful questioning, along with his detailing of times and places, they fought back. Cavanti sat quietly as he had nothing to counter the detective's accusations. He was enjoying the barrage toward Caputo from the twin's passionate denials.

Frank was becoming more and more uneasy with the entire situation. No one could act that well. But Mrs. Jones had identified Margaret. Margaret had flown from Jackson Hole to Minneapolis via Salt Lake City. Margaret had been in Yellowstone at the time of the murders. She had rented cars in her name, she had stayed in hotels, and she had even paid off the marina manager.

Frank weighed his conclusions. He cursed under his breath. Never before had he encountered anything like this. In all his writings he had never come up with such a twisted plot.

Frank called Julia after a quick meal in his apartment. She was excited to hear from him. He told her about the arrest and about his grave reservations. "I still haven't been able to find out a thing about Ilene Samps and Simon Miller's past. I'm convinced that something from those days influenced the Swansen tragedy. I'll have to visit Ilene Samps again."

"Would you like me to go with you? Perhaps a woman-to-woman approach might help."

"Let me try it on my own first." Frank was concerned about Julia, worried that some unknown person might kill Julia as he, or she had killed the others.

Frank called Caputo, expressing his concerns. "Joe, I don't know what your thoughts are after the interrogation, but I'm worried."

"You have nothing to worry about. I sit with criminals every day of the year. No one is ever guilty. They all deny having engaged in any kind of crime. It's so typical it stinks."

"Joe, this case is very unusual. I suggest you go slowly. I don't want you making an ass of yourself. I know the evidence is strong, but I smell a rat. Something isn't clicking. I want to interview Ilene Samps again."

"The 30 day adjournment will be up on Thursday. The DA believes he can get an arraignment within half an hour. I can't fight him."

"I'll be on my way to Chicago first thing tomorrow morning."

"I've given your name as a witness. You'll probably be served this evening."

Frank hung up, picking up the suitcase he hadn't even unpacked and rushed out the door. He didn't bother to hail a cab, walking away as fast as he could, as if he was being chased by a train. He stopped several blocks away to grab a cab. "International Hotel at Kennedy Airport."

The first flight of the day to Chicago was from La Guardia. He was up early to catch the intra-airport bus. His mind was busy trying to figure out just how to approach Ilene. He decided to use Mrs. Crawley as bait.

Once he arrived, Frank called Joe. "I'm in Chicago. Try to get a postponement for the arraignment."

"You have to be in court Thursday."

"I haven't been served."

Joe exploded. "What? You were supposed to be served last night."

"I wasn't at home last night."

"Where did you call me from?"

"A phone booth."

"Shit." The line went dead.

Frank didn't like upsetting Joe. He'd been a good friend, always willing to help with his mysteries when he was working, but he felt his intuitions about the Swansen case were right. The question now was how he could prove it. He knew he needed some solid evidence.

Ilene Samps wasn't pleased to see Frank. "You again? What do you want now?"

"Do you want to see innocent people go to jail?"

"I don't give a damn about anyone. Leave me alone." She started to close the door, but Frank stuck out his foot, jamming the door. "I suggest you talk to me, otherwise you'll have to speak to the police and they won't be so gentle."

Ilene tried to force the door shut but Frank pushed both her and the door out of the way, forcing himself in. "Let's talk in the living room." He closed the door behind him.

Ilene was furious. "I'll call the police if you don't leave."

Frank smiled. "Go ahead. That's exactly what I want."

"You're a beast."

"I know. Now... tell me about your relationship with Julius Swansen and Simon Miller."

"Go to hell." She clamped her mouth shut in disgust.

Frank didn't budge. "I already know about your relationship with Mrs. Crawley and Rebecca." He regretted not knowing Mrs. Crawley's first name. "Both of them told me plenty, except for what happened after your move to Chicago."

"I'll kill those bitches. Get out. I'm not telling you anything."

"I'm beginning to feel that you're covering up for someone. What could have happened that's so awful that you won't talk about it? Eventually I'll find out. You could be held as an accomplice in several murders."

"Get out... get out." She screamed, now completely hysterical.

Frank felt badly for her, but it was a fact that the truth didn't always surface easily. He, too, was upset. He called Julia to tell her about his encounter with Ilene.

"I'm coming to Chicago. I'll call you with my flight details." She hung up before Frank could say a word.

Frank slammed the phone down. "Damn."

Julia was back on the phone in minutes. "I'll be on United flight 792, arriving tomorrow at 1:12 p.m. Can't wait to see you. Love you. Bye."

Frank checked into The Airport Motel, just outside the perimeter of the airport. He was upset, his plans gone awry. He hadn't been able to get a thing out of Ilene. He bought himself a pre-made sandwich and two bottles of beer, in no mood to go to a restaurant.

The night passed slowly. He was restless. His mind wouldn't give him a moment of reprieve. Suddenly it occurred to him that perhaps he should get Ilene, Rebecca and the Crawley woman together. The more he thought about it, the more he liked the idea. He decided to orchestrate a reunion.

Frank felt mentally better the following morning since he had a plan, a scheme to crack the case. He hoped Julia would approve of it. His appetite was back to normal. The small restaurant at the motel was able to provide him with his favorite breakfast of eggs, sausages, and lightly toasted English muffins. He drank three strong cups of coffee and could feel the caffeine zinging through his body.

Just as Frank was leaving to pick up Julia his cell phone rang, Commissioner Fields on line. "Frank, Simon Miller has a sister, Frances Rand at 1239 – 68th Avenue."

"Thanks. You're good."

Frank's reunion with Julia was joyful for both of them. His mental burden about analyzing his confusion about 'love' seemed to have passed. He felt that his emotions toward Julia, once primarily sexual, were now real. He felt his love for Lisa hadn't been genuine. He let out a huge sigh. A feeling of a successful change embraced him. His mind suddenly cleared, his unrecognized selfishness evaporated. He was a new man.

The only unpleasant thought that accompanied his rebirth was that of Julia's crime. He wished she hadn't killed Ms. Smith. But wishing such a change about something that had happened in the past was ludicrous. His hope was that the police would close the case.

After a late lunch, Frank drove Julia to Ilene's house. During the drive, he suggested different approaches, discussing the situation with Julia ad nausea. He parked the car in a neighbor's driveway, not wanting Ilene to see him. Julia knocked on the door and was admitted after a few tense moments.

Julia emerged after twenty minutes, face somber, pointing her thumb downward. Frank was disappointed. Julia repeated the substance of her conversation with Ilene. "I tried everything. The woman is as obstinate as a mule. She could care less if a hundred more people get murdered. I tried working on her conscience – that failed too. I told her she had no heart. She said it had been destroyed years ago."

Frank was unhappy about the outcome. Deep in his heart he'd hoped Julia would succeed, but he wasn't going to be defeated. "I have a plan. I'm going to bring Mrs. Crawley and Rebecca Jones to Chicago. Those three women were best friends during their teenage years. Such a reunion might break the ice in Ilene's heart."

"What if it fails?"

"The last straw would be to convince the prosecuting attorney, or the defense, to bring her in as a hostile witness. I think I can play a certain role in the matter."

"Are you going to call them?"

"No. we're going to go to Minneapolis and see them. I also want to see Frances Rand, Simon Miller's sister. Maybe she knows something."

"I'm glad I took the rest of the week off."

****

Frank chose to visit the Jones' and Mrs. Crawley at night. He and Julia arrived at eight, after an early dinner. Frank felt more comfortable with Mr. Jones, so he called there first.

He explained his plan, then asked Rebecca to invite Mrs. Crawley, who came upstairs reluctantly. Frank went into great detail about the case, telling the whole story. "My interest at first in investigating the murder was simply related to a search for a subject for my next book. All that changed. Too many people have died. I'm afraid for the lives of others. I'm spending my own money on this. No one is coercing me to do this. I believe it's imperative to bring out the truth. That's why I want you three women to get together. I will not attend the meeting as Ilene is very hostile to me. Your presence will bring up the past for her. Force her to talk. Please, help me in this mission."

Mrs. Crawley didn't seem clear on why she should spend her time with people she didn't know. It wasn't any of her business. Frank reminded her that her son had died because of it. Rebecca Jones was far more sentimental about saving lives. Finally, she was able to convince Mrs. Crawley to join her.

Frank felt pleased as he booked their flights to Chicago and made hotel reservations for all of them for the next day. He even offered to drive them to the airport.

They talked very little during the short flight. Rebecca and Mrs. Crawley rarely traveled by plane and were anxious during both take-off and landing. Frank sat in the aisle seat and saw them clasp hands out of fear. They were glad to touch down.

Since they had arrived early in the afternoon, they agreed to go to Ilene's house before checking into the hotel. Frank did the driving from the airport to Ilene's house where once again he parked in the neighbor's driveway. It had been decided that Julia would accompany the two women into the house.

It was several minutes before Ilene recognized the women. They hadn't seen each other in over twenty years, and their teenage faces had changed greatly as they grew older. They disappeared into the house. Frank remained hidden in the car, keeping his fingers crossed, hoping his plan would yield some much needed information.

An hour passed. Frank's anxiety grew by the minute. What could they be talking about? That women could converse for hours about looks, fashion, and their lives since they'd last seen each other never occurred to him.

By the time the second hour went by, Frank was biting at his nails. He had to restrain himself from knocking on Ilene's door. The sun had finally set when the three women emerged. They were talking with fervor. Frank tried to make out the expression on Julia's face, but to no avail. It appeared that she was trying to calm them down.

"What happened?" Frank was almost screaming at them as they climbed into the car.

"There was lots of talk about their past, but whenever Julius' or Simon's name came up, Ilene changed the subject or threatened to kick us out."

Rebecca interrupted. "We found out that Ilene had two children. She wouldn't say who their father was, or where they are at present. Her attitude got worse every time another personal question was asked. I never knew her to be so stubborn."

"I knew it would be a waste of time," Mrs. Crawley stated, voice flat and heavy.

"You're completely wrong," interjected Frank. "Her behavior simply confirms my belief that she's hiding something sinister from her past. I know how to make her talk."

"You failed before. We failed now. What else do you think you can do?"

"We still have courts in this country."

Julia looked at him, a question in her eyes. She wasn't sure how much further to take this conversation with both Mrs. Crawley and Rebecca there. Finally, she said, "Let's have dinner. I'm sure the ladies are hungry. Ilene didn't even offer us a drink."

Frank drove back to city center, his mind already hard at work, deciding on what steps to take next. He'd never been more determined in his entire life. This real, live case he was working on, along with his desire to write the best mystery ever to get him back to the top of the bestseller list, was driving him with an ungovernable force.

It was obvious that neither Mrs. Crawley nor Rebecca had ever eaten in a gourmet restaurant like the one at Chicago's Statler Hilton Hotel. They talked about each and every morsel they put in their mouths. The ooh's and ah's never stopped. Ilene's name wasn't mentioned once.

Frank enjoyed seeing them exult over the food. He'd forgotten what it was like the first few times he'd eaten a really memorable meal. The dessert brought loud applause. They talked about the English Trifle all the way to their rooms, how silky the texture, how intense the flavor.

Finally, as Julia and Frank entered their room, she spoke. "Do you really have a plan? Did you anticipate Ilene's refusal to talk about her relationships with Julius and Simon?"

"Frankly, I didn't know which way the conversation would go. I hoped she'd speak up. That would have saved us time and effort."

"What do you mean?"

"Had Ilene provided us with the information we need, our next step would be moot."

"Do you mean the need to take her to court?"

"Either way the case will go to court. The judge adjourned the case for thirty days. I hope the police managed to get another week's delay. I must call Joe before it's too late." Frank didn't wait for Julia's next question. He dialed Joe's number.

Frank was pleased to find Joe at home. He told him about the latest developments, then said, "You must get the judge to give us another week. I'll return to New York as soon as I've talked to Simon Miller's sister. I need your help in getting the Manhattan DA to agree to work jointly with the Wyoming DA since the same person killed people in both states at the same time. I know this sounds unusual but so is this case."

After a long pause Joe said, "I'll try."

Frank heard the receiver click in his ear. Joe must be really pissed at him. He shrugged it off and sat down to write a letter:

The Honorable Judge Rupert Damon,

It's not my habit to write to a judge about an open case. However, due to circumstances beyond my control, and in the spirit of seeking the truth in a case that might go awry due to indisputable evidence, I ask that you allow a change in procedure. I know that I don't have a legal leg to stand on, but never before has a case of this magnitude, which took place in both New York and Wyoming, been so related to events of some forty years ago.

Should this case be tried in two separate states the defendants are bound to be sentenced twice for crimes they haven't committed. I know exactly how district attorneys and the police work, but in the Swansen case a great injustice will be perpetrated.

I'm going to convince both DA's to subpoena a woman by the name of Ilene Samps. The recent murders are directly related to sinister events which took place in this woman's life. So far, despite all my efforts, Ilene has kept her mouth shut about her past. Only the court can make her speak. That's when the truth will emerge and the real killer or killers identified.

If you recall, I'm the one who brought to you the information that led you to adjourn the Swansen case for thirty days. The police are going to ask you for another week. In the name of justice I ask you to approve their request.

Thank you.

Frank read over his draft several times, making a small change here and there until he was completely satisfied. When he was done he showed it to Julia, then signed it and went downstairs to the concierge to have it overnighted to New York.

"I've never seen you this tense," Julia said. "I'm worried about you. You're taking this case too much to heart."

"I feel like I'm living out a story. I've written several mysteries, all fiction of course, but this case, which started out as a friendly gesture on my part, has turned out to be a fabulous story that I could never have imagined. The Swansen case has turned out to be the greatest challenge I've ever encountered."

"I hope you're right. I'm afraid that the twins are really guilty. After all, all the circumstantial evidence points to them."

"That's why I wrote to the judge."

In the middle of the night, Frank woke Julia. "Rebecca said yesterday that Ilene admitted to having two children. I completely forgot about that. Who was the father? Where are they now?"

"Frank, do you ever sleep? Please."

Frank lay back, mind on a new track. How could he get information about Ilene's children if she wouldn't talk? They were probably married with different names. How could he look for them in the huge city of Chicago? Ilene likely left Minneapolis because of her pregnancy. Was she married then? Was there a father's name on the birth certificate?

Julia was still asleep when Frank arose at the sight of the rising sun. He got dressed and had breakfast. It was only seven. He wanted his watch to move faster, anxious for nine o'clock so he could call Dickson in Jackson Hole, the Manhattan prosecutor, and the twins' attorney, John Cavanti. He returned with a large cup of coffee for Julia. She was amazed. Frank had never been known as a thoughtful person.

Frank called Joe Caputo again, this time at his precinct. He explained his thoughts at great length, pressing Joe to see things his way with a persistence he hadn't felt before. "You must convince the DA to subpoena Ilene Samps. He must get the Chicago police to help bring her to New York. She's a hostile witness but I believe she is crucial to the case. If the twins are arraigned for murders they didn't commit, the DA will lose more face than he can imagine. I'm calling the defense attorney and Dickson in Jackson Hole. I'm leaving for Minneapolis and hope to be back in New York the day after tomorrow." He was vehement about this and felt he had presented a strong case. Joe's response was uncertain. The only promise he made to Frank was to bring it up with the detective in charge of the case.

Frank got Julia to rush the women into having a quick breakfast while he made arrangements for them to catch the next flight to Minneapolis. He called Dickson and Cavanti to explain his plan. Dickson was leery about agreeing to work jointly with his Manhattan counterpart. It took Frank a while to convince him. Frank wasn't sure the New York DA would accept such a proposition, but try he must. By the time he'd completed all his phone calls Frank was mentally exhausted. He sat back limply in his chair, rubbing his temples to banish an incipient headache.

****

After dropping Mrs. Crawley and Rebecca at their homes, Frank instructed the taxi driver to go to 1239 – 68th Avenue.

Frances Rand lived in a single family house on a quiet residential street. The entire neighborhood seemed filled to the brim with single family homes of all different sizes. The only similarity was that each house had a small front garden separated from the sidewalk by a white wrought iron fence.

Frank asked the driver to wait. The door opened as soon as he rang the bell. Frances Rand, a tall, pleasant looking woman in her late forties, a small smile widening an already round face, said to Frank and Julia, "I was expecting a friend. Are you at the wrong house?"

Shaking his head at this question, Frank introduced himself and Julia. Surprisingly she let the two of them in. What a trusting soul. "I'd like to talk to you, Mrs. Rand. I saw your brother in New York recently." Frank made his approach softly, hoping to get the kind of information he needed without antagonizing yet another woman.

"Oh… please, come in, sit down. Can I get you anything? Coffee? Tea? A soda?" They were conducted into an overly warm and overly filled den.

"No, thanks."

"How is Simon? I've tried calling him several times but he doesn't seem to know who I am. What a dreadful illness. It's horrible to lose one's mind, isn't it?"

Frank realized that Mrs. Rand was one of those talkative people who could drive him crazy. He quickly got to the point to try and stem the tide of words. "I'm working on several murder cases. They all appear to be connected to something from the past life of your brother and his friend Julius Swansen."

"I'm several years younger than Simon. I really don't know much about him or his friends. He was always an active boy while I spent time in my room with my doll collection. I had no interest in his boy things."

Frank wondered why she hadn't asked him any questions about his involvement in the case. She seemed quite content to sit and answer his questions. "I'm particularly interested in the period after he graduated from high school. I understand that both he and Julius were dating Ilene Samps and eventually they both were married to her."

"Yeah… they were an odd threesome. First Simon married Ilene, then Julius married her after Simon divorced her. Then Julius divorced Ilene and married her sister Adela. I questioned Simon about it at the time but he brushed me off. It was a hot topic for gossip at the time."

"Did you see Ilene in those days?"

"Sure. I saw her several times."

"Did she have children?"

"I heard something to that effect, but it was just a vague story. No one had the facts. Ilene totally disappeared. I heard she'd gone to live in another state."

"Is there anything you can tell me about Simon or Julius that seemed odd or outlandish to you?"

"I don't know. Simon was rough. I liked him because he was my brother but I hated his behavior. He didn't seem to care about me, his only sister."

"Did he talk about girls?"

"He wouldn't talk to me about his adventures. From time to time I'd hear something from my friends."

"What did you hear?"

She blushed a bit. "Simon bragged about his ability to score with girls. He was quite open about his conquests with Ilene and Adela." She seemed embarrassed to talk about this subject, cheeks still pink and her hands fidgeting with each other.

Frank looked over at Julia who had been silent. "Did I miss anything? Do you have questions?"

Julia turned to Frances. "I know it's difficult for you to talk about sexual matters. We don't like it either. Circumstances surrounding the Swansen murders have necessitated digging into the past. I hope you understand."

Julia and Frank remained silent, letting Julia's words sink in. "I see what you mean. It's hard to talk about a brother who behaved badly."

"We have the general picture but we need more details. When did Simon marry Ilene? Where did they live? Did Simon attend college? How long were they married? Was Ilene pregnant then? You see what I mean?"

"Simon didn't go to college. After he left high school he got a job in a lumber company. He was good with equipment and working with his hands. They got married several months after Julius left for MIT. Julius used to come home for long weekends and holidays. I heard they argued and fought, but I have no details about those encounters."

"Where was Adela?"

"Oh, yes, I forgot about that... I heard the craziest story, that Adela and Ilene had switched places. Simon went wild, threatening Julius. That was the cause for the divorce."

"Did they ever know who was with whom?"

"They were so much alike it was impossible to distinguish one from the other. Even Simon and Julius couldn't tell them apart."

"I was told that Ilene had two children. Did she give birth before divorcing Simon?"

She thought for a moment, hands idly picking at a thread in her sweater. They watched in fascination, waiting for it to unravel. "I don't know. I didn't see much of them at the time. Then she moved away. I wasn't close to any of them because of the age difference."

"Is there any way you could find out about all this?"

"I'll try. I'm still in touch with two of my girlfriends. One is in California and the other in Alabama. We haven't seen each other in years. Maybe they know something."

Frank handed her his card. "Please, let me know as soon as possible. We're going to court in a week." She let them out, still asking no questions about their involvement. They left her standing at the open door, a look of puzzlement clouding her face.

"The only thing we learned is that Simon and Julius fought about the twins. I bet Julius set up a trust for Simon, either because he was blackmailed into it, or just to get Simon out of his life. The open question is who the father of the two children was. We still don't know if that has anything to do with the murders."

Before leaving Minneapolis, Frank called Commissioner Fields to bring him up to date about his meeting with Simon's sister and the upcoming court case in New York. The two men spoke with decided warmth on both sides. Frank had certainly found an ally in the commissioner.

Frank booked flights to New York for the following day.

20.

A message was waiting for Frank when he and Julia returned to New York. Joe had left a note saying Judge Damon had refused to postpone the arraignment procedure despite requests from both attorneys. The court would convene tomorrow morning at ten. Frank swore and stormed around the apartment, mad at the whole world for not turning to his liking.

Frank rushed to the courthouse the next morning. Julia stayed behind in her own apartment, taking care of chores that had piled up during her long absence. She needed a little time away from Frank's emotions.

The court was crammed with spectators and reporters. Members of the press had written many articles about the peculiar murders involving the Swansen family. Speculations were rife, one wilder than the other.

Fortunately, Frank ran into Joe. He needed his help to even get in the courtroom. Joe's associate detective, in charge of the investigation, had already made up his mind about the twins' guilt. He presented his circumstantial evidence to the prosecutor who accepted it hook, line, and sinker. He took in the information that Frank had provided as nothing more than the work of an amateur. Joe hadn't said a word about the situation to Frank until he saw him at the courthouse. Frank was furious, but he seethed in silence.

The arraignment procedure took only a few minutes. The prosecutor presented the charges, spoke about the evidence on hand, and demanded a full hearing as soon as possible.

Judge Damon asked the defendants how they pleaded. He was met with a steady stream of shouted denials. The judge reprimanded the defense attorney, who fought with the twins to have them behave and answer the judge's questions properly. The judge also shouted at the spectators, demanding silence. It was pandemonium.

Finally, silence descended. Judge Damon, now completely upset, spoke determinedly, "In light of your behavior I will put in the records your plea 'not guilty'. You are hereby arraigned for the murders of......"

Frank couldn't listen another second. He rushed from the courtroom, anger pushing him as if a tornado was behind him. He waited outside for Joe and attacked him as soon as he saw him. "You couldn't even convince your commanding officer. I'll bet you anything in the world he's made a great fool of himself. I don't understand the DA. I thought he was much more intelligent." He was literally dancing in place, fueled by his passionate belief in the twins' innocence.

Joe felt badly. "I'm sorry, Frank. He wouldn't listen to me. In fact, he threatened to report me to the captain in charge of the precinct for disrupting his investigation. As a result, I stopped giving him your info. I'm sorry, but I can't afford to lose my job." He had the grace to look ashamed, which in some way cooled Frank down.

"Why didn't you tell me?"

"I didn't want you to stop your investigation. I think you are on the right track. You have more freedom to move than I do."

"What about bringing Ilene Samps to court?"

"The twins' attorney will have to subpoena her and arrange for her transportation."

Frank thought about it for a moment. "It doesn't really matter who brings her in as long as she's presented as a hostile witness. I wrote a long letter to Judge Damon. I hope it'll have some impact on the case. Anyway, Joe, thanks for your help. You're a good friend."

"You should have seen the twins. They almost had to be carried away by the court guards. A juried hearing is scheduled for the 10th of next month."

****

Frank called David Ramsey, attorney for Julius Swansen, who had set up the Simon Miller Trust with Chase Bank. Frank cajoled him into meeting with him as soon as possible and an appointment was set for 2:00 p.m. that afternoon.

As Frank strolled down Madison Avenue, his cell phone rang. It was Susan, from the U.S. Consul's office in Rio de Janeiro. "I've tried to reach you several times, but to no avail. I have the information you're seeking. A Margaret Jones flew into Rio on American Airlines flight 679 from Miami a week before the murder of Matthew's girlfriend took place. She left the day after, on flight 680, going back to Miami."

"Susan, you're an angel. Thanks. I'll keep you posted as soon as I can."

"Well... well... well..." Frank mumbled to himself under his breath. New Yorkers were accustomed to people talking to themselves so he didn't receive a single glance. "Now I'm getting somewhere. Could this Margaret Jones be one of Ilene's daughters?" His mind began racing down a new track.

David Ramsey, a Harvard trained attorney, received Frank with a strong handshake. He was 6" tall, full bodied but not fat, in his mid 60's. His hair was completely silvery and he covered a slightly weak chin with a thin, well trimmed beard. He wore late model, very expensive Prada eyeglasses. "Mr. Galitson, what can I do for you?" He led Frank into a conference area in his vast office where they settled into leather club chairs.

Frank briefed him, without going into great detail, about the Swansen case. "I know I'm getting closer to solving this mystery. I strongly believe that the trust was set up for Simon Miller by Julius, as payment for him keeping his mouth shut about affairs that took place during their late teens and early twenties. I believe that something happened during those years that triggered the recent stream of murders. I'd appreciate any light you can throw on how this trust came to be established."

The attorney stroked his chin with thin, manicured hands. "I'm sure you're aware of the rules of confidentiality between a lawyer and his client."

"Yes, of course, but where a string of murders is concerned, and innocent people may be incarcerated, you'll be dragged into court where you'll spend days. The police don't know about this trust, but if obliged, I'll advise them of it."

"You have a very gentle way of threatening me, don't you?"

"Oh, no… I'm not threatening you. I'm trying to save you time and money. The facts are quite simple. Simon Miller suffers from Alzheimer's. His mind is gone. Both Julius, and his wife Adela, are dead. You have absolutely no risk of breaking confidentiality. Who's left to sue you?"

The two took a moment away from sparring to sip at steaming cups of espresso delivered by a silent male secretary. "What are you planning to do with the information I give you?"

"I can assure you I'll use it only to track down the killer, or killers, and for nothing else."

"You're not a police officer. Why are you so interested in this case?"

Frank realized that David Ramsey was diverting the conversation. "Mr. Ramsey, I have no intention of sitting here, bullshitting. I've told you the facts. Either talk to me or I'll go to the police."

Ramsey paused several moments before speaking. "You're right about one thing. There's no one left to sue me." He paused again, staring at Frank's poker face. "Simon Miller blackmailed Julius, threatening to expose his sexual relationship with his wife and her sister at a time when his company was going public. I managed to get them both in here and we nailed down an agreement. The terms of the trust are known to you."

"What were those relationships? Were there children involved?"

"Yes. Two children were born to Simon's wife."

"How was it determined that Julius was the father?"

"I don't know, but Julius agreed to assume paternity."

"Once the trust was set up, did you hear of anything else that might be relevant to that case?"

"Julius never brought it up again and I didn't ask. It wasn't any of my business."

"I must find those children. Do you have any idea where they might be?"

"Not a clue."

"Here's another matter, totally unrelated to the issue of the trust. I understand that Julius' twin daughters became trustees for his and Adela's trust. Why did he choose the youngest girls, who had no experience, over his older children, Paul and Sheila?"

"That was his decision. He made no explanation."

"The twins were eager to sell the company while the others refused. Why did they want to sell out when the company was doing so well?"

"That's something I could never figure out. They came to see me several times. One day they were desperate to sell and the next they weren't. They blew hot and cold about the decision."

"Maybe they simply came to accept the voice of the majority."

Frank rose. "I appreciate your help. What you've shared with me will remain with me. Thank you." They shook hands cordially before Frank left the office.

Frank walked back to his apartment, mind busy with thoughts. Why did the twins act so erratically when visiting Ramsey? One day for the sale and another against. The unusual teenage friendship between Simon, Julius, Ilene and Adela later turned into marriages, adultery and pregnancies... Frank stopped in his tracks as if he'd run into a wall. Who had they impregnated in high school, the cases that landed them in jail and saddled them with community work? Their teacher, Ms. Roberts, said the girls had abortions – maybe not. If not, where were those children? Why did Simon blackmail Julius if they had been so close in childhood?

The thought of Margaret Jones surfaced. Was Margaret Jones, the woman who flew to Brazil, the same woman who flew from Salt Lake City to Minneapolis? Could it be a coincidence? Both were on location when murders took place. Was Margaret one of Ilene's daughters? Who was the second child and where was she now? No one seemed to know a thing about the girls, except that they existed. Ilene was the link in the chain that had to be broken if the truth was to come out.

A surprise was waiting for Frank as he entered his apartment. The smell of grilled fish was in the air. Julia had prepared dinner, using the grill on the outdoor patio. She looked flushed but supremely satisfied at the look on Frank's face. She let out a giggle.

"When did you learn to cook?" Frank asked, a huge smile on his face. He hugged and kissed her. "You're wonderful."

"I must learn how to be a housewife." She winked. "I hope it's soon."

Frank kissed her again. "I must finish this Swansen case first, then my life will return to normal. I can't wait to complete my next novel. I can feel it in my bones that it will be a best seller."

"You'll be back on the top of the bestseller list. I've always had confidence in you. I love you, you idiot."

Julia's happy smile conquered his heart. The table had been set out on the patio. Julia brought the fish, grilled vegetables and a light salad. Frank filled their glasses with a fragrant chardonnay. "Here's to us."

Julia returned his smile. For dessert she served tiramisu, a delicacy she'd brought in from a nearby bakery.

After dinner they lounged on the patio facing Central Park, a relaxing view. Frank talked about the events of the day, his discoveries, and his plans for the period before the court case opened. "I must go back to Minneapolis to speak to Jennifer Roberts and try to locate Ilene's children. I'll also make a courtesy call on Commissioner Fields. He's been very helpful."

Julia didn't have to pretend interest this time. She was finding the case more intriguing every day. "When will the case open?"

"In six weeks."

"That'll give you plenty of time to write."

"Absolutely. I'll only be gone for two days."

****

Since Joe had informed Frank he hadn't talked to the Manhattan DA about combining his prosecution with that of the Wyoming DA, Frank called him to suggest such an effort. The prosecutor agreed, thinking that combining murders which had taken place in two separate states would significantly strengthen his case. He promised to keep Frank informed. In fact, the prosecutor advised Frank he would be called as a witness for the prosecution. At first, Frank wasn't too happy about it. After thinking it through carefully, he decided it would at least give him a platform on which to present his concerns. He also thought, in the event he found out the real motive for the murders, he might not be needed at all. He decided to continue his investigation vigorously.

Frank took a taxi from the Minneapolis airport directly to the assisted living compound where Jennifer Roberts was a resident. He found her in her apartment. She was pleased to see him, inviting him in without question. "Did you find what you were looking for?"

"Not entirely. I know now that Ilene Samps had two children. I believe one of them is called Margaret. I don't know about the other. According to Ilene's friends she must have given birth in Chicago. Ilene clams up like an oyster when questioned. She's hostile and she could care less if innocent people are given the death sentence. How can I find out exactly what took place in those years? I feel it in my bones that something must have occurred in the past to cause all these murders."

"Is that all?" It seemed to her that it was a pretty tall order to fill.

"There's one more matter. You told me that Julius and Simon impregnated two girls in high school. Who were those girls, and is it possible that they didn't have abortions as you were led to believe? Could it be that those two babies are alive?"

Ms. Roberts remained silent for several moments. "I have a memory like an elephant, but that doesn't mean I was aware of everything that went on in those days. I'd love to do some research. I'm quite curious. I'll call you if I find out anything." She let him out, closing the door quietly behind him, already busy thinking who she could call to dig out some information.

Commissioner Fields was in his office despite the late hour. Frank was pleased that he could see him now, as he wanted to return to New York as soon as possible. He told him about the latest developments and his talk with Ms. Roberts.

"I'll check the birth records in Minneapolis just in case the births took place here. I'll also call my counterpart in Chicago to have him undertake inquiries there."

"That'll be terrific. Thank you."

Frank changed his departure time to the first flight leaving for New York the following morning, then checked into a motel close to the airport. He called Julia, telling her about his two visits. She was delighted to hear he would be returning the next day.

The next two days saw Frank consolidating and reviewing all of the notes he'd prepared, making some needed changes, then he began to write. Meanwhile, Julia returned to work to assist her father at the foundation. He was overwhelmed to have her back.

Frank was starting to pay attention to the new emotions embracing him. His feelings and thoughts about 'love' had undergone a sea change. He felt that his egocentric attitude was now completely gone and he felt comfortable with his feeling of love for Julia. He missed her, even when she was only away for several hours. He asked her to move in with him. Julia joyfully accepted his invitation. They moved in some of her furniture and works of art, along with all of her personal belongings. The rest was donated to the Salvation Army. Both of them were happy. It took a couple of days for them to settle into a routine but both were willing to compromise.

Commissioner Field called three days after Frank's return to New York. "Frank, I have the information you're looking for. Ilene Samps gave birth to twin girls at Chicago General. They were named Anna and Denise. There's no other record of them in Illinois."

"I wonder where they are. They must have social security numbers. That might help us find them."

"I can get that for you."

"Thanks."

Frank was pleased at this step forward, but was uncertain about what involvement the two might have in the murders. He desperately wanted to find out Ilene's secret. He forged ahead with his writing, not allowing his mind to wander.

Commissioner Fields called several days later to inform Frank that there were no records of either girl obtaining a social security number. Frank didn't know what to make of it. He put the issue on the backburner.

The court date was fast approaching. Frank called John Cavanti, the twins' defense attorney. He was pleased to discover that Ilene Samps had indeed been subpoenaed and arrangements had been made to transport her to New York. He could only hope that someone would pry the truth from her.

****

Court was called to order. Judge Rupert Damon emerged from his chambers, signaling to the completely full spectator section to take their seats. He looked to the prosecutor's table on the right, which included both the Manhattan DA and the Wyoming DA, then at the defense team on the left. He allowed himself a small smile when he saw Frank sitting next to Cavanti.

Joe Caputo sat in the spectator section. When he saw Frank sitting up front with the defense team, he rose, wanting to talk to him, but before he reached the small gate in the barrier separating the two sections he stopped, returning to his seat.

The jury was called. The twins pleaded 'not guilty', looking dazed and exhausted. Before instructing the first prosecutor to proceed, Judge Damon explained the peculiar circumstances of the case which provided the opportunity for the two DA's to work together.

The Wyoming DA was first to speak. He talked at length about the murders which had taken place in Yellowstone, the evidence he would present and the witnesses he would call. The Manhattan DA spoke about the murders committed in the city, about his evidence and the witnesses who would provide their own version of the truth..

Prosecutors began calling their witnesses to confirm the presence of the twins in the area of the crimes and the evidence against them. Dickson presented various exhibits such as rental car and hotel registrations and lists of passengers on the relevant flights. The defense tried hard to dispute the evidence during cross examination, but to no avail. By 5:30 the prosecution rested and court was adjourned until the following morning at 9:00 a.m.

Joe was nervous. The arrest warrant issued for Frank by the Wyoming DA was burning a hole in his pocket. He contemplated whether to arrest him now or wait until the end of the trial. If the Jackson Hole DA did nothing about Frank, why should he?

Frank was called as the first defense witness. Cavanti asked questions they had already discussed, but Frank's evidence was mostly based on assumption rather than hard evidence. In cross examination, the prosecutors literally destroyed his responses. Frank had not realized how much a real life trial deviated from those in his novels.

The second defense witness, Ilene Samps, was called. She entered from a side door, accompanied by a female police officer. As she passed by the defense table, she stared at the twins. She emitted a sharp scream, her face turned white and she fell senseless to the floor.

Frank was shocked. He had been watching her entrance carefully. She had been pale, her face clearly showing her contempt, but at the sight of the twins she snapped. Why? What had caused her to faint? The twins! Her twins! Frank grabbed his head with both hands. Was it possible? Was it possible? The question repeated itself over and over in his racing mind.

By the time Frank had settled his mind, Ilene had been revived by court personnel. Judge Damon asked her if she wanted to rest for a day but Ilene snapped that she had nothing to say. He ordered her to take the stand as she seemed fit enough. Ilene reluctantly swore to tell the truth, all the truth and nothing but the truth. Her words grated out through clenched teeth.

Cavanti began by asking about her early relationship with Julius. The prosecutors objected vehemently, claiming the question to be irrelevant. The judge agreed. It soon became evident that Cavanti was getting nowhere. At that moment Frank's cell phone vibrated. He answered cautiously, not wanting to interfere with proceedings. Commissioner Fields was on the line. "Frank, Ilene Samps' twin girls were adopted by a family named Warrenton in Santa Cruz, California, a week after they were born."

Frank leaped from his seat like a man struck by lightning. He called Cavanti over. Minutes later Cavanti asked permission to approach the bench. The prosecutors were asked to join them. Frank explained the circumstances surrounding the death of Lisa Warrenton. A postponement of several days was requested.

As Frank finished speaking, he noticed from the corner of his eye that a woman, who had been sitting in the back dressed in a navy blue business suit and wearing a hat covering part of her face, was running from the courtroom.

Frank didn't waste a second. He jumped over the small gate, chasing her. He caught up with her at the main entrance of the courthouse. He grabbed her arm, forcing her to turn and face him. "Who are you?"

The woman tried to free herself, screaming and kicking. Frank held on to her with all his strength. He looked closely at her face, then it hit him. He pulled her over, grabbing her by her hair. The black wig she wore gave way to show blonde hair. In front of him stood another twin; identical to Margaret and Elizabeth. He gasped aloud and she sneered at him.

Frank held her tight, propelling her back into the courtroom. At the sight of her, the twins, still sitting at the defense table, gasped as did the judge. The spectators went wild. Everyone in the courtroom was in shock, their eyes darting from the newcomer to the twins. Ilene started to scream. No one understood what she was saying. The judge hammered his gavel time and again, shouting, until finally the courtroom quieted down.

One of the guards grabbed at the woman to help Frank, who then shouted at her, "What's your name?"

The confusion in front of the bench was obvious. The judge was as shocked as the rest of the people. He didn't even try to stop Frank, who shouted again, "What's your name?"

"Margaret Warrenton." Was her defiant response. She stood as tall as she could, showing no fear in the situation.

"Was Lisa Warrenton your sister?"

"Go to hell."

Judge Damon woke as if he had been experiencing a bad dream. He spoke to the court officer. "Handcuff this woman. Bring her in front of the bench." The officer complied quickly, not really caring whether she liked it or not.

"Do you have a sister by the name of Lisa Warrenton?"

"Go to hell."

"I warn you young lady, if you choose to continue in this manner, you'll be in contempt of court. I can have you put in jail for twelve months. Answer my question."

"Go to hell." Her color was high, breath coming quickly, her chest heaving with emotion. Contempt for all of them was written large on her face. There was a hint of tears in her eyes.

Judge Damon was just starting to say something when Frank raised his hand. He turned to Ilene still sitting in the witness seat. She also appeared to be completely in shock. "Is this woman your daughter?"

The silence in the room was frightening. Everyone's eyes were on Ilene. Finally, she nodded. "Anna" was the single word she mumbled.

"Was Anna the one who married James Jones of Minneapolis?"

"Yes." She collapsed in her seat, fighting for composure. Her hatred had kept her going until this moment when the truth unblocked her pent up emotions.

The twins looked at each other, speechless.

Frank turned to the judge. "Your Honor, Lisa Warrenton, from Yellowstone, and her sister Anna, had their last name changed when the Warrenton family adopted them. These two women are the murderers, not the women sitting at the defense table. I suggest a full police investigation before this case continues." There was another outbreak of loud gossiping in the courtroom and it took several minutes for the judge to obtain silence.

"Mr. Galitson, you should have been an attorney," Judge Damon smiled broadly at him. "So ordered." To the court guards he said, "Hold Ilene Samps and this woman as material witnesses in our jail downstairs. This court will adjourn till next Tuesday. Members of the jury, you're instructed to return next Tuesday.

You're not to discuss this case with anyone. Violation of this order will put you in jail for one year." On a wave of noise and excitement the crowd finally cleared the courtroom.

Frank's mind was swimming. What if the police failed to get a confession? What was the motive for all the killings? He took himself off to his apartment, thoroughly upset about the myriad complications of this damn case.

Joe called Frank that night. "Your arrest warrant has been dropped. The police commissioner finally put me in charge of the investigation, realizing that I've been right all along, all thanks to you of course. I'll have the women brought to the interrogation room in my precinct tomorrow at nine. You're welcome to join me." Frank was delighted at this huge step forward.

Frank arrived early. He was impatient for the interrogation to start. Ilene and Anna were brought in, handcuffed, accompanied by three officers. Their cuffs were removed as they were seated in the locked interrogation room. They rubbed at their wrists. They both looked exhausted, clothes wrinkled and hair in disarray.

Frank came in with Joe, sitting across from the women. Joe had agreed that Frank could go first. He decided to take a risk with his first question. He wanted to test the waters. He looked straight into Anna's eyes. "Why did you kill Lisa?"

The result of his question was very different from what he expected. Ilene turned to face Anna, face and voice ferocious. She grabbed her hand. "Why did you kill her? She was your sister. How could you have done such a thing?"

Anna shouted, her free hand pointing toward Frank, "She fell in love with this character. She wanted to spill the beans."

Frank seized the moment. "You made it look like a suicide, but you made one mistake."

She almost spit at him, eyes blazing. "Go to hell. If not for you, we wouldn't have been found out."

Frank decided to change the direction of his questions. "What was Crawley to you?"

"I used him to get Jimmy out of jail."

"If you cared for Jimmy why did you divorce him?"

"I'm not telling you anything anymore. You're nothing but an interfering prick. I hate you." Her voice rose almost to a scream at the end of her diatribe.

Frank turned to Ilene. "Tell your daughter that if she cooperates we'll be able to ask the court for some leniency. We have all the proof we need for a complete conviction."

"You know nothing," Anna exploded again, slamming her fists on the table. She made as if to rise but an officer leaned forward, pressing her back into her chair.

"Let me tell you something. Lisa had a facelift to alter her looks. I always wondered what the scar was behind her ears. You entered the Swansen apartment in Manhattan easily. The doorman thought you were one of the twins living there. You stole data for their social security numbers and their drivers' licenses, then applied for new ones. You poisoned Sheila, then strangled and shot her, moving her body to a remote Yellowstone location. Killing Paul was easy, as was incriminating Margaret and Elizabeth in the crime. Your flights, your car rentals, and hotel registrations were all designed to frame the others. And, to complicate matters further, you killed their witnesses as well as the executives of the Swansen Company. But what shook me the most was that you killed your own father, Julius Swansen. Am I on the right track?"

The two women clamped their lips tightly, refusing to meet anyone's eyes. The very air in the room smelled of mutinous rage. No one spoke for a long while, until Frank asked, "Why did you do it? What for? Julius would have given you anything you wanted. He loved your mother more than any other woman. He's the one who forced his best friend Simon Miller to give her up." Frank wasn't sure about all this, but he wanted to strengthen his case. There was a huge sigh from Ilene at Frank's words.

Anna turned to her mother. "Is that true?"

"I'm not your mother. I'm Adela Samps." Frank was amazed at this twist, speechless for a long few moments.

Anna stared at her, in complete shock. "Why were we given away for adoption? Why weren't we told who our mother was?"

"Our situation was far too complicated to raise children. You were adopted through the services of an attorney. We knew where you were and we received regular reports about you."

Frank intervened. "Why all the killings?"

Finally Anna confessed. "We found out about our real family by accident. We tracked down Ilene, believing her to be our mother. We saw what a miserable life she was leading, blaming Julius for forcing our adoption for no sensible reason. The Warrentons were bad people. We grew up fearing for our lives. It was revenge for ruining her life and ours. We were full of hate. We wanted to eliminate anyone associated with Julius, and eventually take over his fortune."

Frank asked only two more questions. "Why did you frame Matthew Swansen and your twin stepsisters?"

"We were going to claim ownership after a year or two. It was important to us to keep the twins alive."

Frank got up, looking at Joe. "The case is now yours." He left the room, partly elated at the end of the investigation, partly distraught over the story of lives ruined for no good reason.

PROLOGUE

As the trial ended, Frank obtained a private session with Judge Damon. He explained the circumstances of Matthew Swansen, Julius' brother, jailed for a murder he didn't commit.

Equipped with a copy of the New York Court's transcription of the case, along with Margaret Jones' confession, and a letter issued by the judge, Frank flew back to Rio de Janeiro. On arrival, he engaged a well known attorney who reopened the Rosita murder case to present new evidence. Matthew was soon released. A haggard but grateful man, he flew back to New York with Frank. Frank invited Matthew to stay in his apartment until Julius' estate and trust were properly settled. It took him days to get used to freedom, fresh air and water and a diet of his own choosing.

Elizabeth and Margaret threw a lavish party in Frank's honor. They gave him 100,000 shares in the Swansen Company as a gift.

To the twins' surprise, Frank, with Julia's help, brought Ilene/Adela to the party. Julia took her to Arden's Salon on Fifth Avenue for a complete redo and outfitted her with some decent clothes. It was almost impossible to recognize the woman who emerged from all this pampering.

The reunion of the twins with their uncle and aunt turned out to be a blessing for the remnants of the Swansen family.

Frank and Julia were married soon after the publication of The Yellowstone Murders, which became a major hit. The novel ran at the top of the bestseller list for months. Frank was satisfied.

Frank and Julia went to Jackson Hole for their honeymoon, this time in full enjoyment of the area and themselves.

They're married to this day.

The Yellowstone Murders

Daniel Rosenfeld/Laura Weldon

6002363R0

Made in the USA
Charleston, SC
01 September 2010